COVER

YOUR

TRACKS

COVER

YOUR

TRACKS

A NOVEL BY DACO S. AUFFENORDE

TURNER

Turner Publishing Company
Nashville, Tennessee

www.turnerpublishing.com

Cover Your Tracks

This is a work of fiction. All the characters and events portrayed in this book are either products of the author's imagination or are used fictitiously.

Cover design: Emily Mahon
Book design: Tim Holtz

Library of Congress Cataloging-in-Publication Data Upon Request

9781684425501 Paperback
9781684425518 Hardcover
9781684425518 eBook

Printed in the United States of America
17 18 19 20 10 9 8 7 6 5 4 3 2 1

For my sister, Audrey Clark

CHAPTER 1

A violent gust of wind rocked the passenger train as it rolled down the tracks inside Glacier National Park. The cars yanked and pulled from one side of the track to the other, zigzagging like pinballs traveling through a narrow chute. Without any apparent reason, the brakes on the train squealed, and twenty-three cars and the powerful engine kangarooed into a hard deceleration.

Margo Fletcher, who was seated toward the rear of the train inside a viewing car, tightened her seatbelt and grasped the arms of her seat. At eight and a half months pregnant, she couldn't afford a fall. Her heart rate shot into overdrive, and her baby shifted as if turning a complete somersault. Her stomach clenched as if she were experiencing a contraction. Unable to mask the pain and the worry, she groaned. She hoped the baby hadn't turned breech, prayed that she wasn't going into labor.

A sandy-haired man sitting a few seats away stood up, holding onto his seatback with only one hand for support. He was built like a pro linebacker, strong enough to keep himself upright. "Are you okay?" he asked her. "The baby?"

She nodded and looked out the window. It would be dark soon. The higher elevations of the Rocky Mountains had been visible only a few minutes ago but were now obscured by a translucent veil of snow. Before she'd gotten on the train, the weather report had predicted light snow, not a blizzard.

When her stomach cramped again, she grimaced. Her neck was moist with perspiration. Surprise deluges of sweat had become common with this pregnancy.

The man continued to stare at her. She met his gaze. He'd been sitting in the passenger car for almost an hour, and as far as she knew, he hadn't so much as looked her way. Not that she cared—she enjoyed the solitude.

"Do you know why we're stopping?" she asked. "It's too early."

His hard stare made her uneasy, although she couldn't say why. More disturbing, he didn't answer her question, which meant either that he didn't know any more than she did or that what he knew wasn't good. When snow slapped the windows hard, Margo covered her face as if the wind and ice had penetrated the glass. The man looked out at the mountains and then across the aisle and down into the gulch. He was searching for something. Or assessing some risk he wanted to keep to himself.

She glanced toward the back of the car. No one else looked unduly concerned. An older couple sat three rows back. The husband seemed to be reassuring his wife, but it was impossible to hear what they were saying. Across the aisle, a group of teenagers were laughing as if they were having the time of their lives on a rollercoaster in a Six Flags amusement park.

Margo turned back around and tried to breathe, which wasn't easy given the stress of the moment and her late term. Her throat constricted. She coughed and searched for her bottled water, which was gone.

They were in the middle of nowhere, and trains didn't make routine stops in the middle of nowhere. Something must've gone wrong, but what? Mechanical failure? Engineer error? Cattle blocking the tracks? That couldn't be right; the train wouldn't stop for an animal. My God, was another train heading toward them? Not possible, not in this age of automation.

Lightning flashed across the sky. Another onslaught of snowfall slapped the windows, and again she recoiled. She hugged her belly and glanced up at the man, who was still standing and looking out the windows. His knuckles were white from gripping the seatback. Why was he still standing there? He should've sat down and fastened his seatbelt.

He cupped a hand over his eyes, as if shielding them from a harsh glare, then sighed loudly.

"What's wrong?" she asked in a quavering voice.

The shriek of the brakes intensified. The man fought to stay upright as the viewing car shook back and forth with hard jolts. In California, they'd call this an earthquake. My God, what if the train derailed?

"Sit down, buddy!" the older gentleman behind them shouted to the man. "Are you out of your mind?"

"My Lord!" The older woman screamed.

"Sir, please tell me what's wrong," Margo implored. "I can't see anything in front of us."

He met her eyes, then shouted to all the passengers, "People, we have a life-and-death situation. We have get to the back of the train. Now!"

What? Walk through a train that was about to careen off the track? He really was out of his mind. But he sounded so authoritative, like a cop.

"What for?" one of the teenagers asked.

"There's no time for a debate," he said. "Let's move!" He looked at Margo. "We have to go now if you want to live!"

CHAPTER 2

Whatever was happening, Margo was *not* about to try to walk, not in her condition. If she fell, the baby could be harmed. That wasn't a risk she was willing to take.

Refusing to take no for an answer, the Sandy-haired man held his hands out to her, bracing himself against the seat with his body. She shook her head. "I can't."

"Listen up, everyone," he said. "An avalanche is heading down that mountain. There's no way the train can avoid it. It will bury us all alive."

Immobilized, she could only stare into his steely blue eyes. The sky lit up with bolts of electricity. The wind had become even more ferocious, and what seemed like boulders of snow bombarded their train car.

The public-address system crackled on. "Ladies and gentlemen, this is your conductor. Everyone, please remain seated. Do *not* panic. We're making an emergency stop. The train is riding rough because the engineer is applying the emergency brakes. Perfectly normal. Please stay calm and remain seated. Doing so is the best way to avoid injuries. Your cooperation is greatly appreciated."

Don't panic? Stay calm? The last thing anyone could be feeling was calm.

"We have to get to the back of the train!" the man bellowed again.

Why in the world would he tell them to get to the back of the train? It didn't make sense. If they ... Then she understood. Getting to the back would be logical only if the train couldn't stop in time. If a snow slide hit them, the train could very well derail. Which meant that, depending on the timing of the avalanche, the back of the train was the safest place to be.

Her fear level spiked a few notches higher. Blood rushed to her head, and her ears started to pound. She hugged her belly. How she wished the act of surrounding her child with her arms would be enough to protect the baby from a potentially fatal train crash.

As an ER doctor, Margo Fletcher made a living staying calm in life-and-death situations. Some of her colleagues whispered that she was detached, a machine—she knew that. She was far from a machine but had spent years trying to cultivate that image at work. Emotion interfered with efficiency. Now, for one of the few times in her adult life, she was paralyzed. She had no idea what to do.

She tried to take the conductor's advice—*don't panic*. Panic resulted in bad decisions. Panic turned otherwise good doctors into quacks.

"Everyone on this train sitting like stone figurines thinks I'm panicking, but it's the other way around," the insistent man said as if reading her mind. "Get up and follow me. Do it for the baby."

"The conductor said to stay seated. That's the only logical thing to do. Look at me. I can't afford to fall or be struck by a flying object." But what if this guy was right? If so, they could die—her baby could die. She made an imperceptible movement to stand but sat back again. If a flight attendant on an airplane had told her to stay in her seat and hunker down, she wouldn't have argued, not for a second, no matter what another passenger said. Why was she questioning the conductor?

Fear continued to immobilize her. All she could do was stare up at the man as the brakes grabbed and squealed, as the train refused to stop. How long did it take for a goddamn train to stop?

The man pointed toward the window and said, "Look up *there* if you don't believe me."

He moved so that she could see out the window, and what she saw almost stopped her heart. Some distance ahead, massive mounds of snow were sliding down the sides of the mountain, like the earth's tectonic plates shifting and crumbling. From their relative position, the avalanche appeared to be moving in slow motion, but logic said that was only an illusion. She flashed to the tsunami that had devastated so many countries surrounding the Indian Ocean back in, when was it, 2004, 2005?

Why wouldn't the train stop?

CHAPTER 3

The elderly woman sitting behind Margo whimpered. The husband patted the wife's arm. Damn it all. There was no more time to analyze and debate the chance of survival. She had one solid fact—that avalanche wasn't stopping; the snow wouldn't slide back *up* the mountain. That left one variable—either the train would stop in time or it wouldn't. Fifty-fifty in her mind. The worst possible odds, because her baby's life depended on the flip of a coin.

Often, in the ER, she had less time and fewer facts than she had now to make a decision that could determine whether another person lived or died. When treating a patient, she could call on objectivity and detachment to guide her. In a medical crisis, she never hesitated. Here, both she and her baby were the patients.

The baby kicked hard, making the decision for them. Margo unclipped her seatbelt and offered her hands to the man. He pulled her upright and helped her face the rear of the train.

The elderly couple sat frozen in their seats, gawping at Margo and the man. The teenagers had quieted but also remain seated. Everyone was petrified. Why were they just sitting there?

The man guided Margo down the aisle, keeping her upright against the violent rocking of the train car. When they reached the elderly couple, he said, "Come with us. It's your only chance."

The woman looked at her husband, who shook his head.

The sandy-haired man turned to the teenagers. "You guys. Stand up and move!"

They ignored him, too, turning their heads away.

"You're crazy, buddy," the old man stammered. "Sit back down. You're putting all of us in danger."

"Listen to him," Margo told the others. "I trust him." She tried to sound self-assured, but the truth was, a part of her didn't know why the hell she was listening to this stranger. Her statistician father would say she was making a snap decision without weighing all the factors. But those other factors weren't accessible now, and she'd weighed what facts she had.

No one moved.

Margo was a doctor who knew how to take charge. She was also a mother risking the life of her unborn child. Maybe she could convince the others. She glanced out the viewing window. The train was closing in on the avalanche. The odds of the train stopping were far less than fifty-fifty. She saw the truth with her own eyes. The odds were ninety-ten against the train—no, against the passengers. Maybe worse than that.

"Please, all of you," she said. "Just look out that window. The mountain is crumbling. Please just look out there. We're going to be buried under tons of snow. The back of the train is the safest place."

When the elderly woman looked out the window, her expression turned to horror. She tried to stand, but her husband grabbed her arm and pulled her back down. "We're supposed to stay in our seats, Evelyn," he scolded.

Evelyn complied. The look of abject terror on her face turned to a look of resignation. Margo had seen that look before—on patients who'd accepted the fact that they would soon die.

"Come with us," the man said to the older man. "Don't kill yourself and your wife. She wants to come. Just look at her. She has the right."

The older man shook his head and held onto his wife.

"Listen to me, man," the man said to the older gentleman. The older man looked away.

The sandy-haired man shrugged. "We're not going to convince them."

Margo struggled as she continued down the aisle. She steadied herself by grasping one seatback after another. She stumbled, but the man caught her and stopped her fall.

"Take it slower," he said and continued ushering Margo toward the back.

Then Margo suddenly realized her purse was locked inside her sleeper cabin. But that wasn't all she'd forgotten. "My coat!" She turned to head back to her seat.

"Wait here, I'll get it," the man replied. He was surprisingly agile for a man his size.

She continued her painstaking journey down the aisle, more slowly now that the man couldn't help her. When he returned with her coat, she hurriedly put it on, and they moved faster, leaving the other passengers behind while also ignoring the conductor's repeated announcements to stay seated. They navigated their way through another car, encountering more worried passengers. The sandy-haired man tried to warn them, but no one would listen.

"We're almost there," he said.

A passenger, a man, shouted, "Jesus Christ, sit down! You two are crazy."

Margo slowed and pointed to the white, sliding mass coming down the mountainside. No one paid any attention to her. She realized that they'd all seen the impending avalanche, knew what was happening, but were in mass denial—denial that the idiotic conductor fueled with his repetitive announcements.

They reached the last pass-through compartment. A sign on the wall read *No Admittance*. The man tried the door, which didn't give. Then, in a remarkable feat of strength, he forcibly opened the door. Cold wind swept inside, so bone chilling that she gasped. A flurry of snow invaded the car. Angry passengers shouted for the man to shut the door and sit down.

"Let's go!" the man said to her.

Margo stood immobile in the doorway. There were no protective walls shielding them from the elements. The only way to reach the last car was to cross an open-air metal platform. She couldn't risk it. One hard jolt or a strong gust of wind, and she'd be thrown from the train.

Across the platform, a sign on that door read *Private. Do Not Enter.* Silly, but the word *private* made her want to turn back.

The other passengers continued to demand that they close the door. Some yelled out obscenities. Some even made threats to harm the man. Fortunately, no one attacked them—not that they would challenge her physically imposing protector.

She blinked her eyes and brushed a hand across her belly. The chilling wind sent rivers of adrenaline flowing through her body. The man extended his arm. She accepted it and allowed him to guide her onto the platform. The back door to the train slammed shut. The wind smacked her in the face, and snowflakes landed in her eyes. God, it was cold. The platform shimmied and rattled. Following this man might very well have been the biggest miscalculation she'd ever made in her life.

CHAPTER 4

The man guided Margo across the platform to the back door of the private passenger car. He tried the door, but it wouldn't open.

"Hold on to the railing," he said.

She clung to the railing with both hands while he tinkered with the door. In the distance, the moaning and rumbling of the avalanche grew louder. Whatever she'd imagined that she might've heard before paled in comparison to this reality. Her insides churned, and she became nauseated.

Miraculously, the door to the last car opened. Why didn't he just break the door down? He certainly had the strength to do it. Leaving the door open, he led her inside and over to a chair. Not only was this private passenger car empty, it was unlike any other car on the train. The space resembled a small studio apartment. The walls were paneled in dark mahogany. The sitting area was furnished with a chenille sofa, leather club chairs, and side tables that matched the mahogany walls. There was a dining area that included a full bar. The luxury car looked brand new, untouched and elegant. How strange it seemed. Didn't this kind of extravagance on railroad trains die out in the last century? Maybe even the century before that?

"Sit down and hold on tight," the man said, then turned back toward the door, which was now flapping in the wind.

Why was he going to leave her alone? That thought, and not the cold, made her shiver. Alone, she was helpless. Trying not to sound panicky, she said, "Where are you going?"

He didn't answer, so she got up and followed him. She'd placed her life in his hands, and she wasn't going to sit passively by and watch him leave.

"Go sit down," he ordered.

She remained standing and kept her balance by holding onto a side table. He didn't argue any further but instead stepped outside the car and onto the platform.

"What are you doing?" she shouted.

He kneeled, then lay facedown and began tampering with the coupling apparatus. She now understood what he was trying to do and why. Was it even possible? One wrong move, one hard jolt, and he'd be thrown from the train. He was either mad or brilliant. She'd settle for either if he could get this done.

"Be careful!" she cried.

Some moments later, the coupling wires flailed in the air, like the arms of a drowning victim. He lifted a lever, which caused a metal bar to flip up. The private car, now separated from the train, went dark. Without electricity, the heat shut off. The wind sweeping inside immediately made the room cold. The man began turning a wheel on the platform—a handbrake, obviously. The car slowed quickly, putting space between them and the rest of the train.

Frigid air continued to rush inside the cabin, stinging her cheeks. What if the main train stopped in time? They'd look like fools, might even be charged with criminal vandalism. She covered her belly with one arm, again needing to feel the baby move, needing confirmation that she'd made the right decision.

Their detached car slowed at a smoother pace, and soon they came to a complete stop.

The man got to his feet, walked inside, and muscled the door shut. Margo stared at him, unsure whether to thank him for saving her life or to berate him for doing something so foolish. The response became clear when she heard the ungodly roar of the approaching avalanche.

"Thank you," she whispered.

Without exchanging another word, they hurried to the middle of the car and watched through the large picture window. The train rounded a tight curve, and moments later its entire length was consumed by a massive white shroud. A fraction of a second later, the harsh sounds of steel bending and grinding and snapping penetrated the air. The tsunami of snow lifted, twisted, and tossed the remaining railroad cars down into the deep ravine as if they were nothing more than toys being hurled onto the floor by an angry child.

Margo feared her heart would stop. She wanted to scream. She did scream.

She couldn't bear the awful sights and sounds, so she turned away, retreated to the couch, and covered her ears. Tears flooded her eyes. All those people. Angry and scared. Shouting, threatening. That older man who'd refused to come with them, his wife who'd wanted to but didn't even though she knew what lay ahead. Those teenagers who barely had a chance to live, just kids.

When the baby nudged Margo's belly, she forced herself to sit upright. She and her baby were alive, but they were also stranded deep inside a mountain wilderness.

All was quiet except for the wind and snow that continued to beat against the side of the car. The storm was worsening. The man walked over to where she was seated. Her head spun, and every inch of her skin was prickling to the point of sharp pain. All at once, clarity returned. She was isolated in the wilderness with a strange man powerful enough to uncouple a moving train car.

"We have to call for help," she said. Instinctively, she reached to her side for her purse that wasn't there. She checked her pockets. They were empty—no phone, no gloves, no nothing. "I don't have my damn phone. I left it in my purse. What about you?"

He patted his pockets. "When I went into the viewing car, I'd just come in from stretching my legs at the last stop. I left everything in my cabin."

She faced the window again and sat staring into the beyond, trying to make sense of what had occurred. She couldn't. She needed to walk, to feel ground beneath her feet, so pushing her weight forward, she stood. "We have to go down there and help while there's still light left in the day."

"No one survived, ma'am."

"You'd be surprised what people can live through. I'm a doctor. I've seen it all." Over the years, she'd learned that human beings were remarkably resilient and often lucky. Survival was always possible. She'd witnessed the impossible. A six-year-old girl came out of a mangled car with multiple fractures, including a partially crushed skull, and made a full recovery when no one thought she had a chance; an eighty-year-old man fell down a flight of stairs and broke only an index finger; patients lived for decades after being told they had stage-four cancer or ALS. No human being wore the crown of God when it came to deciding who lived and who died.

"No one survived," he said.

"You don't know that." Her legs turned to jelly. She wobbled and stretched her arms to keep her balance. Walking on that moving train seemed like a cakewalk compared to this light-headedness. She took a step back and collapsed into the chair. "We need to find out. It's the least we can do."

He shook his head. "Even if you weren't expecting a baby, you couldn't walk down that steep mountain cliff in a blizzard. And it's getting dark."

"I've taken an oath. My duty—"

"I understand how you feel. Disasters like this are hard. I know. I've seen more than my share of death and destruction."

She gave him a quizzical look.

"I was an Army Ranger."

"My God, no wonder you were able to uncouple a train car. We'll go down there together. We did this together, so . . ."

"What's your name?"

"Margo Fletcher." Through all this, she hadn't once thought to ask his name.

"I'm Nick Eliot. Now, Margo, look out the window. Do you see the train?"

She rose up on her haunches and did her best to gaze out the left-side window and down into the sheer ravine to the south. Another blast of wind rocked the car, as if forewarning them of the dangers out there. The snowfall was thick, but she could see where the avalanche had taken out the trees and filled much of the gorge with white. There was no sign of the train. Her stomach roiled and churned acid again, which burned her throat. She used her fingers to wipe away the tears rolling down her cheeks.

"You can't be sure there are no survivors," she insisted. "We can't just sit here waiting for rescuers to arrive. What happened to no soldier left behind?"

It was an insulting thing to say, but the man—Nick—didn't react.

A brilliant flash of lightning filled the sky, followed seconds later by an ear-shattering blast of thunder, the loudest she'd ever heard. Nevertheless, she rose from her seat again and headed toward the door, moving slowly in the dimming light. But this time, she was more determined.

Nick followed her, and when she reached the door and gripped the handle, he grabbed her wrist. "Do not open the door. Think of the baby."

"Please let go of me. It's not for you to decide."

Their eyes met. She drew in a breath, holding it for a long moment.

He released her wrist. "It's true that we leave no soldier behind. But we don't put ourselves in harm's way when it's hopeless, and we don't look for survivors at the expense of protecting the living. But I'll go out there, if only to stop you from putting yourself and the baby in further danger. You have to promise me you'll stay put."

She nodded. Staying was the right thing for the baby.

He gestured for her to step aside and, when she did, he opened the door. She looked down toward the ravine. A fine powder filled the air, and she could see only ten, maybe twenty feet into the distance. She tried to locate the railroad tracks, but everything was now covered in white. How swiftly the weather had changed; how swiftly the snow had blanketed the ground.

Nick stepped outside onto the back platform and shut the door without saying another word.

His footsteps pounded on the metal and down the side stairs. Soon, the ping of metal faded, replaced by the rustle of the wind and the occasional roar of thunder. She returned to her seat but in a fit of remorse sprang up to try and see where he'd gone. There was no sign of him. How would he find his way back with such poor visibility?

Had she sent this man, her protector—her child's protector—on a fool's errand? Perhaps to his death?

CHAPTER 5

Alone in the passenger car, Margo waited for Nick to return. A chill crept over her skin, and it didn't come from the cold outside. She pulled her coat up around her neck and reflexively hugged her belly before tucking her cold hands underneath her armpits. No matter what happened, it wasn't her life that mattered now—it was the baby's.

She thought back to her first pregnancy when she was only seventeen. On the day everything was set in motion, she sat inside a small room, breathing in the stale, antiseptic air. The doctor was instructing the nurse, but what they were saying escaped her. The door flew open, and her father shouted, "Margo, get up and get dressed! Now! We're leaving."

How had he found her? He wasn't supposed to know.

"This is none of your business, Dad!" she said, mortified, instantly teary-eyed.

"You are not going to kill an innocent being!" He glowered at the doctor and his nurse. The nurse backed away as the doctor rose from his stool.

"Sir, you don't have a right to be in this room," the doctor said. "Or to make this decision for your daughter. She's seventeen."

"I beg to differ. She's a minor who lives under my roof."

"Under the law, she's competent to make her choice without parental involvement."

Her father's eyes were so lethal that when he glanced at the nurse, she took another step back. The doctor didn't budge.

"Let's go, Margo," her father repeated, then lunged at her and grabbed her wrist with an aggression he'd never shown before—the act so jarring that she struggled to think straight. Her father didn't believe in violence, or so he'd said, despite having served as an officer in the navy.

The doctor looked at Margo and then took a step forward, jaw clenched.

"I'm okay," she said to the doctor. That was a lie. She was frightened and angry. The fear won out. She was too terrified of her father to argue with him, even though lately she'd been arguing with him all the time. Her decision was made—partially for him but also for herself. Deep inside she really didn't want to go through with the abortion. But she was only seventeen and up until then had seen no other way out.

Shakily, she stood up and looked at her father. "All right, Dad. You win. Can I have some privacy while I get dressed?"

Her father refused to leave the room. He probably thought she'd bolt, or have the doctor lock the door and go through with the procedure. Finally, after she promised on her mother's life that she wouldn't defy him, he relented and went outside.

She didn't go through with the abortion, and even up to this horrid day of the avalanche, she was glad she hadn't terminated that first pregnancy.

Yet she still lost her baby forever.

Her parents had forced her to place the baby for adoption. She was too young, too naïve, to resist her her demands that she sign over irrevocable rights to the child. The Fletchers' family skeleton was now locked away in a hidden closet.

Now, a scraping at the back window of the passenger car startled her. Pushing her weight from the chair, she hurried to the rear and entered the bedroom. A window covered with curtains obscured the view outside. She yanked the panels out of the way and saw that a portion of the back window had been wiped clear of ice and snow. With cupped hands, she peered outside. Nick was standing there, on the tracks. He held a large pine branch that he must've used to wipe the window. He waved his free hand, and she beckoned him to come back.

She returned to the door and waited, anxious to hear what he'd learned, hopeful that there might be survivors. He didn't come. She opened the door and looked into the void. The chilling wind soon forced her to retreat. He should already have walked around to this end of the car. What was taking him so long? Then it occurred to her that maybe he'd never intended to come inside. Maybe he was merely pointing out that he was heading not toward the avalanche site but away from it. If that was the case, it seemed logical that the opposite direction might be the only way down into the gulch. After some long moments of waiting, it was clear he wasn't coming back inside, so she headed to the couch.

The sky became dimmer with each passing minute, and eventually—how long she couldn't say—the outside world turned black. Eerie shadows skittered across the window frames. The metal walls creaked as the car swayed and attempted to resist the harsh winter elements. The longer Margo sat, the more the noises unnerved her. She was accustomed to waiting on test results, for patients to respond to treatments, but this was altogether different. Clearly, her mind was playing tricks. She was safe, but it was hard to maintain clarity. Deep breaths usually helped her relax, and so she closed her eyes and began focusing only on breathing.

Just as she started to settle down, from somewhere outside the car, a loud, agonizing cry pierced the air. Her eyes popped open. This sound was a sound she'd heard all too many times in her job. This was the wail of a man crying out in pain.

Oh, damn. What had she done?

CHAPTER 6

Margo's forehead and chest broke out in beads of sweat. She braced herself on the couch and tried peering out the window. The glass was frosted, and nothing was visible through it. Had she heard a man cry out? Maybe it was only the wind, maybe it was the sound of tree branches snapping, or maybe it was the death rattle of entire trees collapsing under the weight of the snow. More mind tricks. She couldn't be sure. She wasn't sure of anything, except she'd insisted that Nick go out into the wilderness alone and in the dark. If he was hurt, this was her fault.

Her nerves fired hot. She tried to breathe, but the air only caught in her throat. She covered her ears and shouted, "Stop it!"

The volume of her own voice impelled her off the couch. She walked to the door, hoping to find Nick coming up the platform steps. She placed her bare hand on the metal door handle. The frozen steel bit at her flesh. She jerked her hand away. No way she was going to be imprisoned inside this car, not if Nick needed her help, and she couldn't rule that possibility out. Ignoring the pain, she gripped the handle and tried turning it. The metal creaked but refused to give. In desperation, she twisted the knob harder, her hand slipping back and forth. She pulled and yanked, and the door opened a few inches.

A sharp gust of wind met her face, stinging her nostrils. A winter coat and mid-calf designer boots weren't nearly sufficient to stave off this kind of weather. She told herself she'd only feel the first shock of the cold, that she'd surely get accustomed to the temperature. She cupped a hand over her eyes and stared outside into the dark. From inside, it had been difficult to appreciate how much snowfall had accumulated since they'd separated from the train. No matter. She pulled on the door until it opened more.

"Nick!" she cried as loud as she could. "*Nick!*"

No answer.

She secured the hood of her coat and slowly put the weight of her leg onto the platform, which was covered with snow. Her boot sank below the level of the snow. She held onto the doorframe and took another step until she was outside and exposed. The temperature must've been in the low twenties and dropping. Everyone who lived in Chicago understood cold, yet somehow this cold was different—malevolent.

She carefully stepped forward and gingerly grasped the railing at the back of the platform. The mere touch burned her flesh. She jerked her hands away. The cold wasn't the only problem. Her hands were now moist with nervous sweat. She recalled a boy in her fifth grade class back home in Spokane who, on a dare, licked a flagpole in freezing weather and lost a piece of his tongue when he pulled away. Using the sleeve of her coat as a makeshift glove, she grasped the metal again.

A sudden blast of wind swept across the platform, thrusting the hood of her coat off. Her shoulder-length hair flew crazily into the air. Bracing her legs against the railing, she quickly replaced the hood around her head and drew the toggle strings tight.

"Nick? Are you there? Answer me!"

No reply. Of course, he couldn't respond if he were severely injured and lying in the snow.

She inched over to the right-hand side of the platform, the side closest to the mountain. Lightning flashed, and a low rumble sounded in the distance. In that brief moment of light, she caught a glimpse across the snowy barren land where the train had been lost. A hollow feeling shot throughout her body. Never had she felt such loneliness and despair. She leaned a few inches over the railing and gazed in the opposite direction and down the length of the car, where she'd last seen Nick. Another flash of light revealed a shallower depth of snow along the path of the railway tracks. Away from the tracks and toward the mountainside sat a high wall of snow made by the train's front-end cowcatcher, a temporary but impenetrable barrier.

Thunder boomed again and again as if a giant in lead boots was clomping toward her. Flinching, she gripped the rail. As a small child, she'd been terrified of thunderstorms. Her mother would come into her room and hold her until she fell asleep. But when she turned five, her father started saying, "Stop babying her, Isadora. She'll never grow up if you keep running to her." That left only the comfort of a pillow pulled over her head and the sound of her own whimpers.

Sometimes, if the lightning and thunder were particularly powerful, her mother would sneak into her room, saying, "I'm here, sweetheart. It's all right now."

"Mother?"

"Shh, don't let your father hear us."

With age, Margo's fear vanished—or so she'd thought until this night.

Steadying her nerves, she drew in a slow even breath and waited for the next illuminating flash. Soon her mother's responsibility would be her own. She wouldn't allow a little thunder to consume her strength.

When the sky lit up, she looked beyond the wall of snow and up into forest. Evergreens, caked with white mounds, brought back memories of her favorite childhood snow globe, which always sat on the mantle at Christmastime. How she marveled at the ruffled white when she shook the globe—a tangible piece of magic contained in a precious world of its own. Now, as she looked into this forest, all that magic was lost. Limbs and branches, caked with masses of snow, hung so low that a single bump or nudge might rip the trees from their roots or snap their trunks in half. What would it take before the trees came down?

The slightest change in wind, another two inches of snow, thunderous vibrations from the storm?

Lightning flashed again, and oddly enough, the snowflakes appeared to be growing as they fell. She reached out a hand, captured one, and pulled it under the roof of the platform. The single delicate flake was soft, crackly, and nothing like the biting cold. But that wasn't true. As exquisite as this one flake was in her palm, the hard truth was this storm wasn't letting up and, together, all of these lovely snowflakes were perilous. She blew the flake from her hand and again glanced toward the back of the car.

Another flash illuminated the ground, revealing footprints in the snow. The imprints were a foot deep and led away from the car and down the path of the railway.

"Nick?"

He didn't answer. But her shouts were drowned out by a loud clap of thunder. She flinched, then told herself she wasn't the target of this strike. She wanted to go back inside the car, but she forced herself to stand on the platform. In the distance, she heard something—a cry, a shriek, metal grinding, a limb snapping? Had it come from below in the gulch? Were people alive?

She turned toward the opposite side of the platform, which faced the ravine. She considered going back inside, thought of shirking her responsibility. No, she had to check. She had to help Nick and any others who could be injured. It was foolhardy, but she was a doctor, damn it, and an ER doctor at that. She treated trauma cases. She had no first aid kit, but she could clean wounds with melted snow, use the cleanest fabric handy as a bandage, make splints out of tree limbs or furniture parts, and use old-man's beard which grew on trees as an antiseptic. Back home, even during her pregnancy, she'd gone into the field to treat the injured.

But not eight months pregnant.

Clinging to the rail, she started toward the opposite side of the platform to look into the gulch, to listen more carefully. On her third step, her ankle came down on something hard, and she started to slip.

She tightened her grip on the railing, but her legs sailed out from underneath her and slid off the edge of the platform. She landed on her backside but managed to hold on without sliding all the way off. Twenty pounds lighter, and she might have gone off. Releasing one hand from the railing, she felt her belly. Nothing seemed amiss. So she hoped.

She placed her hand on a lower rung, swung one leg at a time back on the platform, and lifted herself up. She wasn't going any closer to the edge near the gulch. Waiting on another lightning strike, she stared into the pitch black that obscured the gulch. When it flashed, she saw nothing more than a white billowy valley. She hoped Nick was wrong, that someone had survived that crash. And yet, there was no sign of life, nor any trace of the train buried underneath the snow.

Then someone or something screeched.

She started toward the platform stairs that faced the mountain. Had the stairs been on the narrow gulch side, she wouldn't have risked it.

The baby moved. "I know, but we have to help Nick or whoever survived," she said rubbing her belly, the sound of her voice maybe for her benefit, maybe for the benefit of her unborn child.

She grasped the railing and started down the stairs. When she reached the ground, she made her way toward the back end of the car, placing a hand on the side wall for support. With each step, she sunk almost knee deep into the snow. She followed Nick's footsteps, but one wrong step could send her tumbling down the embankment and toward the wall of snow.

At the rear of the car, she searched for Nick, calling his name. No answer.

The snowfall abated, and the clouds parted in a few spots, revealing a few stars. The moon hadn't fully risen yet, but the reflection of light against the snow was enough to provide some visibility. She studied the ground, doing her best to make sense of Nick's footprints. Before long, she realized that the path he had taken meandered in various directions. He must've been searching for solid ground. Then she spotted a trail of prints leading away from the passenger car and in the direction of the previous train stop.

What if he'd decided she was too much trouble and had decided to leave her behind? Was he abandoning her or going for help? Surely, help.

She pulled the hood of her coat back to listen. The biting cold stung her ears. She stood perfectly still, trying to hear the voice of anyone nearby. In her mind she felt as if she could close her eyes and step out of this nightmare, but when she refocused all she had was the wilderness, with its whistling wind and creaking tree limbs. A frigid gust penetrated her clothing right to the bone. It was if her long down coat were nothing more than a fine gossamer. She glanced over her shoulder and back. Go back or continue?

The clouds above closed, obscuring the meager light from the sky. Her surroundings suddenly became unfamiliar, and the words *frozen in my tracks* came to mind. Paralyzed, she let out a hysterical laugh that came from a person she didn't recognize.

Lightning flashed. There was Nick. The light disappeared, and he was gone.

CHAPTER 7

Margo started in the direction where she believed she'd seen Nick but stopped when she heard his commanding voice.

"Stay where you are," he said.

She sighed in relief, and all the muscles of her body relaxed. He approached with an uneven gait, and he held a large branch that served as a makeshift cane. Was he hurt or using the stick for balance, a kind of ski pole? Lightning flashed, illuminating his face. The feral glare in his eyes caused her to flinch and take a step back.

"Get inside," he ordered. "It's not safe out here."

Her breath caught in her throat. What was wrong with him? He had no right to be angry with her. When he took a half-step forward, he faltered, and it wasn't just a slip in the snow. He needed her help. And there she was, standing outside in the bitter cold like a lunatic, risking her own life and getting nowhere. He'd warned her to stay inside, and she'd ignored his good advice.

"You're limping, Nick. Come inside so I can take a look at your leg."

"It's nothing. Let's go. You should never have come out."

"I was worried about you."

"You should be worried about yourself and the baby." He wrapped an arm around her, and although he'd been out in the cold for some time, his body warmed her like a comfy woolen blanket. They headed toward the train car and inched their way alongside it until they reached the platform stairs. He supported her from behind as she climbed up. Once inside, he guided her to the couch. Still shivering, she was acutely aware of how reckless she'd been exposing herself and her child to subfreezing temperatures. But she'd heard a scream. It wasn't in her nature or her training to leave an injured person in distress, much less to let another human die in the cold.

"Why did you leave the car?" he asked.

She startled at his harsh voice. Injured people are often belligerent, she reminded herself. "I heard you cry out. I assumed it was you. I'm sorry, Nick. I should never have asked you to go out there."

"There are no survivors," he said in an even voice, the abrupt change in tone jarring. "Only us." He brushed the snow from his pants.

"You're hurt. Let me—"

"I took a step and sank down in the snow. I wrenched my leg on something solid. Maybe a big rock."

"Let me take a look at it."

"It's nothing."

"Nick, I'm a doctor. I could—"

"It's nothing." The words carried a tone of finality.

It wasn't *nothing*. Not the way he was limping, not with his need for a makeshift crutch. But she understood. He was an ex-soldier and probably hated appearing vulnerable, probably didn't want to seem frail in front of a woman, doctor or not. As long as he didn't get worse, she'd honor those feelings.

He found a closet and returned with a wool blanket, along with a box of crackers and a few cans of Vienna sausages that were packed in a welcome basket. "Not gourmet, but a fortunate find. People have survived on a lot less."

"Any bottled water?" she asked. If not, they'd be in trouble. They couldn't drink melted snow, which could be full of bacteria.

He shook his head and sat down. "We'll find a way to purify the snow at some point. Don't worry. We'll protect the baby."

She picked up the tin of Vienna sausages and opened it. Her mother would've been appalled at the dinner menu. Isadora Pratt Fletcher had always been the perfect Southern hostess, a dynamo in the kitchen, a dynamo in general. Typical of a Pratt woman. Margo had inherited the more reserved Fletcher personality from her father, but physically she was a Pratt woman. She looked like her mother, who looked like her mother. They all had dark, thick hair and light-brown eyes flecked with gold. They were tall and medium-framed. Margo's sisters, Heather and Blanche, resembled the Fletcher side of the family—slim, small-framed, blond, and beautiful—a gift from their father's Norwegian descent. Margo had always wondered if her father played favorites because her sisters looked like him.

On the other hand, her mother made her feel as if she were her favorite. She was the one child who would sit and listen, rapt, as her mother shared family recipes or explained how baking had evolved over time. Often her mother would explain the historical relevance of the dishes she'd prepared. Other times, she'd share family stories. Margo's favorite had always been the pioneer bean story. Pioneers ate what was locally grown and, when produce was scarce, they relied on dried beans and pocket soup, which was basically the old-time version of bean soup with a bouillon cube. Her mother's tales were quintessentially her Southern way of preparing her daughters—and probably now Margo's niece—to be a good wife. Etiquette was so important to Isadora that even on a picnic she'd set out cloth napkins, glass tumblers, and stainless-steel dinnerware, whereas other families used paper, Styrofoam, and plastic. Still, her mother might have been proud that Margo had found sustenance in this barren landscape, that these Vienna sausages were amounting to her mother's version of pocket soup.

"What do you think is going on with the rescue team?" Margo asked Nick. "Someone should've been here by now."

"They probably can't get out here."

She began to shiver and pulled the blanket up around her

shoulders. "Doesn't make sense. You'd think that at least some aircraft . . ." She shrugged. There was no use in speculating. At her hospital, the EMTs usually responded quickly, but not always. "So where does that leave us? We just sit here and hope we don't freeze to death?"

"You should eat something."

"I'm feeling queasy all of a sudden."

"You can't go without eating. Not in your condition."

He was right. She had to keep up her strength to make sure the baby didn't suffer. She nodded and forced down a cracker and a sausage. Then he got up and walked back to the kitchen, where he searched through more cabinets.

It was getting colder, and it wasn't from the blood rushing to her stomach after eating the snack.

"There's a bed at the back of the car," he said. "You should go rest, wrap yourself in all the blankets, and cover your face and head. You and the baby will both be fine."

Before pregnancy, she might, out of pride, have insisted that he take the bed. Especially with his injured leg. Now, her baby took priority. As she shifted her weight forward to stand, a loud thump sounded on the platform. Her heart trilled. With the back window of the train frosted over, it was impossible to see out.

"Someone's out there," she said. "Maybe someone else survived. Or it could be someone from the rescue team."

Maybe this nightmare was over. Maybe the rescuers would find more survivors from the main train. Wouldn't it be wonderful if others had survived? She was ready to help the injured, to save some lives. She stood and waddled toward the door. Nick slammed a cabinet shut and charged toward her. Just as she reached for the door handle, he grabbed her arm, which he pulled down hard.

"What are you doing?" she cried. "Let go of me! That hurts!"

He let go and braced a hand against the door. "We have to keep that door shut."

"What's wrong with you? There's someone out there!"

Something bumped the back window again. A blur of movement rushed past the window frame, the form not that of a human being but of an animal. Whatever was out there began scraping its claws across the glass.

"Coyotes," Nick whispered.

CHAPTER 8

Margo was rattled by the continual scraping on the back door but also from Nick's physical aggression. She rubbed her arm, still feeling the pressure from his hand. She wanted to thank him for preventing her from opening the door; she also wanted to scream in his face that he'd better never touch her like that again. Ordering her around like a foot soldier was one thing. Putting his hands on her so roughly was quite another. She'd dealt with uncooperative patients in times of medical emergencies and understood the circumstances. She'd also felt the death grip of her father's hand around her wrist on one of the worst days of her life. This felt different. The savage look in Nick's eyes confirmed that he was quite capable of inflicting physical harm if provoked. She was no match for him.

She backed away and retreated to the couch, needing a moment alone to compose herself. She startled when she turned around and discovered he'd followed her. As soon as she sat, so did he. That was also unexpected. She didn't look at him. Her heart was beating hard, and she didn't want to show him how much he'd upset her. She reminded herself no matter how gruff this man had been he hadn't harmed her, that he'd protected her and the baby. Their situation was perilous, and she needed him to survive.

"I didn't mean to scare you," he said.

She nodded, relieved to hear him express remorse, but his words weren't exactly an apology.

"If we're quiet, the animals will go away," he said. "It's not typical for a coyote to attack a human, not unless the animal is starving or sick."

"Is the door secure?"

"They can't get in. Don't worry, they'll give up."

They sat quietly, listening to the coyotes climb up and down the back stairs, thumping and pacing on the platform. There was growling, scrabbling, and yelps of pain. The animals must've been fighting among themselves. It was hard to determine what was going on with all the commotion, and harder to judge how many animals were out there. Three? Four? As many as ten?

A horrid thought crossed her mind. "What if they break through the glass?"

He put an index finger to his lips and shook his head, which was far better than him putting his hand to her mouth.

They waited, the minutes excruciatingly long. Sometime later, maybe ten minutes or twenty, the tapping of paws on metal stopped, and a welcome silence came. She was glad he hadn't suggested that she go to the back bedroom to sleep. Despite Nick's reassurances, she couldn't shake the irrational thought that the animals would return and force their way inside. If that happened, she needed a protector, someone versed in combat and the art of self-defense. She'd refused to listen to the man's advice earlier, which had almost been a costly mistake. Of course she could trust Nick. She had to trust him. No wonder Nick had been so angry when he found her outside. She'd acted foolishly.

He raked his hands through his hair, leaned back, stretched out his long legs, and yawned. This was their first moment of repose since this ordeal had begun.

She had the feeling he was a person who disliked compliments, and yet she was compelled to offer one. "Thank you for saving me," she said, rubbing her belly. "I mean both of us, all of us."

He nodded.

"I'm curious, did the army teach you how to separate railroad cars?"

"The military teaches you a lot of things. Separating train cars isn't all that hard. There's a cut bar. You lift it. The cars uncouple."

"Yes, but on a moving train?"

"You can't do it when the train is accelerating, but when it's slowing like ours was there's slack in the connection, and you can disengage cars, particularly a passenger car like this one."

His explanation made sense. His capability in the face of danger comforted her. His volatility worried her.

They were quiet for a long while. The cold inside the car lingered like a persistent virus. Her breath was a visible mist. She rubbed the palms of her hands together, a nervous habit she inherited from her mother and one she'd tried to break for years.

"Do you have any idea where we are?" she asked.

"The train stopped moving parallel to the highway, turned northwest, and crossed a creek. Our previous stop was at the entrance to the park. We made one stop, so my guess is that we're about halfway through the mountains. Deep inside the forest."

She shuddered. If he was right, it would be difficult for a rescue team to reach them. Not only was visibility in this blizzard an obstacle, but the terrain was rugged and treacherous. She wrapped the blanket tighter around her body, but it did little to stave off the cold or her mounting dread. Fatigue nipped at her from the inside out. With eyes closed, she listened to the snow striking the windows and tried to repaint that idyllic scene she'd seen through the picture window of the viewing car. So beautiful; so deadly.

"Margo, go to the bed and get some sleep."

Her moment of repose broken, she opened her eyes. She didn't want to be alone, even one room away. "I'll sit with you. I'm not giving up hope that a rescue squad will find us tonight."

He grunted.

On second thought, she might be safer alone. But she stayed put.

CHAPTER 9

As a child, Nick Eliot didn't attend preschool or even kindergarten. "He can play at home," his father, Michael, had said. "That's all they do in kindergarten. He'll get exposed to the corrupt Establishment soon enough." Michael Eliot hated the government because he'd been drafted into the army and forced to fight in Vietnam.

"You can't trust anyone," Nick's mother had said. She'd run away from home as a teenager. She refused to say why. She met Nick's father on the streets of Phoenix, and after Nick was born, they had moved to Flagstaff.

If not for JJ, Nick's imaginary friend, Nick would've been all alone.

Then Nick turned six and started first grade. His father drove him to the school five blocks away and pulled into the carpool lane.

Nick was petrified, but he wouldn't show it.

"Let's go, JJ," Nick said.

His father took a deep, impatient breath. "You'll have to lose Jumping Jack. The other kids will laugh at you if you don't. They'll call you a baby."

Other grown-ups were getting out of cars and escorting their kids his age toward the school building. His father only pulled forward in the drop-off line.

"Daddy, come in with me."

"You need to learn independence to get by in this world. Go on, you don't need me to walk you in. You're a big boy now."

A rush of anxiety punched young Nick in the chest, hitting him so hard he could barely breathe. "But I don't know where to go."

His father glowered at Nick. "Figure it out, man. It's the way you learn to depend on yourself. If you depend on others, you'll be nothing but a stooge in life."

Nick hesitated.

"Get out of the car now, dammit!"

Nick's throat constricted; he tried to swallow. He wouldn't cry, he couldn't cry—not in front of his father. "When will you be back to get me?"

"Your mother will take care of that. I won't be off work yet." Nick's father was a copy editor for a small, local, alternative newspaper.

Just then, a security guard reached for the handle to open the car door.

"Bye-bye, Dad." It was the first time in his life Nick had called his father *Dad* rather than *Daddy*.

The school building looked like a scary monster that ate children. Nick walked a few steps in the direction the other people were going. Then he turned around and looked for his father's car. He wanted to run back to it.

His father had driven away.

The school bell rang.

Nick hurried toward the giant brick building.

"JJ," Nick shouted. "Where do we go?"

The security guard walked up to him. "Hey kid, you must be in first grade?"

Nick shrugged.

The guard grasped Nick's hand. "Come on. Let's find your classroom, JJ."

Nick was afraid to correct the man.

The security guard escorted Nick to a classroom filled with children seated at their desks. The first grade teacher, Mrs. Walters, interrupted her lecture on rules and assigned Nick a desk several rows from the front. He wanted to ask where JJ should sit, but he stopped himself, remembering his father's warning. JJ would just have to sit on the floor. Nick settled into his seat, taking in the classroom. The chubby boy sitting in the desk to his left had brown hair, a pug nose, and a silly smile. Nick later learned that the boy's name was Donnie Hollis.

Donnie looked over at Nick, nodded toward the teacher, and whispered, "She's a mean one. A wicked witch. My dad would say wicked *bitch*."

"Donnie, be quiet!" the teacher said, not yelling but certainly not talking in a soft voice.

"She's real nasty," Donnie whispered again. "I bet I know what she's going to talk about. The Native Americans. I'm part Indian, you know. The Indians scalped the white men. Cut the skin right off their heads, hair and all, while they were alive. I had Mrs. Walters last year too. I'm repeating first grade. It's cool, I'll show you what to do."

Nick didn't understand what Donnie meant about repeating a grade but decided it made sense to stay close to someone who knew what to do. Nick made sure to say practically nothing the entire day. Words got you into trouble.

Mrs. Walters started moving in the boys' direction, her shoes pounding the floor like bricks hitting pavement. Then she sent Donnie to the principal's office. She gaped at Nick for a moment, and he feared he would have to follow Donnie, but she shook her head slightly and went back upfront.

The teacher spent the rest of the day on counting, the alphabet, and the history of their great state of Arizona, which had the third largest population of Native Americans. Mrs. Walters had a lot of rules, but not as many as Nick's father. School wasn't fun like his mother had said it would be—except for the part about the Indians. At recess, Nick stood alone with JJ, unsure of how to join the other kids' games. When the day ended, Nick packed up his things and went to the carpool line. He waited with the security guard until the last car was gone.

"Where's your ride?" the guard asked.

Nick shrugged. He was too upset to speak.

The guard shook his head, but his face was kind. "Wait right here, kid. I'm going to find someone from the principal's office to call your parents."

Nick nodded. As soon as the guard went inside, Nick ran toward home—or in the direction he thought was home. A pit bull barked at him from behind a fence then growled and butted its head against the gate, baring sharp teeth; three older boys pointed and laughed at him; a homeless man reeking of bad smells lunged at him, laughed hysterically, and ranted about someone he called the governor. Nick soiled his pants but made up his mind that from now on he would be like the brave Native Americans—a tracker who would kill his enemy.

When he reached home, his mother was sitting at the dining room table, reading her fortune-telling cards. She looked up, not at Nick but at the clock. "What are you doing?"

"You weren't there."

"How did you get home? I hope you didn't get in a stranger's car. You never get in a stranger's car."

"I waited for you, and then I walked home. A dog barked."

"Oh. I didn't realize how late it is. Well, you got home yourself. Good." She frowned. "What happened to your pants?"

"Nothing."

"Did you pee your pants again, Nick?"

He shrugged. "There was a dog and this man—"

"Damn it. Go take them off and put them with the dirty clothes. I'm sick of cleaning up after you." She went back to her tarot card reading. Just as Nick was about to go to his room to change his clothes, his mother called out to him, "Your father talked to me about JJ. You can't have an imaginary friend in school. Just like you can't pee your pants."

Nick stopped and looked around the corner. "JJ won't ever come back, Mommy. I scalped him dead."

CHAPTER 10

Margo must've dozed off, because the force of her own snoring woke her. "Is the rescue team here yet?" she asked Nick in a froggy voice.

"No."

Her arms were cramped from clinging to the blanket too tightly. She stretched them as she asked, "Do you have any idea how long it's been?"

"Just over three hours."

"They should've been here by now."

"I've been wondering if the train was due to stop at the next station."

"What makes you say that?"

"Trains don't always stop at every station. It's possible the train was scheduled to bypass the next junction if there were no passengers boarding or getting off. Which would mean the authorities might not even know the train crashed."

"The authorities have to know about the wreck," she said. "Everything is computerized these days. If people can hack into someone's refrigerator or sprinkler system, then a train certainly has software that can send out a distress signal. Not to mention that the engineer or conductor would've alerted someone with the railroad that the train was making an emergency stop. That we were running headlong into an avalanche."

"After I left the army, I became a consultant for private industry. Technology has its limitations. In this storm, I wouldn't be surprised if communication cut off before the avalanche occurred. I hope I'm wrong. Either way, we need to conserve our strength if we're going to make it through the night. You especially."

Before she could reply, he rose from his seat and began searching around the cabin.

"What are you looking for? Maybe I could help."

"Sit and save your energy. I'm looking for a flashlight or some flares."

"Flares would be great."

"Unfortunately, not the way you think. With the trees and the snow, a rescue squad couldn't see a flare a mile away. But we could use the flares for light and fire." He began rummaging through cabinets inside the kitchen area and out of the blue, he asked, "Why were you on the train?"

Was he trying to get her to talk so she'd take her mind off their dire situation? Or was he nosy? Maybe he was just making conversation? Whichever, it felt good to talk like normal people did. "My niece is getting married. I'm headed home for the wedding."

"A flight would've been easier. Much shorter."

"It's a short flight from Chicago to Spokane, true, but my doctor won't let me fly."

"So you took a jarring thirty-one-hour ride instead?"

She didn't appreciate his sarcasm, but she answered anyway. "My doctor said I could take the train. If I had a problem, I could get off. Where were you headed, Nick?"

"Seattle."

"And you live . . .?

"DC area. You must be close to your family for you to put yourself and the baby through the train ride."

"We are close," she lied.

They had been close, once. The kind of family that would take Sunday drives in their father's brown-and-banana-puke 1967 Ford Country Squire station wagon, paneled in wood—a car he'd owned since his youth.

"It's a classic," her father would proclaim. "It's got versatility and space that new cars don't. And it's safer than any new car on the road." Her father was obsessed with safety. He actually made and installed seatbelts for the back seats, even the far back, instead of spending the money to have them professionally fitted.

Cheap, she used to think. She was so embarrassed to be seen in that car. Several times during rides through the city, she'd duck below the windows so her friends couldn't see her.

After the third time, her mother pulled her aside and said, "You know your father didn't have much growing up. He joined the navy to get out of Tacoma, used it to get an education, and earned his PhD. I call that impressive for a man whose parents didn't even go to college, whose father made picture frames for a living. You should understand why he's so frugal."

Right now, Margo would've loved nothing more than a Sunday ride in that car.

Nick was still searching through the cabinets. "Brother's daughter or sister's daughter?"

"What?"

"Your niece's parent. You must have a sibling."

"I have two sisters. Heather is older. The younger one is Blanche."

"Are they both married with kids?"

A bitter taste formed in her mouth. "Heather is married; she has a daughter. That's the niece who's getting married."

"Just the one?"

"Yes. Blanche doesn't want children, or so she says. She's an engineer and loves her job. Why do you ask?"

He shrugged. "Your older sister is married and has a kid, and you're going to be a single mother. I wonder what that feels like."

How presumptuous. She wanted to call him out, but refrained from going too far—he'd saved her life. Yet, she had to draw boundaries. "I never said I wasn't married. Not that it's any of your concern."

He stopped what he was doing and took a step back. "No reason to get upset," he said. "It's not that hard to figure out."

Apparently the army had never taught him manners. But he was right. There was no man in her life.

He returned to the living area. "You know how I know? Not once have you mentioned a husband or a boyfriend."

"We've been too busy trying to survive to talk about that."

"Almost anyone in your situation would've mentioned it, would've said he'd be worried, upset. And the fact is, you still haven't denied that you're going to be a single mom."

She remained silent. It was no business of his if she chose to have a child when she had no husband or significant other.

"You think I've overstepped my bounds," he said.

"You *have* overstepped. What about you, Nick? You haven't mentioned a wife or a girlfriend. Why were you heading to Seattle?"

He regarded her with a look of amused condescension. "You should rest. Let's call it a night. I'll stay out here and keep watch."

She folded her arms across her upper chest. "Heading to Seattle to visit family, Nick?"

"I don't have a family. Is that what you wanted to hear?"

"Everyone has a family."

"Not me. They're all dead. Even those who still walk the earth."

"What's that supposed to mean?"

"Exactly what it sounds like. Anything else you want to know?"

She rose from her seat. "Take my blanket, Nick. I'm sure there are more on the bed."

He accepted the blanket and placed it on his lap. "Do you need some help getting to the back?" he asked. "It's dark."

"I'll be fine. Wake me if anything happens."

He nodded. "Wrap the blankets tight. Like a mummy."

She made her way to the bedroom compartment and maneuvered her large body underneath the sheet and comforter, pulling them over her head and wrapping them around her as Nick had suggested. Fatigue overwhelmed her, yet sleep didn't come. The howling wind and the rumbling and clapping of thunder kept her awake. So did the memory of Nick's behavior, the judgmental prick.

She thought of her family. Did they already know about the train's catastrophic loss? If so, they would believe that she'd perished along with the other passengers. Sure, they'd mourn her. They loved her in their way. Would they feel remorse for having stolen from her?

CHAPTER 11

The morning light seeped in through the edges of the bedroom curtains. The dawn always woke Margo, no matter how late she'd stayed up or how much she'd struggled to sleep the night before. She opened her eyes, and the reality of their dire situation rushed back in. She threw the covers back, sat up, and glanced around the private chambers. Luxurious, yes, but now hollow, mocking luxury. There was even a private lavatory, a godsend for a pregnant woman.

When the baby moved, the tension eased, but not the hunger pangs. Nick might be abrasive, but he was right to remind her that she had to keep up her strength for the baby's sake. When she tossed the covers aside, the chill inside the room assaulted her. She went to the living area. A blanket lay neatly folded on the couch. Nick was gone.

Why hadn't he awakened her to tell her he was leaving? Her heart beat faster. Where had he gone?

Shuffling from window to window, she tried to see out, but ice on the glass obscured her vision. She tried the back door. The handle turned, which meant that Nick had already loosened it when he left. She pushed the door open, looking for footprints but finding none. How quickly the snow blanketed the ground, obscuring every trace of humanity. Pale gray clouds hung low in the sky. The snowfall was light but endless.

A snowflake fluttered down and landed on her nose. In minutes, the sky darkened to an ominous gray, and the snowflakes began to clump. A strong gust of wind strummed the tree limbs as if they were guitar strings. She turned to go back inside, checking the ground to make sure she wouldn't trip—which was how she noticed the blood in the snow. But what kind of blood? Animal or human?

She shut the door and waddled to the kitchen to find something to eat. A tray holding a single envelope sat on the counter. She opened the envelope, maybe because the contents would make her feel as if she were in contact with the outside world. The note, in the seller's own handwriting, revealed that the passenger car was being delivered to a customer. The note gave Margo hope. Scores of people, some rich and powerful, would wonder what had happened to the train. She placed the note down on the tray.

A wave of guilt overwhelmed her. All those dead passengers, not to mention the hundreds of grieving friends and family and coworkers. Why had she and Nick survived? How unfair. She caught herself. She had one obligation—to survive and save her baby. She couldn't mourn the others. Not yet.

She began opening cabinets, looking for sustenance. The kitchen was stocked with dishes and utensils but no food. She tried turning on the faucet over the sink—no water. If there ever was water, the tank was now frozen. Or maybe the lines had broken. She twisted the knob on the stovetop—no heat. No surprise. If the stove had worked, Nick surely would've made that discovery last night.

She returned to the living area, sat down on the couch, and, wrapped in a blanket that didn't come close to staving off the cold, waited. She wished she didn't need Nick so much, but she did. To pass the time, she blew vapor rings in the air, a silly game that reminded her of when her mother bought home candy cigarettes for the kids. She and Heather pretended to smoke, feeling like sophisticated actresses. That fun ended when their father caught them. He deplored the idea of his daughters consuming sugar and pretending to ingest nicotine.

"Line them up, Isadora," their father had said in a raised voice.

Then he gave a lecture on the evils of smoking and on the agony of tooth decay.

The Fletcher girls often heard those three little words—*line them up!* The lectures were bad enough, because they were not in fact lectures but berating sessions. Worse, their mother was also a target. Even as a young girl, Margo understood that her father was humiliating her mother. Not until she became an adult did she understand that her mother tolerated his behavior to protect her daughters. That was what mothers did—protect their children at all costs. That was what Margo would do with the child she was carrying.

Sometimes her mother would push back, however, and Margo would feel pride. Using her charms as a Southern belle, her mother would say in a gentle tone, "The girls are only having fun, Anthony. They're children, not sailors to be commanded. Not everything in life runs with mathematical precision."

But their father treated them as mathematical components anyway. As a statistician, he worshipped numbers, certainty, and the rational. Instinct and intuition were dirty words. Sucking on candy cigarettes that could rot your teeth and teach you bad habits wasn't rational behavior.

When Margo was a sophomore in high school, her father opened her purse and discovered an unopened pack of real cigarettes. She was tempted to blame her friend Bree for sneaking them in there, but that would've been a lie. She had gotten them from Bree, but she'd asked for them. So she informed her father with teenage bravado.

"For your insolence, you'll sleep in a tent outside for the rest of the week," her father had said. "Until the smoke and tar and nicotine are purged from your body." Never mind that the pack was unopened, proving she hadn't tried a single one.

Despite her mother's pleas, Margo did sleep in the backyard for the remainder of the week. Of course it rained. She had to use the hose pipe as a makeshift shower. That was humiliating enough, but the worst of the punishment was the survival-kit potty. Now, as Margo sat in this orphaned train car, she wished she'd learned a lot more about camping out.

The wind and snow pounded against the walls in a broken rhythm, like the sound of a deranged psychiatric patient beating his head and fists against the walls of a padded cell. The train car rocked with the wind, sometimes violently. Occasionally, the sound of tree limbs arching and cracking rose above the howl of the wind. The snow's weight tested the limits of the trees.

At last, there were footsteps on the back stairs. The door opened. Nick was carrying a plastic bag in one hand. His upper cheeks were scarlet from too much exposure to the cold and, through his thick day-after beard, a deep scar on his left cheek and another small one in the middle of his forehead stood out. Odd that the scars hadn't been noticeable when they first spoke on the train. She hadn't considered his age before this. From his present appearance, sun damage and elemental exposure aside, he was likely in his mid to late forties.

"Are you all right?" she asked.

He nodded and walked inside the room with a soldier's rigid gait, obviously trying to avoid limping. He went into the kitchen and put the bag in the sink. He shook his arms and shoulders, causing the remnants of snow to fall from his coat.

Before she could ask about the bag, she noticed that his left pants leg was ripped at the seams. Underneath, his calf was covered with a white cloth.

She rose from the couch and started toward him. "You're bleeding. You should've told me last night."

"I'm fine."

"Let me take a look at it."

"I've already dressed it. It's nothing."

She stood before him with hands on her hips. "You've said that one too many times. I insist."

"If it'll make you feel better, take a look." At the kitchen table, he raised his pants leg. A cloth was wrapped around the lower calf and secured it with a string he must've found inside the car.

"Is that a whipping knot?" she asked.

"Yeah. It allows the leg to bend. How did you know?"

"Sailors use it. Mostly with ropes. I've done some sailing in my day."

He didn't grimace as she removed the soiled cloth stuck to his leg. Under the bandaging, he presented with a four-inch laceration to the outer leg—a sheer tear, almost like a knife wound. There were smaller lacerations that appeared to be bite marks.

"I thought coyotes don't attack humans," she said.

"As far as coyote behavior goes, generally they don't attack unless they're hungry. And, in this cold, I'm sure food is scarce." He took a deep breath.

Infection and rabies were the biggest concern. There was no way to deal with those issues now. He must already have considered these possibilities. No need to reiterate the obvious.

"The wound needs sutures," she said. "The laceration is long, and you don't want to rip it any more than it is. I could tear out a seam on a couch pillow and use the thread. I just have to find something to substitute as a needle."

"Negative. If you'll get a clean towel, let's wrap it up for now. It's not that bad."

Manly patients were a dime a dozen in the ER. They weren't easy to persuade, so the worst approach was to argue with them, because they only dug in harder when pushed. If he didn't want stitches, so be it. He'd reconsider if the injury worsened, of that she was sure.

"You're the patient," she said.

Without responding, he sat with folded arms and an annoyed expression. What appointment was he late for? She re-bandaged the leg. The procedure must've hurt, but he showed no sign of pain. Only when she finished did he let out a long sigh of relief.

A new sort of rumbling sounded in the distance—the wind?

Nick bolted out of his chair, walked to the kitchen sink, and retrieved the plastic bag he'd brought inside the car. He reached under a cabinet and found a frying pan. From another drawer, he found silver-ware. He shoved the items inside the bag and started out of the kitchen.

"What's wrong, Nick?"

"We're no longer safe here. Grab a blanket and whatever else you can carry. And I mean for a long trek."

The rumbling grew louder and louder and turned to a low decibel roar, as if a wave had crashed onshore. The sound was decidedly *not* thunder, because it didn't stop.

A spike of electricity shot up Margo's spine.

"The mountain is completely unstable," he said. "Avalanches are happening all over the place. We've got to leave now."

She began to shake uncontrollably. "No. It has to be safer in here than outside."

He bent down and firmly gripped her arms. "We have to go. Now. It's not a choice."

"You're hurting me."

"Margo, listen to me."

She didn't move; she needed to think, to calculate the odds.

"We're sitting right below a massive horizontal plane of snow," he continued. "It's coming down any minute—any second, as a matter of fact. If that happens, and we're inside here, we're going down the mountain just like the train."

"Give me a minute to think!"

"Quiet. Sound is a factor."

The rumbling intensified, and still she stood paralyzed. He gently but firmly pulled her toward the door. When they passed the couch, he grabbed the blanket, and when they reached the door, he yanked it open. As soon as they were outside, the cold attacked them. Vibrations reverberated through their bodies, the sensation coming at them from everywhere and nowhere. Margo tried to breathe, but the air was beginning to fog with a fine white powder, which burned her lungs when she inhaled. She coughed, trying to catch her breath.

Not missing a beat, Nick reached for the hood of her coat, pulled it up and around her face, and secured the toggles tight so her nose and mouth were covered.

"Come over to the stairs. I'm going down first." He let go of her and jumped to the ground. "Hold your arms out to the side and jump. I've got you."

She was tempted to retreat back inside the train car, her safe haven. Her father's face flashed through her mind, as it always did when she needed to make crucial decision and didn't know what to do. What would her father have calculated now? Never mind what he'd do. This was all instinct—hers.

CHAPTER 12

M argo stood on the platform, looking between the snowy ground and Nick. He motioned for her to jump. Walking down was too hazardous; there could be ice underneath the snow on the steps. The jump was about five feet, doable even a few months ago. Not now. With her pregnant belly and bloated limbs, she might as well have been leaping from the top floor of a skyscraper. The wind, honed by the bitter cold, sliced through the air. The dull rumbling nearby continued to build. A sudden crackling, like eggshells breaking in a boiling pot, reverberated through the canyon, the sound out of place and menacing. White talcum flooded the air, becoming thicker by the second.

Without further thought, she held out her arms and took that leap of faith. Nick caught her under the armpits and stopped her from falling. When he let go, she almost lost her balance but managed to right herself. Tiny ice crystals stung her eyes and cheeks. She blinked hard and bent her head down, trying to shield her face.

Taking one of her hands, Nick led her along the outside of the tracks and toward the rear of the passenger car. The rumbling intensified, propelling her along as fast as she could go. Moving away from the passenger car, their no-longer-safe haven, they followed what appeared to be the path of the railway tracks—away from the train wreck. With each step, she sank almost knee-deep into the snow, sometimes going so deep that she touched a railroad tie with the sole of her boot. The wind shifted and blew in their faces, the gusts so ferocious that she was forced to lean forward to prevent a fall. Nick kept shouting over his shoulder, urging her on. He didn't have to. Although her lungs burned and she was gasping for breath, nothing could stop her. Her mind swirled as if lost in an indiscernible dream in which she was a bird with a broken wing trying to fly, trying to escape a would-be predator's jaws.

When Nick slowed, she caught her breath well enough to shout, "Where are we going?"

"To safety."

She prayed such a place existed in this wilderness, because it looked as if they were heading toward oblivion. They plowed ahead. Nick quickened the pace again, and the pain in her chest and legs intensified, but it also served an important purpose—the pain reminded her that she was still alive.

A loud boom, like a cannon shot, assaulted them from behind. She didn't dare look back. Nick picked up the pace and shouted for her to hurry. She found a hidden reserve of energy that let her go faster. Fear could be an effective fuel.

She pushed forward but, after going five to ten yards at most, she tripped on a raised railroad tie or a large rock and fell to her knees. Without Nick's help, she regained her footing and continued on. Then a wave of terror hit her having nothing to do with this new and unexpected avalanche—well, nothing directly. She couldn't remember the last time she'd felt the baby move. *The baby's fine*, she told herself, repeating the mantra over and over. *The baby is fine.*

Muscle fatigue turned to muscle failure. She stumbled several times. She began to cough.

"Inhale through your nose," Nick called out without looking back. "Exhale through your mouth. Saves energy."

The avalanche was rapidly approaching, its roar no longer a dull rumble but rather an agonizing groan, as if the entire mountain were in unbearable pain. Was it possible for a human being to outrun a vicious, soulless giant?

They started around a bend in the tracks. She had to look back, to stare death down. When she glanced over her shoulder, there was nothing but white. No trees. No sky. No ground. Not a trace of the passenger car. Only white, a void. The snowy mountain had devoured everything.

"Hurry!" Nick shouted. "We're almost there."

She tried to run to *there*. Where was there? A place Nick had made up to spare her the agony of accepting their impending death, to keep her hopes up until the last possible second?

He urged her forward, and by the time they staggered around the curve, the dense fog of white gave way to a light haze. The white particles were dissipating.

"Over there!" Nick shouted, pointing with his free hand. "The snowshed."

Could it be? Safety at last.

Fifty yards ahead was a railroad tunnel that resembled an enormous, metallic carport with a slanted roof. In all the flurry, they accelerated their pace—a mistake. She stumbled and went down to her knees, jarring every organ inside. The impact pounded the air from her lungs.

Whumph!

That ominous sound again. The taunt of thousands and thousands of tons of frozen powder about to slide down the mountain and bury them propelled her back on her feet. She took a step, but, damn it all, she tripped again.

Nick helped her stand and without warning swept her off her feet as if she were a slender child. He carried her toward safety, half-jogging and half-sliding. A loud clap of thunder boomed, competing with the roar of the avalanche. They'd never make it to the shed. There wasn't time now. A white mass of snow slid toward them, creating a massive wall that was littered with broken tree trunks and branches and boulders, all of which were being tossed about like toys in a sandbox.

She turned her head away—there was no reason to pay homage to their executioner.

The snowshed was too far away. No way could they outrun the avalanche.

Please, God, make it painless. Don't let my baby be impaled by a broken limb or survive longer than I do, entombed in my lifeless body.

Nick abruptly stopped running and set her down. Clinging to her hand, he pulled her from the railroad tracks and down the right-of-way embankment, not *away* from the avalanche but *toward* it.

"What the fuck are you doing?" she screamed.

"Trying to save our lives!"

Then she understood. Going in this direction was their only chance to avoid being thrown into the gulch. They took four more steps before the first wave of snow struck them like a wrecking ball, knocking them to the ground. She lost her grip on Nick's hand.

"Swim on your back uphill!" he called out. She tried to swim, windmilling her arms, but she was soon buried under snow. Her head throbbed. She gasped for breath.

The image of her unborn child flashed through her mind. She wished she'd found out the gender. A moment later, her body felt weightless, not buried under tons of snow but suspended in pure white light. She was no longer cold, no longer shivering. Was she dead, was this a dream? Would she wake in the viewing car of the train, freshen up at the next stop, and get ready to face her family? The baby moved. She wasn't dreaming.

Snow surrounded her entire body. She was buried alive! How long had she been like this? Sheer panic gripped her. She couldn't breathe. No, wait. Yes, she could. How was that possible? Because the hood of her coat had created a temporary air pocket. The same was true with the mounds of snow. There were plenty of pockets inside the snow, which wasn't solid like cement. She stilled a moment. Though she was encased in snow, she could hear sounds—not the mountain's rumble, but the crackle of snowflakes settling. If that was true, really true, she couldn't be that far from the surface. Swimming on her back uphill had kept her closer to the surface! Giving her a chance to survive.

She flexed her muscles without moving her limbs. Nothing seemed to be broken. She shut her eyes tight and pushed her arms up and away from her body. The only way out was to dig. As she pushed, her knuckles bumped against something rough. The object was only a foot, maybe two feet, away. She groped at it—the thick, scaly bark of a fallen tree. With her hands and fingers, she dug and clawed at the snow until she determined that the width of the tree was about two feet. She twisted and turned her torso, hollowing out the snow around her. Then she bent her knees, pushed against some compacted snow, and hoisted her body closer to the trunk, which she grasped with both hands. Little by little, she pulled with her arms and moved her knees back and forth until her feet were resting against the trunk. Her limbs became the new branches of the tree. She pushed upward and began to follow the line of the tree trunk toward the surface, careful to avoid the splintering shards from broken branches. Inch by inch, she moved higher along the trunk. The snow beneath the tree wasn't as compact, so it was easier to move through. She climbed upward five or more feet and finally broke free of this grave and into the gray light of the day. She inhaled deeply, savoring the sting of the frigid air. She was so exhausted, so shaken, she could do no more than crawl. But she'd never been happier to crawl in her life. The air was clear, and a fresh blanket of snow covered the landscape for as far as the eye could see.

Nick—where was he?

"Nick? Can you hear me? Nick?"

There was no sign of him. In a frenzy, she began kicking the snow. Realizing the futility of the act, she dropped to her knees and with cupped hands dug down a couple of feet, all the while shouting his name. He must've been buried close to where she was.

She paused to think. There must be a better way. A bird chirped nearby; she recognized the call of a chickadee. How peculiar that anything had survived the avalanche, although she had. She turned and saw the bird pecking at an exposed branch of a downed tree, probably because she'd lost her nest. How sad but also inspiring, because now

Margo knew what to do. She quickly began searching for something she could use to peck at the snow. Not far from where she had been buried, she found a four-foot branch with a sharp point at one end. With it, she began poking the stick into the ground, hoping to locate Nick.

"Nick!" she shouted.

Unexpectedly, one of his hands reached through the white mass.

"Oh, thank God."

She dropped the stick and dug out the snow around his hand. A few moments later, his other hand broke through. She continued to dig until reaching the top of his head, which was covered by his coat. He must've pulled it above his head at the last minute to create a makeshift hood with its own pocket of air. Otherwise, he would've suffocated. She worked until he was able to use his own arms and hands to unearth himself.

When he broke free, he rolled onto the snow. He collapsed down to his back and closed his eyes, presumably taking a moment to breathe a sigh of relief. Then he reached inside his coat and with some difficulty pulled out the plastic bag, the contents of which were still a mystery. Hell, the contents of Nick's entire psyche were a mystery.

CHAPTER 13

By age thirteen Nick had achieved the independence his father had demanded of him at the start of first grade. It had been four years since he'd relied upon his parents to prepare his lunches or send him to bed or to do much of anything for him. He rode his bike to school and ran around the neighborhood as if it were an adventure board game and he was the ace player. Even at this young age, he distrusted others, especially his own parents—which explained why he had no friends. Oh, kids wanted Nick to be their friend. He was a good athlete, smart, and a leader. But he chose not to let anyone get close. Friends made life too complicated. Still, he knew where every kid lived and what all the families were like—who went to the Catholic church, who went to the Baptist church, who went to the town's one synagogue, who believed in God, and who didn't believe in anything but a bottle of Jack Daniel's. He knew which parents coddled their kids, which beat their kids like his did, and which did worse. He knew which kids were liars, which were naïve, which were brave, and which were wimps. Knowing about people's secrets was more than just power; it was like touring the proverbial sausage factory.

Nobody knew Nick's secrets. He made sure of that.

Nick did keep that first kid he met, Donnie Hollis, around though. But Donnie was a friend in the way a dog was a friend—you kept them around for companionship and sometimes protection. The kid could be unintentionally amusing; he was, in a canine way, blindly loyal to Nick, and in a pinch, loyalty was something Nick could use to his benefit. Nick also kept Donnie around for another reason: Nick's father hated Donnie and his family, and Nick liked nothing more than to defy his father.

"The Hollis family is bad news," Nick's father had told him at the start of first grade. "The father is a criminal. Served five years in the state penitentiary for armed robbery. The son is only seven and is already following in his father's footsteps. Stay away from Donnie Hollis."

When Nick's father caught Nick talking to Donnie one day after school, the belt had come out, which only made Nick more determined to hang out with the kid. Now, in eighth grade, Donnie was at best a clown and at worst a pain in the butt. Last year, he'd been suspended from school for smoking cigarettes in the boys' bathroom. By the start of the following year, the kid had graduated to weed. In short, Donnie was still a loser.

"Hey, Nick," Donnie said. "I got a new video game. Come on over. We can hang out and play it."

"I've got homework," Nick said. "If I don't get it done, my father will freak." Never mind that Nick's father hated the educational system. God forbid if Nick ever flunked a test and embarrassed his parents. Besides, knowing Donnie, that video game was stolen property.

"You're such a dweeb, Nick."

"You try living with my father."

Donnie chortled. "At least yours isn't in the pen."

Nick thought, but didn't say, that he wished his father were locked up in some prison. Instead, he asked, "Do you miss him?"

Donnie shrugged. "Nah." But his face got all screwed up, as if he'd been struck with a bout of indigestion.

"Hey, if you got some Cokes at your house, I'll come over," Nick said. Nick not only wanted a Coca-Cola; he also wanted to check out Donnie's mother, who was hot and often indifferent about modesty.

Donnie raised a single eyebrow. "We could sneak a few." Then he laughed wickedly.

They went the seven blocks across the parkway to Donnie's place, a run-down house in the bad part of town. Nick's father passed by the place on his way home from work, so Nick hid his bike behind the bushes in case his father came home early, which wouldn't be unusual. There would be a price to pay if his father caught him at the Hollis house.

The two boys walked into the kitchen through the back entrance, a screen door that hung precariously loose on its hinges and was patched in places with silver duct tape. Donnie's mother was sitting at the kitchen table reading the *National Enquirer*. She had the television tuned to a gossipy talk show, with the volume turned up way too high.

When the screen door slammed shut, Mrs. Hollis lowered the paper and said, "Hey, honey darlin'. You have a good day at school, sweetheart?"

Donnie nodded.

Mrs. Hollis pointed to the television. "Turn that TV down, honey. I can't stand those commercials." Donnie lumbered over to the television and adjusted the volume.

Nick, who had been standing in the doorway, walked farther inside the room. Despite the time of day, Mrs. Hollis was dressed in a lime-green, gauzy nightgown and fuzzy slippers, as if she were a character in one of her soap operas. Nick's own mother wore an oversized T-shirt and sweatpants to bed, but Mrs. Hollis's nightgown was all lacey and short, exposing her legs up to her mid-thighs. Nick snuck more than a peek. If Mrs. Hollis noticed, she didn't care.

"Come give Momma a hug and some sugar, son," she said to Donnie, holding her arms out wide.

"Mom, I've got a friend here," he replied, his pale cheeks turning red.

"Oh, you can always hug your momma," she said. "How are you, Nick? My goodness, how you've grown. You're such a handsome young man. I bet Nick wants a hug." Without waiting for a response, she rose and wrapped her arms around Nick, who felt himself blush and tingle.

Mrs. Hollis laughed and took her seat. "I'll start supper in a bit, Donnie. We're having macaroni and cheese."

"Cool," Donnie said.

She looked at Nick. "You can stay for dinner if you like, sweetheart."

"No thank you, ma'am," Nick said. "My mother is expecting me home. And I have homework. I'll just stay a little while."

"Homework," she said, glancing sidelong at Donnie. "You hear that, Don? Nick has always been such a smart boy. That's because he works at it. You could be just as smart as him if you worked at it."

Donnie frowned. Both boys realized that no matter how hard Donnie worked, he could never be as smart as Nick. Donnie led Nick away from his mother's too-gooey spider's web. Nick took another quick glance at Mrs. Hollis's thighs, and the boys sprinted to Donnie's room. A fluffy black cat was sitting in the middle of his bed.

"Get off!" Donnie shouted at the cat. "You're getting fur everywhere, you dickwad."

"I didn't know you had a cat." Nick reached a hand out to pet the cat. The cat shot a paw out and scratched Nick's forearm, drawing blood.

Nick pulled his arm back. Though the scratch hurt, he forced himself not to show pain. He'd become good at hiding pain.

Donnie flung the cat from the bed. "You think that's bad, the little fucker scratched me when I was sleeping two nights ago. Fuck, I hate him."

"I see why, man."

"No shit. Try living with all that hair and piss. And the litter box where he takes a dump, don't even start on that. I'd like to skin the little shithead alive and feed him to the rats."

Nick studied Donnie's face for any sign of sarcasm or hyperbole. He found none. "Why don't you do it, then?"

"I'm thinking about it, dude."

Just as Nick thought. Donnie didn't have the guts.

"Hey, you watch wrestling?" Donnie asked.

Nick glanced around the room. "Nah. My dad's got all these rules. He doesn't like wrestling."

"That sucks. Maybe you ought to skin *him* alive."

"I'm thinking about it."

Donnie flashed an awkward smile, but there was worry in his eyes.

"I was joking, man," Nick said. Not that the idea didn't appeal to him. Nick had more than once lost skin when his father hit him. "Hey, what about those drinks?"

"Okay, I'll be right back." Donnie left the room and returned with two cans of soda in his pants pockets. He handed one to Nick, who popped the tab and took a long drink, savoring all the sugary bubbles.

"You look like you've never tasted a soda."

"Only a few times. My parents don't approve. They think it's poison. A corporate conspiracy to weaken the masses. A way to gouge the American working class."

"Shit. Your parents are weird. And cheap."

Nick agreed but resented Donnie for saying so. He took another swig of his drink as he thought about his father, not enjoying the soda quite as much. It was dangerous for Nick to step out of line, and he was tired of being his father's punching bag. He couldn't wait to finish school and leave his parents behind.

"What are you going to do when you grow up?" Nick asked. He'd never asked Donnie this before. Maybe it had not occurred to him until now that Donnie would even grow up.

"I want to be a wrestler. What about you, dickwad?"

Nick took a swallow of his drink instead of punching Donnie. He'd learned long ago that the best way to stay out of trouble, to get what you wanted, was to suppress the impulse to give in to anger right away. Retaliation could wait. Although, he'd fought Donnie once, but only after Donnie had attacked him. Donnie thought Nick and two other boys had been laughing at him, which was only in part true, because the other boys had been. After Nick bloodied Donnie's nose and used his superior speed and reflexes to body-slam Donnie to the ground, the older boy tapped out. He didn't challenge Nick after that; on the contrary, he tried harder to be Nick's friend. But this confrontation resulted in a lesson most bullies had already learned—no one should cross Nick Eliot.

"So?" Donnie asked.

"I'm joining the army."

"Why, man? You want to go around shooting and killing people?"

"Yeah. I do."

"Or get your ass shot off? My dad was in the army. Got kicked out. They got a lot of rules. You have to say, yes, sir, I'll shine your boots, lick the floor, kiss your ass, whatever you say, sir." Donnie laughed. "I'd rather be kicking someone's butt in the ring."

"All that's fake, anyway."

Donnie's face turned red. "No, it isn't."

Nick shrugged.

Donnie's mother knocked on the bedroom door.

"Donnie, it's time for dinner, baby." She pushed the door open. "Your friend can come back another day. I called his mother to see if he could stay, but she said to send him right on home." She looked at Nick. "Maybe next time. I'm real sorry, honey."

Nick's anger rose. Mrs. Hollis wasn't the only one who was sorry.

Later that week, Donnie told Nick that the Hollis's black cat had disappeared. Nobody knew why.

"That's terrible," Nick said. "I didn't think you had the guts."

"Fuck you, Nick!" Donnie said and stormed away.

CHAPTER 14

Nick lay prone on the frigid ground, gazing up at Margo with empty eyes. His light hair and beard were white with snow, and for a moment she wondered if he'd actually died in the disaster.

Was she only imagining that he'd survived? That *she*'d survived?

He moved, took a few deep breaths, rolled onto his stomach, and struggled to get up on all fours. The wind had relented for now, as if it, too, had been swept away by the avalanche. The air was still filled with white particulates, and the snowfall persisted. Strangely enough, Margo felt warmer. The act of surviving had many unforeseen benefits, apparently.

How had they lived through this avalanche? She knew how. Nick had led them down the embankment and inside its protective pocket. Otherwise they would've been tossed over the cliffs when that raging wave of snow struck. He had also told her to swim against the snow, which somehow had kept her closer to the surface. The man was brilliant, or lucky, or a little bit of both. No, a lot of both.

"Are you hurt?" she asked.

He shook his head. "You?"

She felt a thrill at the sound of another human voice. "I think I'm fine."

He got to his feet and stood on wobbly legs. "We have to get off this fresh snow. It's unstable."

They walked east, away from the avalanche site. It was hard going whenever they hit a patch of soft, deep snow. At least they were no longer running for their lives. All the while, he carried his plastic bag.

"We should head toward the highway," she said. "That's where we'll find civilization, maybe the rescue team."

"Impossible in this weather. It's miles away. We couldn't make it even if we were both in top form. You're not, and now I'm not."

"Why not go as far as we can? If we follow the tracks, we'll surely meet up with the rescue team. They have to know about the wreck by now."

"No one is anywhere close to here, even if they've figured out what's happened, which isn't a given."

"But a helicopter or a search plane."

"We're in a mountain forest. A major blizzard is obscuring visibility, the train wreckage is completely covered up. As to us, we're like straight pins in a shag carpet. No one in the air wouldn't be able to see us unless they were directly overhead. But whether they can or can't doesn't matter at the moment. There's more snow coming. Our only option is to wait out the storm in a safe place."

She looked at the sky. The clouds no longer seemed so ominous, and there were actually large patches of blue beginning to appear. But the absolute certitude and command of Nick's voice stopped her from questioning his judgment. He hadn't been wrong yet.

"Where?" she asked. "That shed you were taking us to is buried under snow, if not totally crushed under the weight."

"Somewhere safe. I'll know it when I see it."

At first blush, it seemed like an absurd comment. But she'd come to trust him.

He took the lead, helping her over the tougher obstacles and through heavy snowdrifts. They didn't travel far before his limp returned.

"Nick, your leg. Let me take another look."

"It's nothing. Like I keep telling you. Don't mention it again."

She wanted to insist, but when he turned around and looked at her, she recoiled at his uncompromising glare. He took two steps toward her, scanned the area, and pointed.

"See it?" he asked.

She nodded. A steel roof protruded above the snow—the far end of the snow shed's roof. Unbelievable—part of the structure had actually survived the avalanche. "I can't believe it's still standing. And above ground."

"Salt-box design. The slanted roof directs rain and snow to slide over the metal surface and drop into the gulch below."

They trudged to the entrance, which was almost completely blocked except for a small opening above the level of the snow. Nature had formed a ramp, which led up to the opening.

"Wait here," he said. He climbed up the slope, lay down on the ground, and began kicking at the snow. Soon the opening was wide enough for them to get inside.

He returned to her and extended a hand. She placed hers in his, and he helped her up the snowy ramp.

At the opening, she asked, "Is it safe in there? You don't think the roof will collapse, do you?"

"It's built to withstand the weight of snow."

"This much?"

"That's the idea."

She peered inside the shed, able to see because of the light seeping in between the slats on the outer wall that faced the gulch. Thankfully, the integrity of the structure appeared intact and undamaged. Even better, the interior looked dry. Beds of rocks lined each side of the railway tracks. But the cliff side of the tracks was only two feet from the outer wall and not far from the mountain's edge. She shuddered at how close to the drop-off the shed was located.

"We stay on the side closest to the mountain. It'll be fine."

She recalled a silly movie she'd seen years ago about an asteroid striking earth and wiping out all of humanity, leaving behind only nature. At the moment, it sure felt as if she and Nick and this tunnel were the only remaining artifacts of human civilization. A lot could be said about the shed and mankind's ingenuity.

He helped her climb inside the shed and down to the ground. It was warmer in there. But the wind howling through the cracks was loud and haunting—louder than the sounds outside.

"Now what?" she asked.

"We need to build a fire before it gets dark. I'm going to gather wood and twigs."

"I'll go with you."

"It's too dangerous. You'll only slow me down."

"You have an injured leg. You need help, and besides it's really my choice."

He stared into her eyes and then looked down at her belly. "Is it your choice?"

She reflexively rubbed a hand over her abdomen.

"I'll be back soon," he said and, without waiting for a response, walked away.

Now alone, she felt like a kind of prisoner—not because she lacked the freedom to go where she wanted but because she lacked the stamina. The light faded in and out. When it dimmed, she looked toward the entrance. The sky, once filled with splotches of blue, was now beginning to cloud over and had turned a darker shade of gray. The air was getting colder. She walked around to warm up, but it didn't do much good.

"Where the hell is the rescue squad?" she cried. Her voice echoed against the metal walls. She hadn't screamed with such force since she was sixteen years old and attending a picnic on the river hosted by her father's university. An abandoned snowshed and her father's faculty picnic—what an odd connection to make. Or maybe not so odd. Because on each occasion, she feared her life was over.

CHAPTER 15

Even at the ripe old age of sixteen, Margo was still excited to attend her father's annual university picnic at Riverfront Park. The event, for faculty and their families only, was always held in early September, just before classes began. Almost always, the weather was still warm, and she looked forward to all the planned activities—badminton, softball, and without question the whitewater rafting. Not only was the event fun, but it also marked one of the few occasions when their father seemed to bend some of the rules, if only slightly. Was this because he enjoyed the picnic or because Professor Anthony Fletcher didn't want to play the martinet in front of his peers?

On that day, he pulled the old Country Squire into the lot parking lot and stopped near the attendant, a young blond woman wearing cutoff jeans and a halter top.

"Hi, Professor Fletcher," the woman said in a German accent. "Go to the third row, make a right, and take the end spot by the woods. The shade will keep the car cool."

"Thank you, Ms. Stuhlmeyer," their father said.

Margo wanted to hide under the seat. She was riding in the way back next to her little sister, Blanche. Greta Stuhlmeyer was their father's graduate student, a mathematical whiz. Not only was Greta brilliant and really pretty, but she was nice. Margo liked her. She didn't act snooty or nervous like a lot of the other students. She was at the park now because the grad students got to work the picnic grounds in exchange for the right to hobnob with the faculty.

Their father gave a perfunctory wave to Greta then pulled the car around to the parking space.

"I'm going to get a halter top like Greta's," she whispered to her older sister, Heather. "The boys will love it."

"You'll do no such thing!" their father said. "No daughter of mine is going to dress like a slut while she's living under my roof."

Margo couldn't believe she'd overheard.

"Oh, Anthony, stop," their mother said. "She's a teenager. It's just talk. Leave her alone." What a surprise that Margo's mother had come to her defense.

They parked the car and went to the gathering. Margo didn't have to hang around her parents or sisters. She found some friends and was having a great time. But just as she was about to go river rafting, her mother called her over.

"Margo, honey, do me a favor. Go back to the car and get my purse. I left it under the front seat."

"Why can't Heather go?" Margo asked.

"Because I asked you to," her mother replied.

Margo groaned and then sprinted to the station wagon, determined not to miss the bus taking the kids over to the river-rafting site. She got to the station wagon and was about to reach for the door handle when she froze. A shrill gasp and a deep groan emanated from the car's interior, as if someone were hurt and in pain. Jarring horror-movie clips began flickering across her field of vision, as if she were watching a damaged film that had been cut and re-edited. Was she witnessing a murder? No, not that. Large, full breasts flapped up and down and hit the seat. Her father's flat, bare, old-man's ass—how did she know it was *his* ass?—bounced crazily, as though he were playing some silly game of leapfrog, only he was missing his jumps. Her father was bouncing off the backside of the girl, not just any girl, but Greta, his graduate student. That halter top that Margo had so admired lay over the bench of the front seat. What? No. How stupid her dignified father appeared. So fucking stupid. Disgusting. The groans of those strangers inside their family car rose an octave.

She wanted to cry, to scream, to murder them both. She wanted to run away. Instead, she steeled herself and calmly walked over to the front passenger side door, inserted the key, and opened the door. She got her mother's bag from underneath the seat without looking back.

"Margo." It was her father's voice but not any father she recognized.

"Mom forgot her purse," she said and shut the door.

She raced back to the picnic area, tossed her mother's purse on the picnic table, which was set to perfection, and she kept running until she was two blocks out of the park. At an intersection, she screamed so loudly and so long that she stopped traffic.

She'd been saddled with her father's duplicity for the rest of her life. She didn't tell her mother, didn't tell anyone, because it would've been her word against her father's, and her father's word had been, and to this day still was, the law. And even if her family had believed her, wouldn't the consequences have been worse? She would've broken up her family, and Blanche was so young. How could she do that to her sister? How could she break her mother's heart? And so she became an involuntary co-conspirator in her father's infidelity—his crime—and had remained silent all these years.

Now, imprisoned in this snowshed, Margo felt the same kind of deep rage at her circumstances—lost, defenseless, and devastated by life's unfairness. She picked up a rock and hurled it at the wall as hard as she could. The sharp ping reverberated throughout the tunnel. She picked up another and threw that one too. Then she screamed in frustration. She was filled with a combination of anger, fear, guilt, and the desire to run as hard and as fast as she could to get away from this place. The baby shifted along the front of her belly.

Protect the baby.

She wrapped her arms around her stomach and started singing "I See the Moon," an old lullaby her mother sang to her and her sisters:

Over the mountain, over the sea,
Back where my heart is longing to be
Oh, let the light that shines on me . . .

What she would give to hear her mother's voice again.

There was a crunching in the snow near the shed's entrance. She turned, expecting to see Nick. Instead, a scrawny but large male coyote padded inside, his head down, his ears back, and his teeth bared.

Adrenaline fired through her veins. She stifled a scream. Show no fear, she told herself. She looked for a stick, a shard of metal from the tracks, anything she could use as a weapon—rocks! She bent over and, as quietly as she could, filled her coat pockets. She stood and threw a rock at the animal, not coming close to hitting it. The coyote growled and advanced. She raised her arms, waved them wildly, and shouted at the animal, hoping to frighten him into retreat.

The coyote approached cautiously but with a look of predatory determination.

She wasn't about to let a crazed animal harm her unborn baby. Rearing back, she threw another rock, which missed but came close enough that the animal veered away slightly. She hurled more rocks and screamed at the animal. Her screams came reflexively now. The coyote didn't leave but instead turned in a circle and confronted her again. She stomped a foot and hurled another rock, this time hitting him on the snout. The animal yelped, then hopped back and to the side.

Some of the rocks made contact but most of them fell to the ground. She was angry, not only because of the coyote, but also because she might not survive out in this wilderness even if she got rid of the animal. She was so goddamn angry.

The next rock struck the coyote in the head. The animal yelped, arched its back, and turned around but, to her chagrin, he circled back. He was bleeding. When she saw the blood, she let loose with another stone barrage. Still the coyote wouldn't flee. He was thin, and there was drool around his muzzle. Coyotes rarely attacked humans, Nick had told her, which meant that this one was probably rabid. Or desperately in need of food. She reached into her pocket to reload but found that she'd run out of ammunition. When she bent over to scoop up more rocks, the animal charged. Her hands scraped across the ground until she found another rock. She straightened just as the animal was upon her. Before she could throw the rock, the coyote lunged and sunk its teeth into her coat. The animal yanked and growled. Using her free hand, she hit him in the face with a rock. He wouldn't loosen his grip, wouldn't go down. As strong as the animal was, she wouldn't go down either, wouldn't expose her neck to his teeth.

With a sidearm motion, she struck the animal hard right below his left ear. The crack of rock against skull echoed throughout the shed. The coyote whimpered and let go.

She stomped a foot and raised an arm, brandishing the rock. Instead of turning tail, the coyote growled as it stepped back a few strides, about to regroup for its next attack.

The light at the shed's opening dimmed. Nick Eliot stood at the entrance.

CHAPTER 16

Nick worked his first job at age fourteen, throwing newspapers. At fifteen, he lied about his age and was hired on as a weekend dishwasher at the Howard Johnson's—nasty work, but it paid well for a fifteen-year-old, and besides, one of the perks was a free meal. At sixteen, he graduated to custodian and jack-of-whatever trade, working at the local gun-and-tackle shop. He learned to shoot and fish, thanks to the store's owner, who took him out on weekends. By the time he was seventeen, he'd earned enough money to buy his first car, a faded-green Pontiac GTO junker that barely got him around town.

One Friday afternoon in late May, he was driving toward the outskirts of town. Donnie Hollis was in the passenger seat. They were heading toward a run-down Little League baseball field, but not to play baseball.

"Over there," Donnie said, pointing.

Nick drove into the baseball field parking lot and parked his car. The field was on the edge of the forest.

"Where?" Nick asked. "I don't see anything."

"Look at the pine tree, dead center." Donnie opened his car door. "Come on, let's get closer."

"You're definitely morbid, dude." But Nick got out and followed.

Donnie led him across left field to the tree line and pointed. Nailed to a tree, in a crucifixion pose, was a dead cat, which had been skinned from the neck down. Last week, the skinning victim had been a squirrel. The sight was gruesome but also oddly fascinating.

"Now that takes balls, even though the guy doing this must be one whacked-out crazy motherfucker," Donnie said with more than a tinge of admiration.

Nick shook his head. "You do this Donnie?"

"Me? Hell, no."

"You wouldn't admit it if you did. Who would?"

"My crazy mother says it has to be a witch doctor. New Orleans voodoo and black magic have finally made their way to sunny Arizona, she says. I think she's right for once." He paused to spit. "This look like voodoo to you, dude?"

Nick studied the dead cat some more, then said, "What do I know about voodoo? I do know I've seen enough."

"Guy like you who likes to hunt and fish, never thought Soldier Boy would be a wuss." Donnie began clucking like a chicken between laughing and flapping his arms.

Nick put a hand on Donnie's shoulder and shoved him. "How many times do I have to tell you not to call me Soldier Boy before I have to use something other than words to convince you?"

Donnie stepped back and raised his hands in surrender. "Okay, okay, Nick. Don't go wacko on me." He heaved a huge sigh. "Wow, those little punks showing up here tomorrow to play ball will sure go bat-shit crazy when they see that dead cat. Seriously, what kind of sick fuck does this kind of crap so little kids can find it?"

Nick stared at Donnie. Why did he still tolerate the guy? Maybe because all Lone Rangers, no matter how solitary, need a Tonto. "You tell me what kind of guy would do this, Donnie."

Donnie shook his head but then smiled. "Hey man, I've got a hot chick lined up for you this weekend. Caroline from St. Mary's High. Me and Debbie are picking up a bottle of Jimmy B. We're heading to the lookout Saturday afternoon."

"I've got to work," Nick said.

"Debbie told me the chick puts out, goes all the way if she likes a guy. Debbie told her all about you." He grinned. "She likes big guys, smart guys. Can't wait to meet you."

Nick shook his head.

"Dude, you know how those Catholic girls like to screw. You have my word, she's hot shit. She'll be pissed if you don't show."

"That's your problem. I'm sure you can handle them both."

Donnie chortled, but his eyes showed hurt, as if he, not Caroline, had been rejected. As Nick had said, that wasn't his problem. His involvement with Donnie Hollis would only go so far. Nick didn't hang out with Donnie on the weekends. The kid didn't know how to stay out of trouble.

"Come on, Nick."

"No can do." The truth was that Nick wasn't interested in the whores that Donnie dug up. Once a girl like that dug her claws into a guy, they never let go of him, not a guy with a wallet. Besides, Nick had some last-minute studying to do. Tomorrow morning, he was taking the GED exam, and after he passed he would get out of high school early. He was done with school, done with his parents, done with Arizona.

Donnie pulled a pack of cigarettes out of his front pocket. His mom now let him smoke. For that matter, Mrs. Hollis let him do anything he damn well pleased. No way would Nick's parents even consider allowing him to smoke even though he would be eighteen in a week.

"Here," Donnie said, tapping the pack to kick up a cigarette.

Nick took one. Why not? Donnie lit his own and then Nick's. Nick inhaled, trying not to hack and cough. For the next half hour, they stood around blowing smoke rings and shooting the breeze. Then it was time to find the mouthwash.

After Nick finished the exam the following day, he pumped his fist. He'd aced it. He was sure of his results as soon as he completed the test. He wanted to celebrate, and for a brief moment considered calling Donnie and telling him that he would go out on the date with Caroline. But Donnie, like his father, seemed always to be on the cops' radar, and Nick didn't need any trouble. Nope, nothing would interfere with his plans to leave home, and that exam score had just assured his ticket.

Sunday morning, Nick's mother knocked on his bedroom door. "Nicholas, wake up."

Nick threw back the covers. "What is it?"

"Get out here, now!" His mother was upset, which meant his father was upset. It wasn't the first time one of his parents had rousted him out of bed for some imagined infraction.

"Okay, all right. I'm coming," he said.

Nick opened the bedroom door and looked down into his mother's face. The days when she'd stood over him like some ogre had long passed. He'd surpassed her in height by the time he started the seventh grade, and now, at six-four, he towered over the small-framed woman, who stood five-four in heels.

"Get dressed," she said. "The pigs are downstairs."

"What?"

"Some maniac nailed a dead squirrel to the oak in our front yard, and some bigger idiot called the cops."

Nick drew in a long breath. "What do I have to do with this?"

"You tell me, Nick. The cops say you were seen at the little league field a couple days ago admiring another one of these atrocities. And now there's a dead animal nailed to the tree in our front yard. You figure it out."

Nick dressed and greeted the officers with a polite good morning. His father, arms tightly crossed and lips pursed in anger, stood next to the cops. His father was probably angry for two reasons—because Nick was a target and because he hated cops.

Nick, his parents, and the police all sat down at the kitchen table.

"I'd like to ask you a few questions, Nick," one of the officers, the older one with the graying hair and leathery skin, said.

"I'm not going to let him become a victim of police oppression," Nick's father said, his chest puffed out and his fists clenched in the posture of a protective parent. When an outsider attacked Nick or Nick's mother, Mr. Eliot would come to their aid. In these instances, infrequent as they were, Nick would, despite himself, feel fleeting warmth toward his father. "Our son has nothing to do with this."

"It's okay, Mom and Dad," Nick said. He raked his hands through his hair and looked at the police. "How can I help you, officers?"

"Seems the front yard of your house was the location of the latest animal killing," the older cop said. "You were seen at the baseball field looking at a dead cat. Do you know who's doing this?"

"No idea."

"You went to the ballpark just to take a look," the officer said. "How did you know about it?"

"I didn't," Nick said. "A friend insisted I go see it. He thought it was funny."

The cops exchanged a quick look.

"*He* thought it was funny," Nick repeated. "I thought it was totally creepy. Disgusting."

"Except there's a problem," the older cop said. "You said there were two of you. There wasn't a report of two teenagers. Just one, fitting your description."

Nick glanced at his parents. His mother was chewing on a thumbnail. His father looked as if he wanted to take off his belt, except such punishments had stopped a year ago, after Nick grabbed the belt out of his father's hands and wrapped it around the old man's neck—he didn't keep tightening the belt for long, only long enough to make his point.

Nick shook his head. He was going to join the army, volunteer for combat. If he did well enough, the government would pin a medal on him. He couldn't let these accusations about a dead cat spoil it for him.

"The fact is, officers, I was out there with Donnie Hollis," Nick said. "He was the kid who insisted that I go see the spectacle."

"Donnie Hollis?" the older cop asked. "Figures."

"Hollis is your pal?" the other officer asked.

"I wouldn't call him that, sir. He's a kid I've known since first grade, so we go way back. We're very different. You should talk to Donnie. He'll confirm that both of us were out there. And if I'm not mistaken, and I mean no disrespect, officers, it's no crime to look at a dead animal. If it was, people would go to jail for looking at roadkill."

Nick's father grunted and leaned over in his chair, fire in his eyes, but he backed off when Nick's mother put a hand on her husband's forearm.

"You saw this, and you didn't report it?" the cop asked.

"I mean, yes, I should've reported it, I guess," Nick said. "But I really don't want to get involved. You know Donnie can't . . . never mind."

"Don't be a smart-ass," Nick's father said. "Don't."

"Donnie can't what?" the officer asked.

"He can't stay out of trouble," Nick replied. "I don't think I have to tell you that he's been in juvie more times than I can count. I didn't want to get him into trouble."

"We've never liked Donnie Hollis," his mother said. "My Nick has always felt sorry for the boy."

"I can't lie," Nick said. "Donnie Hollis has been talking about killing animals since he was twelve, thirteen years old. I remember going to his house, and his mother had this beautiful black cat, and Donnie hated the cat and said he'd like to skin it. The cat disappeared not too long after that."

The police exchanged another glance.

"What do they say?" Nick continued. "The killer always returns to the scene of his crime? Donnie keeps asking me to go see these things. I hadn't gone before yesterday, when I finally gave in. He said it was like going to a slasher movie, weird entertainment. I'm sorry I went. Earlier this week, he asked me to double-date with him and his girlfriend,

Debbie, and some other girl he said he went out on a limb to fix me up with, but if truth be told, I don't like the reputations of these particular girls and, anyway, I'd had to come home to study. It pissed Donnie off. Still, I can't believe Donnie would ..." He shrugged. "It's strange that Donnie knew about these dead animals. I asked him how he knew, and all he said was that everyone knew about the skinnings. Then he kind of grinned. I hope I don't get Donnie in trouble."

"You think he's behind these animal killings?" the officer asked.

Nick shrugged. "I told you about his mother's black cat, but all I can say is that he gets weird ideas. You know." He paused. "I wonder if ..."

"What do you wonder?" one of the cops asked.

"I wonder if it was Donnie who reported me because I wouldn't go out on that double date. He said if I went along it would help him get laid by his own girlfriend, you know what I mean? So when I didn't go, he was really pissed at me. Said I was cock-blocking him. So maybe he reported me for revenge. He does stuff like that. Who else but Donnie would claim I was at the Little League field alone?"

The cops nodded at this explanation. They asked some follow-up questions, most of them repetitive to try to trick Nick into saying something inconsistent. When he didn't contradict himself, the two officers conferred.

"That's all we need," the older officer said. "Animal control is on the way to remove the squirrel."

"That's all right," Nick's father said. "My boy here is going to take it down. It'll be a reminder of who his real friends are. Won't it, son?"

Nick didn't look at his father, just nodded at the older cop, who nodded back. It was obvious the cop realized what Nick had known for years—his father was a limited, insignificant man, bitter and useless. Nick was also sure his own life would be quite the opposite. He would do something significant.

As soon as the police left, Nick's father called him back into the kitchen. On the table was the large fancy glass-cut ashtray, the one that sat at the center of the living room coffee table when an occasional guest visited. This couldn't be good.

"Sit down, man," his father said.

His mother, standing near the stove, knitted her brow and said, "This is for your own good, Nick." Then she high-tailed it out of the room like the wimp she was and watched from the door to the living room.

His father started to speak but then looked at his mother. "Maybe this isn't such a good idea."

"Get it over with," she replied.

"The cops did you a favor in not pursuing the underage smoking that you did down at the ballpark," his father said. "Five hundred in fines and up to thirty days in jail. Well, your mother and I are going to impose our own penalty."

Nick sat down. "I don't follow."

His father tossed a pack of his Marlboro cigarettes onto the table. "Oh, I think you do. Open the pack."

Though Nick had the physical advantage of youth over his father, one visit with the police had been enough. He was not about to involve the authorities in their messed-up family life. If he'd wanted to do that, he would've made it happen years ago. He opened the pack and set it back down on the table.

"No, take one," his father said.

Nick shook his head. "Jesus, you got kids out there doing heavy drugs, and you're pissed off over cigarettes? Unbelievable."

"Take one."

Nick did as his father asked. He would play the game, but he would do so according to his own rules. His father walked over to him, opened the matchbook, pulled one off, and lit the match.

"Put the cigarette in your mouth," his father said, and held the flame to the end. "You want to smoke? You're going to earn the privilege. Now start smoking the goddamned thing, and when that one is finished right down to the very end, keep going. You finish the pack right here and now, you earn that privilege."

Nick smoked six cigarettes, one right after the other, making sure to blow as much smoke as possible into his father's face. He liked seeing his father's outrage combined with his unwillingness to get physical. Nick's head hurt the more he smoked, he felt sick to his stomach, and if he smoked one more, he might hurl his innards. But it was all worth it, and he continued until he'd smoked the entire pack. He pushed his chair back to leave and he noticed his father holding up another pack of cigarettes. He'd had enough. Nick pushed the ashtray toward his father, stood, and said, "I never liked them anyway. Keep 'em for yourself."

"Your smart-ass attitude will get you in trouble once you're out in the world. You'll be shoveling other people's shit your whole life."

Nick stared at the jerk. Shoveling crap—that was exactly what Nick's father, had been doing his whole life.

CHAPTER 17

Margo cowered, her eyes shifting between Nick and the attacking coyote. The baby shifted, and her heart bounced erratically in her chest as if it were a ping pong ball made of lead.

"Stand back, Margo," Nick shouted and dropped whatever he was carrying except for a long stick.

She stumbled back but managed to stay upright. She retreated farther while keeping a vigilant eye on Nick and the animal.

Nick growled an ungodly sound and raced inside the shed and toward the rabid animal with his upper lip curled in a sneer and his eyes aflame—not a sight Margo had ever witnessed. The coyote wheeled around and confronted Nick, then snarled in return and advanced, baring its teeth. The animal feinted right in what seemed like a taunting move. Instead of shrinking back, Nick advanced on the animal, brandishing the stick as if he, too were taunting his antagonist.

As Nick engaged the animal, Margo filled her pockets with more rocks and moved toward the fight. She was preparing to throw a rock when Nick reared back, dropped to one knee, and in a smooth, almost balletic motion speared the animal clean through the throat, like a fisherman harpooning his catch. It happened so fast that all she heard were the sounds of bones fracturing. In its death throes, the animal gagged, jerking its head back and forth at odd angles. For a moment it looked as if Nick was smiling with pleasure. She shivered. No, he must only have grimaced. She wanted to turn away from the gruesome sight but was too stunned to move.

Nick kicked the coyote's flanks hard, and it fell to the ground. The sharp point of the stick protruding from the back of the animal embedded into the earth. A moment later, Nick grasped the coyote's head and broke its neck. If it hadn't already been dead before, it was now. Almost casually, Nick wiped his hands on the ground and stood up.

He looked up at Margo and said, "Pretty gruesome. But you're a doctor, so you're used to blood."

"Blood. Not violent death."

"You've had patients die, right? Or do you save everyone?"

"As I said, I've never been there to witness the violence. Only the aftermath. And I still hate to see people die."

"It still bothers you?"

What an absurd question to ask. "Every time."

"What was the first?" Now he'd asked a morbid question. He seemed fascinated, engaged, a strange reaction for a man standing over the carcass of an animal he'd just killed.

She didn't want to talk about this, but she also wanted to erase this gruesome attack from her mind. This was also the one of the few times Nick had reached out to her to communicate—an important development in their ability to survive, perhaps. So she told Nick the story of her first day as an emergency-medicine resident. She'd walked into the hospital in Evanston, Illinois, not knowing what to expect, even though as an intern she'd been treating patients for some time. Residency meant responsibility. The ER was packed on that first day, but the cases were routine—a child who had fallen off a swing and needed stitches, people with influenza, a high school athlete with torn knee ligaments.

Her shift had ended at eleven p.m. She walked into sterilization to clean up before leaving the hospital. Matthew McCann, the supervisor of emergency medicine, was there, scrubbing his hands before attending to another patient.

"Dr. McCann, I'm Margo—"

"I know who you are, Dr. Fletcher," he said without looking up. His tone was abrupt, all business. "I'm one of the staff doctors who hires the new residents. How was your first day?" Under his green bouffant scrub cap, his dark-blue eyes bored into her.

"My day was long. Interesting. Everyone was racing at two hundred miles an hour, and I was going seventy."

"You started getting the knack of it by the end of your shift."

She hadn't realized he was watching her.

"Word of advice," he continued. "Don't overanalyze. Read the situation and react."

She nodded politely, accepting both the compliment and the advice. "Are you still on shift, Dr. McCann? You came in before I did."

"I'm supposed to be done. But an eight-year-old boy fell off his bike and cut his knee on some broken glass, so I'm going to patch him up. Won't take long."

The sirens of approaching ambulances sounded in the distance. They both stopped and perked up their ears.

"More than one," he said. "We're shorthanded. I assume you'll work past your shift." It wasn't a question, but it also wasn't quite an order. She was dead tired. Not only had they been unusually busy for a Wednesday (according to the nurses), but first-day jitters had taken a toll. She feared she wouldn't be at her best. Still, even if she had a choice—and that wasn't clear—she wanted to stay. This was what she wanted to do with her life. She began scrubbing in.

There had been a multiple car pileup on the interstate. Matthew assigned her the less severe cases—level four triage. Her first patient was a six-month-old infant with a head laceration. The EMT had applied a bandage to the right side of his head to stop the bleeding. A minor injury—until the child stopped breathing just as the orderlies were about to wheel him into a room. As the attendants rolled the stretcher, she took the child's hand to measure his pulse. The hand was like ice.

She looked up at the EMT. "How long have his hands been cold?"

"They weren't until now."

She checked the child's respiration. There was none. Read and react, Matthew had said. She turned to one of the nurses. "We need to intubate."

The nurse sprinted out of the room and soon returned with an infant intubation kit. Because of the child's age, it was difficult to choose the proper-sized instrument. Margo carefully inserted the tube past the tongue and down the baby's windpipe. The baby's chest began rising and falling. Success—the baby was intubated and receiving an adequate flow of oxygen. The infant reached out, and she placed her index finger in his palm; his fingers wrapped around it.

She left the examination room, walked into the hallway, and was about to enter the next room when someone shouted out her name. She hurried back to the baby. A yellowish fluid—cerebrospinal fluid—was seeping from the baby's right ear. An indication of a cranial fracture. Why hadn't she seen it before? Trying not to panic, she sent the baby to pediatrics. Now it was up to the pediatric neurosurgeons. She wanted to get on that elevator and follow the baby, but that was impossible. There were other patients in the ER to treat. She watched the elevator doors close and walked back to her post, shaking off the feeling of futility.

She treated more patients that night, and at shift's end she met up with Matthew McCann again in the scrub room.

"Thanks for hanging around, Fletcher," he'd said. "Go home and get some sleep."

She marveled at Matthew's calm throughout the night. He never raised his voice, never lost control. It was four in the morning before she clocked out. On the way to her car, Matthew called out, "Margo, hold up a minute."

It took her a moment to recognize him, because he was no longer wearing his scrub cap, and his thick, straight, flyaway dark hair fell into his eyes. When he caught up, he flipped the hair out of his face.

The mannerism was youthful, so different from the person she'd been working alongside for hours. "You got out the door before I could catch you," he said.

"Everything all right, Dr. McCann?"

"No. I have to tell you something. You did an excellent job with the baby who suffered the cranial fracture, but the injuries were too severe. The pediatric team did all they could."

She nodded slowly, but hearing this news was like taking a knife to the heart. She'd learned early on in her internship that there were patients who would make it and others who wouldn't. She'd seen death, had already learned to view it as the worst part of the job. But never had she witnessed a baby die. She would never forget his tiny hand wrapping around her fingers. She willed herself not to cry, the restraint taking every ounce of emotional strength she had.

"Do you ever get used to this part?" she asked.

"Never. And you shouldn't. It helps to talk about it though. Let me buy you a cup of coffee later this week. Someplace else where no one can call '*stat*.'"

"Yeah, later in the week would be good."

Matt McCann was right—she'd never gotten used to death. And unlike Nick, she wasn't used to killing.

Now, Nick brushed the dirt from his hands.

"Sad story," he said. "I've seen those close to me die. Comrades in arms." He shrugged. "Are you all right?"

She nodded. "I owe you my life, Nick."

"You owe me nothing. I defend what's mine and ask nothing in return. I learned a long time ago life is simpler that way." He relaxed his brow, the lines disappearing. "You should rest."

What an odd thing for him to say: "Defend what's mine." Was he implying that she belonged to him? Or was this just an expression of a former soldier sworn to defend his country and its citizens? Regardless, she had a better understanding of what it was like to be a soldier, always on the ready for the next horrific attack, willing to kill or maim almost by reflex and, then, when the threat was gone, to return to normal as if nothing had happened. Doctors had to be detached, but they also cared about life. It wasn't only a matter of reacting to friend or foe—doctors treated everyone, even murderers. How odd their connection. They shared a common thread yet were attached to opposite ends. Nick's brutality, his ability to kill, lingered a beat too long in her thoughts.

"Rest," Nick repeated. "Take care of the baby."

He was right. The baby came first. She gestured at the coyote's body. "I'll get rid of it."

"Are there more out there?" She laughed, though nothing was funny. "Of course there are."

"After I dispose of the animal, I'll light a fire. I'll leave the carcass close enough so that the others know we're dangerous. I think they'll get the message."

She looked around for the best place to rest, glad not to have to worry about the ground shifting. She'd take the hard ground over that any day.

"Where are we going to build the fire?" she asked. "I'll clear the area."

"You should rest."

"I need to help. It'll help me unwind, and that's good for the baby."

He paused but then nodded, pointing to a spot. "Close to the entrance. It'll keep away other animals."

She walked over and began clearing the rocks with her feet while Nick carried the dead animal outside. It must've weighed forty pounds, and despite its emaciated state, there was plenty of flesh on its bones. Nothing they could eat, not if the coyote was rabid. Her stomach churned, and not only from disgust. Strange that she should've felt hunger. No matter, the baby wouldn't go hungry, not as long as she was alive.

When Nick returned, she said, "That coyote was sick. Don't you think?"

He nodded, his eyes and face expressionless. That's it? No comment or explanation? No emotion?

Her stomach grumbled again, and she remembered what she wanted to ask him. "What's in that bag you're carrying?"

"Dinner. You have anything against eating hare?"

How delightful that sounded, a surprise but somehow not unexpected. She wanted to shout with joy but couldn't. That damned coyote wasn't the first animal he'd killed out there.

CHAPTER 18

A few days after the police questioned Nick about the dead animals, he took a ride down to the army recruiter's office on South Woodlands Village Boulevard. Nothing had ever been easier than signing on the dotted line. Two weeks later, he passed the physical examination and got the results of his background check—no problem. He was in. He wouldn't receive his uniform until he went to basic training, but he found a military surplus store and bought used army fatigues, a pair of Oakleys, and a dog tag. A barbershop was nearby so he walked in with long hair and out with the shortest buzzcut.

Wearing the uniform, Nick returned home later that evening, when he knew his father would be there. He rang the doorbell and waited on the front porch as if he were only a visitor, a stranger. Then it occurred to him that he *was* an unwelcome visitor, an unwanted stranger. This had never been his home, but rather a place where he ate, slept, urinated, and defecated.

His mother opened the door. She wore her typical frown. Inattentively, she asked, "Can I help you?"

Nick cleared his throat.

His mother did a double take. "Is this some kind of joke? Get in here before the neighbors see you."

"Yes, ma'am, it is me, Private Nicholas Eliot. And furthermore, I hope the neighbors do see me."

"This isn't Halloween, and you're too old for dress-up." She hesitated. "Don't call me ma'am." She pushed open the door. "Inside. Now."

"No thank you, ma'am," Nick said.

She stomped her foot. "Stop playing games."

His father came to the door. "Nicholas? What the hell is going on? Why are you dressed in a uniform?"

"I've enlisted in the army."

"So you've joined the imperialist military?" his father said sarcastically. "Well, isn't that smart. I knew you didn't have any common sense."

His mother's jaw hung slack, and her dull eyes darted back and forth between Nick and her husband. This was precisely the expression Nick had hoped for.

"What about your things, son?" his father asked. If Nick hadn't known better, he would've thought his father didn't want him to leave. "Your clothes, your music albums, your posters, your books."

His father hadn't referred to him as "son" in twelve years.

Nick stared into his father's eyes. Did this man really care about him, or was this an act, intended to break Nick down?

"Do what you want with them," Nick said. "I came to say goodbye. I'll find a place to crash until I head out for basic training."

His father said, "Don't do this, son. Please. Come back inside, and we'll talk."

"Negative."

"The army takes a man's mind and body."

"Let him go," his mother said. "I'll make his room into an art studio. I've been waiting forever to get back to my crafts."

Before his father could say another word, his mother stormed away.

Nope. He definitely wasn't coming back, but at least he had respect enough to tell his parents goodbye, even if they didn't wish him well.

Good riddance.

CHAPTER 19

After Nick and Margo built a fire near the entrance to the snow shed, Nick took the hare from the plastic bag. What amazing presence of mind on his part to have grabbed a pan and a table knife and a spoon from the passenger-car kitchen. Even better, in Nick's hands, the utensils doubled as makeshift weapons. What were the odds that a person sitting in the viewing car would be a former member of the Special Forces? If Nick were some ordinary guy, they wouldn't be eating wild hare for an afternoon meal. They would be lying dead with the other passengers, buried under tons of snow.

He removed the animal's entrails but left its extremities and head intact. Using the knife, he made an incision across the horizontal plane of the hare's back and slipped a finger underneath the skin. He pulled the skin apart a couple of inches. With his bare hands, he twisted the feet until the bones snapped and then cut off the paws. He grasped the head and twisted until the spine snapped. He separated the head from the torso using the sheer strength of his hands, and through the incision, he pulled off the rest of the skin.

Though he was adept with survival skills, it was still remarkable how he was able to cut through flesh and bone with a dull knife. He and Margo had spent hours together, mostly in crisis mode, and it was clear how he operated in a disaster. That said a lot about his abilities as a soldier. But what did she know about him as a person?

"Have you always been a hunter?" she asked as he placed the meat in the pan and set it over the fire. "Who took you, your father?"

He looked annoyed. Somehow, she'd gone too far. "I've hunted since I was a teenager," he replied as he began butchering the meat. "There was a boy in the neighborhood, Donnie Hollis, who used to murder animals. His idea of fun. Went from field mice to squirrels. He eventually got caught by the authorities when he started killing the neighborhood cats, including his mother's. He liked to skin them, tack the remains to the trees in odd configurations, and then he'd put them where people could see his work, even the little kids. Said he was warding off the gods of evil, or performing voodoo rituals, or whatever. Story changed depending on his mood. He thought he was part Native American. He wasn't."

Her skin prickled. What did that have to do with his history as a hunter? Why hadn't he stopped at *teenager*? There was no reason for him to describe something out of a scene from a bad horror film. Did he want to shock her, to make her uncomfortable? Why? If Nick wasn't making this all up, did he have a hand in those ritual killings? She didn't dare ask. The answer would be meaningless. An insane person would say yes. An evil yet rational person would lie and say no. For her own protection, her own sanity, she resolved to assume that Nick had no involvement in the gruesome business. She needed to trust him. The alternative was too terrifying. Whatever her thoughts, she was vulnerable.

She looked at the deep scars on his face. Though curious, she wouldn't ask about those either. He'd been a combat soldier. Answer enough.

"Hugo Manning, the owner of a gun-and-tackle shop where I worked as a kid, taught me to hunt," he continued, as if his thoughts had gotten back on track. "Hugo said there were only two reasons to kill an animal. One is to eat, and the other is to defend yourself. Killing for sport is wrong, an insult to nature. When my son is born, I'll teach him the same."

"Not your daughter?"

"My daughter too. I knew this soldier who . . ." He shook his head, as if catching himself. "Feminism or not, it's still true that most girls don't like to hunt the way boys do."

"That's a generalization."

"Do you like to hunt, Margo?"

"No."

"How about your sisters?"

"They don't hunt either." She didn't add that her father, although a former naval officer, didn't have the hunting gene, either.

He twisted his lips into what at first she thought was a rare smile but on second thought might've been a smirk.

Flames flared up along the side of the pan. The meat crackled and sizzled. She'd never eaten rabbit, had always been a bit squeamish about it, but now nothing had ever smelled better. Hunger altered taste, that was certain.

"How'd you catch the . . ." She started to say rabbit, but that reminded her of a cute bunny who'd lived in their backyard. "The hare?"

"Luckily, the snowfall let up long enough for me to follow fresh tracks in the snow, which led me to its hideout."

"A warren, they call it?"

He shook his head. "Rabbits live in warrens. Hares live above ground and prefer thicker underbrush for cover, which makes them easier to snare."

"Very impressive."

"Hugo was a good teacher."

They paused, the anticipation of consuming the food growing. Her stomach growled, then she bent forward and sighed.

"What's wrong?" he asked. "Baby okay?"

She nodded. "I can't stop thinking about all those people on the train. I wish we could've done something."

"You shouldn't focus on that. Only wastes energy that you need to survive. There was nothing we could do. Those people are out of the reach of anyone but their maker—if people have a maker."

She sat up and began rubbing the palms of her hands together. Her mother's habit or not, the act was relaxing. "I believe we have a maker."

"I thought doctors relied on science, the rational."

"You sound like my father. He's a statistician. He thinks everything fits into a slot. Yet, he's very religious, often to the point of . . ." She stopped. Nick didn't need to hear about her parents' conservative religious views and their opposition to abortion. "I see it this way. Sometimes there are gaps in the rational. From my experience, God fills those gaps. That's what doctors learn."

He turned the meat, the grease popping and splattering. "Why did you become a doctor?"

She stopped rubbing her palms. "My sister Heather is eight years older than me. She got married young. Nineteen. She and her husband, Charles, wanted to have kids early, but she has polycystic ovarian syndrome. It's a hormone disorder that affects the ovaries—essentially the ability to mature and release eggs into the fallopian tubes is reduced. There's treatment, but it's not curable. Her whole treatment protocol fascinated me. Anyway, I knew I wanted to help people."

"Your parents must be very proud of you."

She scoffed. "My mother is. My father was against my going to medical school. He hates doctors, believes all doctors are frauds. Especially after my sister Heather went through one too many fertility treatments without success. He thinks mathematics and science are the only respectable professions. Oh, and the clergy, they're respectable too. Doesn't stop him from going to a doctor when he gets sick though." That she'd blurted out these words startled her. She didn't usually speak so candidly about her family with friends, much less to a perfect stranger. And yet, this was exactly what she needed to do.

Nick shrugged. "I've known some bad doctors myself. Incompetent or not, physicians like yourself enjoy playing God."

"That's a silly stereotype."

"The civilian doctors do. The docs in the army are different, combat teaches them that. They know they're not God."

"They do God's work."

He nodded and took the pan from the fire. When the meat was cool enough to touch, he tore a leg and thigh from the carcass and handed her the piece. "Well done. Just as ordered."

She thanked him and took the meat. She'd never been a fan of well done, but wild game had to be fully cooked to get rid of parasites.

As soon as she took a bite, her appetite returned. She devoured the meat, even went so far as to lick the bones.

"And now you want to be a mother as well as a doctor," he said. There was something disapproving in his tone.

She set the bone down. "It's the natural process. Don't you want children, Nick?"

"I told you I'd teach my son to hunt. That answer the question for you?"

"It's a luxury that men have," she said. "The ability to wait. There's never a *too late* for a man." What she didn't say—what she never said—was that, for her, there'd been both a *too late* and a *too early*.

CHAPTER 20

On the day Margo's father burst into the women's clinic and hijacked her right to choose, father and daughter drove home in silence. Margo's mother was in the living room when she and her father walked inside the house. Blanche was at a friend's house on a playdate. Margo dreaded seeing her mother's face. She'd tried so much to be like her, the perfect, chaste Southern belle. But after that day at the faculty picnic when she caught her father and Greta, chaste was the last thing she was. A cliché, of course, but a cliché that was spurred on by rage and teenage hormones.

They all sat down. Her parents on the couch, and Margo in the Inquisition chair—a hard early American wood-slatted chair without arms.

"How did you find out?" she asked, thinking the best defense was a good offense.

"What difference does it make?" her mother asked.

"Heather," she said. "It had to be her. I'll never forgive her." Margo had told only two trustworthy and loyal friends in the whole world—her older sister and her best friend, Bree. And Bree would never tell.

"Heather did you a favor," her mother said, for once taking the lead. "How far along are you, Margo?"

She squirmed. "I'm not really sure."

"How many periods have you missed?" her mother persisted.

"Three, maybe more."

"Who's the boy?" her father asked.

"Does it matter?"

"Of course it does."

"I don't know." Margo was filled with the contending emotions of humiliation and defiance. How could a young girl explain that she'd hooked up in a tent with some guy at the *Sasquatch!* open-air concert who'd said his name was Keystone and who you couldn't find in a gazillion years if you wanted to—which she didn't.

"Now, here's what's going to happen, Margo," her mother said. "Your father and I have made a decision. You can't very well stay here and finish out high school. We live in a small community. We have Blanche to think about. So, you're going to Alabama to live with your Grandmother Emma. She's agreed to homeschool you for the remainder of this school year. You can enroll in public school the following year and get your diploma there in Birmingham."

Margo shook her head. "I don't believe you guys. You're forcing me to have this baby, but now I'm nothing but damaged goods who's being exiled?" She was such a child. If she hadn't been, she would've walked out and made her own choice.

Her mother rose from the couch and walked over to Margo. "It'll all work out fine, honey. There's always a silver lining." She leaned down and embraced her. Margo's arms hung limp at her sides.

"No need to worry," her mother continued. "Everything has been arranged."

And, boy, hadn't everything been arranged. Immediately after the birth, the baby was signed, sealed, and taken away.

Margo looked at Nick now. He was staring at her. That she hadn't expected, and it forced the words from her when she said, "We should get an early start down the mountain and toward the highway first thing in the morning. Sleep when it gets dark, get up when the first light appears."

"That's not going to happen."

"I don't follow."

"We're snowed in. Simple as that."

"I have to get to a doctor. No one has to tell me my blood pressure is way too high right now. It's been high for weeks. I'm at risk for preeclampsia, which means my baby's life is at risk. I have to get back to civilization."

"Impossible. Like I said, we're snowed in. Try to stay calm. Worry isn't good for you or the baby. When I was out today, I spotted lodgings."

She was so relieved she gasped and clapped her hands like a delighted six-year-old. Real shelter meant survival.

"Let's get going," she said.

"We go when I say it's time."

Was he playing some kind of sick game? "And why not?"

"You've been through enough today."

"I'll be safer in a warm place. I say we go."

"And I'm telling you *no*. Are we clear?"

She startled at the threat in his voice. His mind was made up. There would be no convincing him to leave. She glanced toward the opening of the shed. Beyond it was a dark void. There was no leaving at night without him, that was certain.

"I'm sorry, Nick, but I'm confused."

"It's dark. If we leave here now, we could be attacked by the whole pack of coyotes."

"You said packs of coyotes don't attack humans. The one that attacked me must've been rabid. We should get out of here."

"You're pregnant, hormonal. That makes you vulnerable. Do you really want to take an uncalculated risk?"

He sounded like her father, but he was dead right. Research indicated that dogs might be able to detect cancer in humans. If so, why couldn't an animal detect the hormonal changes and smells associated with pregnancy? And besides, nature was unpredictable. What if the attacking coyote wasn't rabid? It wasn't just one lone coyote who'd appeared on the platform of the passenger car. The window was frosted over so they couldn't get a head count, but no doubt the skirmishes involved many animals. He was taking a rational stance, while she seemed to be thinking illogically, which was unlike her.

After a pause, she said, "You're right. Thank you for helping me."

He glanced up as though they hadn't been conversing at all. "Like you said before, the military teaches no soldier left behind."

"The military and the medical profession agree on that. How far away are the lodgings?"

"Half a day's climb for you."

"Up into the mountains? That's the wrong way."

"No choice. It's the only shelter for you and the baby."

"No one will ever find us up in the mountains. We might as well be digging our own graves."

"If we stay here much longer, we'll be committing suicide. No telling how long it'll be before anyone makes it up here. Why can't you understand that, Margo?"

Why was she arguing? In part because she was her father's daughter and prone to arguing, and in part because as a doctor, she knew she needed medical attention. There were no doctors *up* the mountain. But any further argument might set him off. She couldn't afford to do that. She was vulnerable enough.

She took a deep breath. "I'll let you know in the morning if I'll go. Pregnancy is playing a real number on me. I'm tired more often, need more rest. And I've got to get to a medical facility. No matter what I decide, the baby demands that I get some sleep. You should sleep too."

"I'll stoke the fire to make sure we sleep free from the smoke."

After pulling up the hood on her coat, she stretched out on the ground near the back of the fire, lying on her left side facing the warmth. Nick added another large stick to the fire and poked the flame. He left the shed carrying the dirty pan and returned after he cleaned it in the snow. He cleared a few rocks she'd missed and then lay down. She stifled a gasp as he inched closer, cupping his body against hers. This she hadn't expected, and her heartbeat kicked up again. She told herself it was fine, that this was survival. He didn't need to ask permission. He was cold too. Likely colder, because his coat had only a high collar and no hood.

She and the baby were safe. This was all that mattered.

Just as she was drifting off to sleep, he wrapped his arm around her body and snuggled in even closer. She opened her eyes but didn't speak. But that wasn't the biggest surprise. No. That came when he placed his arm around her belly, on her child. She wanted to jerk his hand away. She didn't like strangers touching her, and she didn't want him to touch her baby. But she didn't dare make a move.

CHAPTER 21

Not until he joined the army did Nick realize he would be grateful to his father for something. His father had taught him to follow stupid, arbitrary rules and still get by, and in Nick's years in the army, those awful lessons served him well. It didn't take long for him to rise from Private to Sergeant First-Class, in charge of his own platoon. After the terrorist attacks on 9/11, he was shipped out to Afghanistan for his first actual combat. He took to it. The death of his comrades didn't debilitate him but made him much hungrier to kill America's enemies. He had a knack for that. So, he applied to become an elite Army Ranger and was accepted. As part of the 75th Ranger Regiment, he led a special operations combat group in night missions in the Kabul Province. He was awarded several medals for valor and bravery under fire.

During one of his tours of duty, a female soldier, Specialist Andrea White, was attached to his unit. She was a Black Hawk helicopter pilot with combat experience. Among other things, she'd served in Kabul during the insurgency. She'd been part of quite a few special ops. Her military record was outstanding. She had an important and dangerous job—flying the soldiers safely in and out. The unit's last pilot had taken a bullet to the forehead, and the copter had crashed, killing passengers and crew.

On Specialist White's first day, they raided a terrorist sanctuary that had been identified by satellite imaging. Someone had apparently tipped off the enemy about the attack, because the terrorists had lay in wait. The exchange of fire was intense. Specialist White earned the respect of the unit when she maneuvered the aircraft away from a ground-to-air strike that looked certain to hit its target. She took some shrapnel in that battle—only a flesh wound. She could fly the chopper and fire a weapon better than most men, and she never complained, even when in pain.

Specialist White was easy to work with, partly because she was so competent and partly because she followed orders without question. About six weeks after she became attached to the unit, Nick went out to check on the progress of repairs to a chopper. She was there with the mechanic, working on the engine. Without looking up, she said, "Hey, Sergeant. What do you get when you cross a rooster with an owl?"

The mechanic glanced at Nick with apprehension. It was well known in the unit that Nick didn't appreciate cutups.

"I have no idea," Nick said.

"A cock that stays up all night." With her upturned nose and brown hair bundled with a red bandana in a tight bun on the top of her head, Specialist White looked innocent, childlike, as if she herself didn't get the joke. Such a contrast to her cool efficiency while piloting a copter.

The mechanic flinched. Everyone in the unit knew that that Sgt. Eliot disliked jokes in general, and he disliked raunchiness even more, especially from a woman.

But Nick roared with laughter. He respected Specialist White because she stood her ground and didn't put on a false act about who she was.

That summer, Taliban forces launched a nighttime attack near Tora Bora, detonating explosives in a tunnel near a military compound that was surrounded by civilian houses. The insurgents had overrun dozens of security outposts and, in intense fighting, killed scores of Afghan military personnel.

Nick, the mission's team leader, walked into the barracks, where his soldiers were just turning in for the night. "Let's rock and roll. We've been called in for air and ground support."

By the time his squad members—consisting of fully equipped special ops and aircraft's crewmembers—took their positions, Specialist White and her copilot had already powered up the chopper.

"Are we a go, Specialist White?" Nick asked. He always addressed her by rank as a sign of respect—so that his men would respect her too.

"Armed and ready, Sergeant," she replied. "Sixteen Hellfires mounted, another sixteen at the ready. Coordinates set." Then everyone else confirmed their positions.

"Confirm headset communication," Nick said. They all gave a ready, set.

"Fly her in low," Nick said. "Everyone, keep your eyes open and guns ready."

Thirty minutes into the flight, Private Reed, the radar tech, said, "Sergeant, I'm picking up activity. Looks like the insurgents have ground troops of fifty or more. Are we free to engage, Sergeant?"

"Not our orders," Nick said. "Hold fire. Continue toward our target."

A moment later, flashes of light illuminated the sky.

"Incoming fire!" Reed cried. "Do we have permission to engage?"

"Take her up and out of range, Specialist White," Nick said. "I'll radio in the request to engage."

Bullets continued to pepper the chopper, though only with rifle fire and not something more deadly. The chopper had been built to withstand this type of strike. White piloted the helicopter upward as Nick made the call.

Command center responded, "Continue toward your target."

"Everyone hear that?" Nick asked. "Keep her moving, Specialist White."

A moment later, there was a huge explosion and a flash of light.

"We've been hit," Specialist White said in an even voice. The helicopter had been struck by a surface-to-air rocket. "We've lost engine power."

"Can you get the engines restarted?" Nick asked. Beads of sweat formed on the back of his neck, and his breath accelerated. *Keep calm*, he told himself. Show your soldiers what it takes to survive. Weakness means sure death.

"That's a negative," Specialist White replied.

"Rotators still attached?"

"Yes, Sergeant. I'm taking her into autorotation to maneuver us down. Everyone hold on. It'll be bumpy."

Nick looked at the faces of his crew. They were a good group, an elite fighting force. Fear was natural, but with these soldiers, as with him, fear fueled strength. "Any chance we can make it over to Jalalabad Airport?"

"That's a no-go, Sergeant," Specialist White said. "Engines won't start and autorotation isn't designed for flight. We have to set her down."

Nick got command back on the radio. "We're under attack, north-northeast of Jalalabad." He gave them the coordinates. "We're hit and going down. Need immediate assistance. Insurgents number fifty or more."

"We just got intel that insurgents are targeting the airport," command responded. "Do what you can, rescue is thirty minutes out. Keep in communication. Good luck."

The helicopter shook violently. Over the horrible sputtering of the dying engine, Nick shouted, "When we land, stay together. Reed, take whatever communication equipment you can carry. We've got to find cover before the insurgents reach us. I'm calculating an ETA of twenty minutes before we're met by enemy forces. We'll head up and to the northeast. Try to find cover in a cave."

"Everyone hold on," Specialist White said.

They descended as if attached to a parachute. The chopper swayed back and forth like a child's swing. Yet not for one moment did Nick think they'd crash—he had that much faith in Andrea White.

"How we doing, White?" Nick asked.

"We're close to landing. Pulling up on the collective right now.

Should give us enough upward thrust to make the landing."

"Everyone check your headset," Nick said and waited for his crew to confirm.

Specialist White set the chopper down in the sand with little more than a hard bump. No one was injured. One of the men pulled the door open, and everyone rushed out. Nick led the unit up a rocky foothill to what looked like the entrance to a cave. There was a crack of gunfire, and two soldiers went down. Nick estimated that the shooter was two hundred yards away.

"Snipers!" Ranger Anderson shouted. Too loud. "I'm—"

"Anderson?" Nick asked.

Anderson didn't respond.

The rest of the soldiers hit the ground and crawled uphill, searching for cover. In those sandy hills, the only place to hide was behind mounds of sand and dirt, which provided little protection from bullets. If only they could reach the caves. When more gunfire rained down upon them, the Rangers had no choice but to hug the ground.

"Where are they?" Nick asked.

"I'm seeing movement below," one of the men said. "They're coming in our direction."

"Disperse and flank," Nick ordered. The men broke up into pre-designated groups. Seven men headed up and toward the east. Nick led the others up and toward the south in the direction of the cave.

There was a large explosion, followed by the sound of fire from automatic weapons.

"Head count!" Nick said. Two soldiers who had headed east failed to respond—which meant they'd been killed or wounded.

"Keep moving," Nick commanded.

The groups scrambled farther uphill. Five soldiers, including Nick and Specialist White, continued south toward a small pile of rocks. There was only room enough for two soldiers to take cover. Nick ordered the better marksmen to hold their positions behind the rocks. He motioned for the other man and Specialist White to continue down the ridge with him. The cave was still another fifty yards away.

"Hold your fire so we don't give away our position," Nick ordered.

The other group leader spoke through the headset. "Sergeant, it's Reed." His voice was strained. "They're coming at us. There's no cover."

"Everyone, all units, bury yourself under the sand, we're going blackout," Nick said. The soldier with him buried himself as fast as a sand crab. Specialist White, a pilot, not a special-forces soldier, was slower. Only her legs were buried by the time the other ranger had covered himself. Then Nick noticed a crevice that might be the opening to another cave. He kicked the sand off his body and gestured for Specialist White, who was still burying herself, to crawl with him.

Specialist White motioned that they should continue burying themselves, but Nick shook his head and pointed two fingers to his eyes and back out toward the insurgents. He motioned for her to keep moving and took the lead.

Gunfire continued. His troops were sitting ducks if the insurgents discovered their whereabouts. Nick hoped that the others were now deep under sand surrounded by air pockets—what they'd been trained to create—and not suffocating. Nick had seen more than his share of soldiers die attempting this maneuver despite the rigorous training.

He crawled to the cave's opening, the gunfire withering. The Taliban insurgents were getting closer. He and Andrea White were pinned down.

Nick reached for Specialist White's arm to signal her to stay back. She was shaking like a leaf in tornadic wind. He understood. He wanted to shake like a leaf himself, but he controlled himself—always could. If their whereabouts were discovered, they both knew that they were as good as dead—or worse, prisoners who would be tortured, beheaded, and used for terrorist-recruiting propaganda. He drew her into his arms and tried to comfort her.

The gunfire continued sporadically, the shooters hoping to get lucky and hit the Americans' hiding spots. Where were the coalition reinforcements? They should have been there by now.

Specialist White finally said, "I don't want to die like this. Not a coward holed up in a cave, hiding. I won't let them capture me. I know what they do to women prisoners."

"No. We're not going to die, and they won't capture us. And you're no coward, Andie. Why did you join up?"

"Excuse me, Sergeant?"

"It's Nick. You and me, Andie and Nick. Tell me why you joined up."

She flinched at a round of enemy gunfire that kicked up dirt and sand near the entrance to the cave.

"Tell me why you joined up, Andie," Nick said. "That's an order."

She looked at him as if he were demented but answered. "I . . . I know I'm supposed to say it's because I wanted to serve my country, but really, I like to fly. My grades in school weren't good enough to get me into the Air Force Academy, so after I graduated from high school, I enlisted. I grew up in Nebraska, part of a farm family, and, believe it or not, I learned to fly a crop duster when I was fifteen. Too young legally, but no one stopped me, because I was good. Besides, I'd been driving tractors since I was twelve. Repairing them too." She went on to tell him how she was an only child. Her mother had left when she was an infant, and then her father dropped her off with his parents and split himself. She never saw him and didn't care. Because she'd had to work on the farm, she'd had little time for socializing. Only a couple of boyfriends. High school relationships—nothing serious. And then she joined the military.

"What did you raise on the farm? Corn, I'll bet."

When a loud explosion shook the cave, she moved closer, which hadn't seemed humanly possible until she pressed harder against him. He hadn't taken his arm from around her since he'd placed it there to protect and comfort her.

"Corn, yeah. But also sorghum. Insurance against the gluten-free fanatics."

"No roosters?"

"Maybe one. Some chickens and livestock too. How about you,

Sergeant? Why did you join?"

"To get away from my parents," he said. "My father was a mean son of a bitch and made no bones about it. My mother was just as mean but tried to hide it. They never wanted me. Or maybe they wanted me but discovered I was an inconvenience. They were clueless. I raised myself. I did want to serve my country, to make a difference. To rid the world of enemies. And make no mistake, Andie—you are serving your country. Doing great. You're going to do great for years to come."

Her eyes glistened, visible even in the dark. He tightened his arms around her. "Thank you, Sergeant."

To his surprise, he kissed her hard, and she kissed him back. The strangest of places on earth, the strangest of times, but the purest of emotions. Together, they stayed hidden, holding each other.

A short time later came the wonderful sound of Blackhawk helicopters; the American forces had pushed the insurgents back. The rest of the unit rendezvoused back at the downed chopper. Five of the fifteen on the helicopter had suffered fatal wounds—five more to fuel Nick's anger against the enemy. None of the dead were left behind.

And fortunately, Andie had survived.

They never mentioned the incident in the cave afterward, although there was a palpable connection between them. They couldn't have a romantic relationship—it was unprofessional, a serious violation of the rules. Two months later, Nick's unit returned stateside, and Andie was reassigned to another unit and stayed on in Afghanistan—skilled pilots were in high demand. For Nick, the memory of that night in the cave remained buried. He assumed he'd never see her again. He'd get through it. He'd grown accustomed to being alone, to treating every encounter with another person as temporary. As to matters of the heart, the military had been Nick Eliot's only mistress. Until now.

CHAPTER 22

Margo woke at dawn, rested but sore. The fire from the previous night had died down, providing little warmth. Nick was already up and moving around at the other end of the shed. One step ahead, he was collecting objects, maybe to make another one of his makeshift tools. She pushed her weight upright to a seated position and waited for him to return, carrying scraps of wood.

"I didn't hear you get up," she said.

"Early prep pays off. Learned that early in life, developed the habit while in the military. As a doctor, I'm sure you do the same."

"My father would agree with you. Can't tell you how often I heard my father say 'she who hesitates is lost.' A byproduct of his time in the navy. Us Fletchers, we lived on one hell of a regimented schedule."

Nick stopped and looked at her, waiawaiting ting an explanation.

"Right," she said. "Family dinners were always served promptly at six-thirty—hands washed, napkins in the lap. Once the table was cleared, there was nothing to eat until the next meal. There was no such thing as a late dinner or even a snack. He would say, 'You stay on a schedule to learn responsibility.'" She'd said enough and didn't need to go into how he'd held her and her sisters and her mother accountable for any infraction of his rules. The problem was that her father's rules weren't always that clear until they'd been violated.

Nick nodded and continued toward the fire.

She drew in a deep breath, expecting to fill her lungs with pure mountain air. Instead, she inhaled smoke and started coughing. "Never understood why anyone smoked cigarettes." She coughed a little more, thought of the effects on her lungs, and her worry about the baby returned. Then turning a one-eighty, the urge to laugh came out of nowhere—a little smoke was the least of their worries.

Nick placed another log on the fire. More smoke filled the air but was soon replaced by a robust fire, but she had another coughing fit.

"Move back some," he said.

She stood and stepped away from the flame, while he kneeled beside the fire and poked at it.

"I've always hated campfires," she said.

"Never heard anyone say that before."

"I know there's no empirical evidence of this, but it seems to me that people who love campfires so often become smokers. Not my parents. And we weren't around many campfires. My mother hates them too. My father is still the ultimate health nut and was before it became a fad in the late seventies. He's in his sixties, and my sister says he still runs daily, lifts weights, and plays racquetball three times a week. That's when he isn't cross-country skiing. He says he learned to appreciate the value of physical fitness in the service. I've never disagreed with his philosophy of maintaining a healthy lifestyle. Maybe that's the only thing he and I agree on. If my father hadn't insisted that I join the Girl Scouts to learn what it was like to be a part of a troop—his way of inserting his military background into my life—I would never have been around a campfire. I hated the smell of those Girl Scout campfires. Once we'd eaten s'mores, I was done. But I loved everything else about being outside in nature." Why was she babbling about fires and smoking? Had the smoke gone to her head?

"I'm fine with campfires and don't smoke. My father was a chain-smoker, my mother an occasional, and they weren't outdoors types, at least after I came around."

So much for her theory about smoking.

"Fire is survival," he added. He stood up. His considerable height always felt surprising. "I'm going out, see if I can round up some breakfast."

She stared at the flames. She again feared being alone. Last time the coyote had stalked her.

"The fire will keep you safe," he said. Beyond his survival skills, the man was quite perceptive. "The predators don't want any part of fire. Like I said, fire is survival. I won't be long. We'll wrap up here and head up the mountain."

She nodded, although her pulse quickened. The idea of heading up the mountain still made no sense.

Alone, she paced the interior of the shed, trying to decide what to do. Sure, a cabin would be safer than this shed. Better than using a hole in the ground as a toilet and dirt to bury the waste. But real safety was down the mountain. Nick understood the outdoors. Why couldn't he get them down?

As a child, Margo once asked her father why he'd become a professor of statistics rather than a businessman.

"Business relies on too much guesswork and luck to be successful," he replied. "I prefer hard-and-fast rules in life, like what the military offered. Academia has its own hard-and-fast rules." His answer was one of the most personal responses he'd ever shared. If only there were hard-and-fast rules now.

Tired of pacing, she returned to the fire to warm her hands. The wind howled through the rafters of the shed, causing the metallic walls to creak. Solitude amplified her growing sense of unease. Before the avalanche, she couldn't have imagined that, in this day of technology and air travel, a person could get lost in a remote wilderness. Oh, she'd read of lone hikers getting lost in the forest, even dying, but she'd been riding a large passenger train. Why weren't the authorities there yet?

A howl in the distance made her flinch. She listened, but the sound didn't repeat. She thought of climbing up and looking out the opening of the shed but stayed near the fire. Out of caution, she collected some rocks, filled her pockets with them, and returned to the safety of the flame.

Not until early afternoon did Nick return. He'd slung the carcass of some creature—a large bird—over his shoulder, the bird's skinny legs serving as handles. He didn't speak, only walked closer, and dropped his kill near the fire. He brushed the snow from his shoulders and warmed his hands over the heat.

She wanted to ask why he'd been gone so long when he said he'd be back soon. But he seemed to be in a bad mood. Maybe he was tired. Best not to ask questions and to stay upbeat. "I hope that's what I think it is," she said with a smile. "Thanksgiving was a few weeks ago, but I'd call that a lot to be thankful for."

"Not a turkey. Pheasant," he said in a monotone voice.

"I'm impressed. I can't imagine how you found such a thing out here."

"Not every animal hibernates. You'd be surprised at what lives in these hills during winter—elk, pikas, sheep, among other things. I found this bird roosting in a tree. Sheer luck. I'm going to grab some more wood."

It was more than luck; everything this man had accomplished resulted from skill.

When he returned, he stoked the flames and separated some of the hot embers to keep the fire smoldering. Once again, he went through the process of dressing his catch. He grasped the bird and then met Margo's eyes as if daring her to try and look away. He broke the ligaments that connected the wings to the body, placed the bird on its back, spread open its wings, and placed a foot on each extremity. Again, he glanced at her, said nothing, and returned to work. His silence seemed a command that she stay quiet too. He grasped the bird's feet, bent his own knees, and bounced gently a few times. Then he forcefully pulled up on the bird's legs. In this one fluid motion, he removed the feet, head, legs, guts, feathers and skin, exposing the pink flesh of the meat. He twisted the wings off the carcass and pulled off the breast meat, which he tossed inside the pan. Then he set the pan on the fire.

When they sat down to eat, he broke the silence. "You were restless last night," he said. "You talked in your sleep."

Her cheeks flushed. "I hope I didn't say anything unpleasant or embarrassing."

"You talked about a Martin, or maybe a Matthew."

Her cheeks heated and must've turned beet red. Her inner thoughts, her most personal memories, were not anything she wanted to divulge to this man. "What did I say?"

"Couldn't make out much, but you seemed to be arguing. I told you it was all right, that it was just a dream, and you fell into a deeper sleep." He paused. "Were you having a fight with an ex-boyfriend?" Nick liked to pry yet clearly didn't want to reveal much about himself.

"I don't remember. But I'm sure I wasn't arguing with anyone."

He held up his hands as if to say *none of my business* but continued, "I did understand one thing. You complained about being pregnant, said you hated it."

Her mouth dropped open. "You misunderstood."

He shrugged. "You said the words as clear as day. Several times. You also said you wished the pregnancy had never happened."

Unnerved, she drew in shallow breaths. "As I said, I don't remember my dreams, but I'm sure I never said anything like that. What you think you heard has nothing to do with my baby. But here, wide awake and in the light of day, I'll tell you that I'm thrilled I'm going to be a mother. I went to great effort to become a mother, even with no one in my life." She wasn't just talking about what she'd gone through this past year. No, it went farther back than that.

CHAPTER 23

Summer nights, rain or shine, Margo and her Grandmother Emma would sit on the front porch sipping Chamomile tea. Her grandmother said the tea would calm Margo's nerves, would help cool her from the inside out. The theory never quite made sense, but Margo never questioned it. Her grandmother didn't like to be questioned about anything. An outside observer watching the two women sitting on that porch would've admired the quaint tradition, but it was hell for Margo.

There was nothing calming at all about those evenings. Rather, her grandmother would repeatedly criticize and lecture Margo about making poor decisions. How many times, how many different ways had her Grandmother Emma made it clear that she disapproved of what Margo had done—got herself knocked up, though of course Emma would never use such words? And how many times did she have to hear that if her grandfather—William Pratt the third, fourth fifth, or whatever it was—were still alive, he would never have allowed her to step foot in their home. That he would've disowned her for being an immoral unwed mother. That their ancestors were instrumental in the Birmingham steel industry and didn't own slaves (what her grandmother failed to mention was that the workers in the steel mills were treated as miserably as slaves, that they'd elevated their status above the commoners, that they had their pride.

It wasn't all bad. The family home was impressive enough, located in the Mountainbrook subdivision where all the blue bloods lived. And it was big enough to sometimes escape the presence of her grandmother. The house had been passed down through the generations.

Her grandmother also disapproved of Margo's mother's choices. "Your grandfather William and I never quite understood why your mother didn't marry a Southern gent," her grandmother would say. "There were so many nice young men she was introduced to. She abandoned her heritage for a man in a uniform who became a professor. A college professor doesn't make much money." Her grandmother sniffed, the way Southern women do when they get their noses out of joint.

Yet, improbably, Emma was a good teacher. During Margo's homeschooled junior year of high school, she learned quite a lot. Her grandmother focused heavily on American history and language arts and even had quite the knack of making mathematics understandable in a way that teachers in Spokane didn't.

Just before the baby was due, Margo's mother and Heather came to Birmingham. Margo was excited to see them. It had been months. The next day, Margo went into labor.

She was so scared. Scared of the pain, scared of the emotional feelings she might have for the baby, scared of the aftermath. In later years, she remembered the bright lights and the needle the doctor placed in her spine for the epidural. Some oral medication she was administered made her brain fuzzy. She most vividly recalled hearing her baby's first cry. As soon as the umbilical cord was cut, the baby was whisked away. Only Grandmother Emma remained inside the delivery room, while Margo's mother and Heather followed the baby to the nursery.

"What did I have, Grandmother Em? A boy or a girl?" She felt as if her words had come from the lips of someone else, that Margo was just an observer.

"A girl. Healthy. But let's not worry about that. Let's get your strength up, and then you can get back to being Margo." Her grandmother patted Margo's arm in a rare expression of tenderness. "You forget this ever happened. You, Margo Pratt Fletcher, you're going to be just fine."

Margo was numb and stayed that way for many years.

Now, she wanted to tell Nick, *I went through a lot to be a mother.* She'd gone through the birth of her first child. She'd undergone IVF three times before this pregnancy took. She didn't hate being pregnant. She'd loved every minute of it, even those awful moments of morning sickness, and heartburn, and high blood pressure, and the constant peeing.

"I've made a decision," she said. "I'm not going up the mountain, cabin or no cabin. It's illogical to move farther away from civilization in my condition." Why had she decided this? Because going down the mountain made sense. But she had also made the decision because Nick had overstepped so far that she questioned his judgment.

He didn't look up from the pan of meat. His silence spoke louder than the sizzle of pheasant and the wind sweeping into the shed and the crackling of the snow on the roof.

She brushed some small rocks out from underneath her bottom and legs. Damn it all. "Aren't you going to say something?"

"What is there to say?"

"When the weather clears up, we should follow the train tracks down the mountain. If the snow is deep, we can take a detour. You know how to avoid avalanche areas. We'll find our way to safety."

He scoffed and shook his head. "So much for trusting my survival instincts."

"I do trust them. But I'm also a survivor."

He stood and meticulously wiped his hands as if settling an internal struggle. "Right now, your instincts are wrong."

"Why?"

"If you go down the mountain and take one wrong step, you're sure to fall in your condition. And when you fall, you'll die."

"That's dramatic."

"You'll break a limb or fall inside a sinkhole or simply get wet and die of hypothermia. With the snow build up, a sink hole could be twenty, thirty feet deep or more. That's not drama, that's reality. If you were experienced in the wilderness, chances are you'd never make it down alive. The fact is, you don't know what you're doing. You think you know, your ego tells you that you know, but you don't."

Was this truth or some kind of manipulation?

"I'm experienced, Margo. You've seen enough to know that. I'm not willing to take the kind of risks you're talking about. If you do what you're suggesting, you'll be committing suicide and murdering your baby."

He wasn't making sense. "I wouldn't be surprised if the railway crew is hard at work as we speak. We can stay on the tracks until we meet up with them. If we don't find them after a while, we'll turn around and come back here."

He shut his eyes for a moment and drew in a deep breath. "I'm not going to argue with you anymore." She understood—he knew what he was doing, had foraged for food, had rescued her and the baby several times over. But his plan was illogical. She wasn't helpless, no matter how much he tried to make her feel that way. He must've forgotten that she'd unburied herself from the avalanche and had dug him out from under the snow. She was a survivor and a rescuer, too, and the thought of going *up* the mountain was what seemed suicidal. They could face the same risks going up as down. Why not hedge their bets and head toward civilization?

They ate their meal in silence. She kept trying to understand his side of the argument, but she couldn't make sense of it. Was he also using the silence to evaluate her plan? Doubtful. He was naturally silent, and clearly stubborn.

When they finished eating, he packed the pan and utensils in the plastic bag along with the uncooked meat he'd gleaned from the bird.

"Come on," he said.

"What?"

"Let's go outside for a moment. Look up and look down."

He helped her to her feet, and they left the shed. The cold assaulted her, but at least the snowfall was light.

Nick pointed upward. "That's where I've found shelter. No place else. Read the signs."

She shook her head. He wanted to leave the railroad tracks and head straight up into the mountains, a direction that led farther into the wilderness. She looked east, in the direction she believed was down the tracks and back to civilization. After only ten yards, the tracks vanished under the snow. Still, if she used her common sense, she could continue down and out of the mountains toward a town or maybe even a ranger station. She looked west, where the snow piles from the avalanches were particularly high and imposing. Her home in Spokane lay west. How daunting.

"Follow me," he said. "I'll take you to shelter now. I'll go first to smooth the path. Stay close and watch your step."

She stood a moment considering whether more talk would change his mind. He didn't wait but began walking up the mountain. The hair on her arms rose, but not from the cold and not from the intensifying snowfall. Assess and react, Matt McCann had taught her.

"Thank you for everything," she called out. "Be safe, Nick."

He turned around and fixed his steely glare on her. For a moment she feared he'd come back and drag her alongside him. But he stayed put.

"I have a question," he said. "Would Matt or Marty or whoever you were talking about in your dream agree with what you're doing?"

"He would want me to assess the situation quickly and react. I've done that, and I'm going down the mountain to find the rescuers. Please come with me."

As soon as he turned his back to her, she took her first step and headed down the tracks. A rush of excitement swept over her, and she soon found a large stick to use as a staff.

I'm doing just fine.

CHAPTER 24

After Margo gave birth to her first baby, she spent the next two years learning to make her own decisions. Reliance on others had usually meant disappointment. She'd lied to Nick when she said she didn't remember her dream. She was yelling in the nightmare. At Dr. Matthew McCann. Reliance on Matt had too often resulted in disappointment, and as she made her way down the mountain, she wondered whether Nick's mention of Matt had influenced her decision to go it alone.

By the end of her second year of residency in the Marshall General Hospital ER, she and Matt didn't spend many nights apart. The first cup of coffee turned out to be the first of many such meetings. They talked and laughed, and he gave her tips on how to deal with hospital politics and unusual trauma cases, like the infant who had died on her watch. From that day forward, life came into sharper focus. The relationship was a risk, sure. After having dated several med students and a paramedic, she came to believe that relationships with other medical professionals wouldn't work. The guys were either competitive, egotistical, envious, as overworked as she was, or all of the above. Matt was different, or so she thought.

They kept their personal relationship low-key. The last thing she wanted was a bunch of people gossiping about how she was getting special treatment or how Matt was acting inappropriately as a boss, when neither was the case. There were only a handful of friends who knew they were together, and they were not hospital employees. At work, they were entirely professional. Dr. McCann was the boss and a mentor and nothing more.

On the day everything started to change, they were scheduled to have dinner at The Walnut Room. She was excited, girlish, because it was Christmastime, and she suspected he would propose marriage. She was more old-fashioned than she let on. Maybe her grandmother's traditional Southern sensibilities had instilled a sense of decorum when it came to saying *I do*. Or maybe, sad to say, it was the anticipation that her father would condemn her if she lived with a man she would never marry.

She dressed, making an extra effort to look sexy, slapped on bright red lipstick (Matt's favorite), and found the pair of stilettos she'd purchased on a whim a week earlier.

She arrived at The Walnut Room fashionably late. The water fountain in the center of the room was now covered, and on top sat an enormous Christmas tree. Its boughs were trimmed in white and silver and sparkled with white lights. The tables situated around it were covered in fine linen and decorated with ornaments and white poinsettias. Overhead lights were dim, romantic. Cheery music played. Waiters rushed in and out, delivering the delectable holiday dinners. Everything was perfect. She couldn't have asked for more.

She checked in with the maître d', who directed her to Matt's table. He was wearing a suit, a rare sight seen only on occasions like charity fundraisers.

When she got to the table, he kissed her, and they sat down. He was smiling, buoyant, like a little boy anticipating Christmas morning. He'd already ordered champagne, a bottle of Taittinger.

"I have something I want to say to you," he said, reaching across the table for her hands.

Her palms were actually sweating.

He drew in a nervous breath, released it, and said, "I've been offered clinical chief of emergency medicine." He burst out in an ear-to-ear smile. "I thought this was the perfect opportunity to celebrate."

Margo forced a smile. She was happy for him, but she was also disappointed.

On cue, the waiter came over and poured two glasses of champagne. When they touched glasses, she tried to stop her hand from shaking. *Grow up, Margo. Next time.* Then she reacted.

"I have news too," she blurted out. "I'm taking the position at Lurie." Lurie was a children's hospital in downtown Chicago that had offered her a position as an attending physician in the ER.

He looked confused. "You're taking it? I thought you decided not to."

"You know I want to work with children, Matt."

"Congratulations, Margo. I guess tonight is a celebration for both of us." This time, his smile was forced.

She lifted her glass. She'd told him she was going to turn the job down and spend another year at Marshall General. That earlier decision, right or wrong, was solely because she wanted to be near Matt. He was an amazing mentor. She adored that about him. Matters were much clearer now. So what if they worked at different hospitals? They would be okay. Except, as it turned out, they wouldn't.

In the dream that Nick overheard, Margo was pregnant, and she was shouting at Matt—but not for the reason Nick thought. She wanted to have a life with Matt. She wanted his children. But she and Matt always seemed to be moving in opposite directions. They'd never raised their voices at one another, but in the dream, they didn't hold back. She was going to tell Matt that she was pregnant, but she'd miscarried, and like Heather, had become infertile. The dream wasn't about hating her current pregnancy—it was about loving it and fearing she wouldn't survive this ordeal to see or touch or hold her baby.

Now, as she trudged eastwardly downward through the heavy mounds of snow, ever hopeful, continuing onward back to civilization, the landscape seemed like nothing more than a foreign language written in pine trees on snow. Her internal sense of time had slipped from her grasp, and the sun seemed as if it were about to fall from the sky.

Her best guess said it was sometime after three o'clock in the afternoon. But again, it was hard to be sure of anything. No matter. If she walked east, west, or south, traveling down, eventually she'd meet up with the highway, which couldn't be all that far away.

In the first half hour, she avoided the deeper snow by using her stick to judge its depths. Then, she came across the kind of sinkhole that Nick warned her about. That didn't stop her. The trick to avoid falling into the deeper snow was to simply go around it—retrace her steps, veer wider into the forest, and exit back out to where she believed the railroad tracks to be. If only she could run. The mind so often wants what the body can't deliver.

How odd that, in all this madness, her feet hadn't felt the cold until now—a benefit of the pregnancy—and that was likely because of the physical exertion.

Encountering wild animals—coyotes, in particular—remained foremost in her thoughts. No longer did she believe that a coyote wouldn't attack a human. Attacks might be rare, but they happened. With each step in the right direction, her determination continued to build. She didn't worry about Nick. Nick could take care of himself.

She was careful not to move toward the mountains, because mountains weren't linear and there were few tunnels cut through the rock. She focused on where the light in the sky was most intense and estimated where the east was. She continued to use her stick to judge the snow's depth. She took every precaution. The next few microseconds changed all that when she stepped onto what seemed like hard, compacted snow. Like an eternity lost, God turned off the clock of time. Her every thought and movement became suspended in super-slow motion.

Her body pitched forward, and she dropped her stick. She tried to raise her arms to find balance, and that might've worked if she'd had the strength to shift her weight back to the left foot. She didn't. Her left knee bent and fell onto packed-down snow, but the right leg sunk deep into a soft patch, and her right foot broke through something hard and continued down even deeper but never hit bottom. Her mind swirled as she tried to grasp what had happened.

Snow. Ice. Water.

In this temperature, any error could be fatal. Wet feet meant frostbite. She'd never be able to get her foot dry again. Her heart pounded as if she were at the end of a long sprint, and she did her best to balance her weight.

Don't panic.

One misstep and her entire body could go down. There was only one way to get out of this. She raised her arms, leaned back, and set both hands down behind her, driving them deep into the snow, hoping to gain enough purchase to hold her weight. She repositioned her bent knee to steady her body. With the large belly, it was almost impossible to maneuver. But, she managed to dig deeper cavities with her hands. She eased onto her rump, not slipping forward. Inch by inch, she drew her right leg out of the snow. Minutes later, the leg was free, and she was safe.

After a few slow breaths, she looked at her right leg and found no rips in her pants, which, mercifully, were dry. Her boot was wet, but her foot felt dry. What had just happened? The terrain appeared to be level. There was no indication of a drop-off. She lowered her hood and listened. The wind stilled enough for her to hear the soft trickling of water. She glanced to her left and studied the tree lines. There was a twenty-foot gap in the forest, which was separated by boulders protruding through the snow. Of course. She'd walked into a stream. She'd been so focused on studying the terrain that she'd missed the warning signs around her.

She picked up the walking stick, used it to locate stable ground adjacent to the stream, and carefully inched forward. She was on her way again until the stick sunk lower. When she pulled it up, the tip was wet, and fragments of brown sediment clung to its edges. What had she missed this time? Looking around, she appeared to be free of the stream. But the water and debris indicated otherwise. That left a few possibilities—a sinkhole, a tributary, or an underground creek.

"Dammit!" she screamed but fell silent. Loud sounds triggered avalanches and might attract unwanted guests.

Now what?

Go back to the shed and set out again at first light? Everything inside her said to keep going down the mountain. Going up was irrational. But there was no way she could safely cross the stream. That left a compromise with nature; she'd continue along the bank of the stream because it was heading down.

One step at a time. It wasn't long before the sky darkened and snow began falling, but not heavily enough to dissuade her. She wiped the snow from her cheeks and pushed forward while shielding her eyes from the snow. Just ahead was a break in the terrain. Could it be? Had she reached the highway? She hastened her pace down, making sure to remain on solid ground. As soon as she emerged from the cover of the trees, she discovered her mistake. Civilization was nowhere. No sign of a highway, no sign of railway tracks. She now stood on a precipice gazing into a vast landscape of mountains filled with only trees. Ten feet in front of her was a sheer drop-off—a frozen waterfall. The beauty was breathtaking, the discovery heartbreaking. How could this be? She'd been so careful to go in the right direction.

Angry heat raced through her veins, threatening to rip her soul from her flesh. Exhausted, she wanted to sit down. That, too, would be another mistake.

Damn the snow, damn her mistakes, damn her loneliness, damn her stubbornness. Damn it all.

She faced the mountain that held her prisoner. "Is there no reasoning with you, you beast? You impenetrable mass of stone. I know why you're here. You want to judge me, don't you? To strip the very life from me and my child? Well, forget it. I won't let you. I can, and I will persevere. I'm going to beat you."

She looked into the sky. How long had she been walking? How long would it take her to get back to the shed? It didn't matter. She started the climb. Five steps later, a severe cramp in her abdomen struck—a sensation she hadn't experienced in years. She walked two steps more. Impossible to continue.

She sat down, pulled the hood over her face, and eased down onto her side. The cramp slowly intensified. *Please let it only be Braxton-Hicks contractions.* She drew in deep breaths, waiting and praying that the contraction would pass and that no more would come. To distract herself from the pain, she lowered her hood enough to see up into the trees. The wind had picked up considerably. There was only the wilderness, not city billboards, horns honking, or the other sights of a city that could be so distracting. She rolled her head from side to side. The branches swayed in circles and then back and forth as if a symphony conductor were directing their movement. For a moment, she lost herself in thought, imagining which melody the trees were playing. Maybe Mozart, Brahms? No, Bach. Whips of wind nipped, and a clump of snow fell into her eyes, robbing her of this brief reprieve. Groaning, she grasped her stomach.

Change the focus.

She closed her eyes and imagined a warm sunny day—a picnic lunch with her child in Millennium Park where they'd visit the Bean sculpture and make funny faces in its mirrored surface. They'd skip, play tag, and race one another until they were out of breath and then flop down. They'd lay arm in arm as they gazed into the sky and watched white puffy clouds dance by, tracing images of dragons and dogs and birds and whales. When they'd caught their breaths, they'd scramble up to their feet and race hand in hand to the hotdog stand, where they'd order foot long dogs and ice cream for dessert. They would proudly live the wonderful clichés of a happy family, mother and child. Snowflakes fell on her nose, another reminder of the cold, although she kept her eyes closed.

Margo flashed back to the tiny hand of the six-month-old baby who'd died on her first day of work in the ER and cringed. Mother Nature surely didn't intend to take Margo and her child, not now, not yet, not as they lay in earth's cradle.

Finally, the contraction passed. When no more came on, she braced herself and got to her feet. As soon as her equilibrium returned, she began her retreat. Maybe tomorrow a rescue squad would arrive and find her at the shed. With Nick gone, she'd have to survive on her own.

Nothing was impossible.

CHAPTER 25

Three years passed before Nick reunited with Specialist Andrea White on another deployment to Afghanistan. She was reattached to his unit as part of a cultural support team as well as a helicopter pilot.

"Good to see you, Sergeant Eliot," she said.

"Long time, Specialist White." His jaw tightened in an attempt to remain distant and professional. The memory of their intimate encounter in the cave on the night their chopper went down had never left. The hard truth was that a day hadn't gone by without his pining for her. And though he never believed he'd see Andie again, looking at her now, he couldn't imagine going through life without her. Why had he remained distant? She had, too, but he was her superior, so what choice did she have?

"You can call me Nick, Andie," he said.

"Thank you, Sergeant," she replied. It was a game they'd played since the day they survived that first battle.

"I've been keeping up with your career, Specialist. You've done well. From helicopter pilot to cultural support team member. You even learned to speak Pashto, I understand."

She blushed, her fair cheeks turning an intense scarlet. "I had a lot of lonely nights after I left your unit, Nick. I had to fill the time with something. I missed you."

"Same here, Andie."

There was an awkward silence. Without cracking a smile, she said, "So, a farmer buys a rooster named Randy to service his two hundred hens. When he gets the rooster into the barnyard, he tells him, 'Randy, I want you to pace yourself. You've got a lot of chickens to service here, and you cost me a lot of money. Have fun, but take your time.' The farmer points him toward the henhouse, and the rooster takes off like a shot. WHAM! Randy nails every hen in the henhouse, three or four times. Randy runs out and sees a flock of geese down by the lake. WHAM! He nails all the geese. Randy runs to the pigpen, the cow pasture—soon, he's done every animal on the farm. The farmer is distraught, worried that his expensive rooster won't even last the day. Sure enough, the farmer wakes up the next morning to find Randy laid out flat in the middle of the yard, buzzards circling overhead. The sad farmer shakes his head and says, 'Oh, Randy, I told you to pace yourself. The buzzards are coming for you now.' Randy opens one eye, winks, nods toward the sky. 'Shush, dude. You keep talking and you'll scare them away.'"

"Funny," Nick said, laughing. "Do you have any more?"

"A whole bag of them."

"Why don't you come to my barracks tonight and tell me some?"

"Is that an order, Sergeant?" she asked, smiling one of her cute little grins.

"It depends. Do you want it to be?"

"You know how I love taking orders from you, Sergeant. On and off duty."

"Then you'll be in my room at nineteen hundred hours. Prompt."

"Yes, Sergeant."

Nine months into Nick's deployment, fatigue set in. He wasn't due to return stateside for another three months. He'd never put in for mid-deployment leave but, now, he needed to spend some alone time with Andie. They were both eligible for R&R, but they couldn't be seen asking for the same dates. So they staggered their requests and were fortunate to receive a week's overlap.

A few days before the trip, four dainty knocks sounded at his door—Andie's distinctive knock. He wasn't expecting the visit. She opened the door and peeked inside.

"Sarge, got a second?"

Nick sat up. "Sure. Anyone see you?"

"No, no. All good. I'm not staying. I just want to give you something."

She tiptoed to the bedside and set an envelope on the side table.

"That's not what I think it is," he said. "Because if it is, it's not necessary."

"Hey, we all write letters just in case something happens."

"We're not going into combat, Andie."

"I know. That's why it's better to do it now, so it's not filled with last-minute emotional drivel."

He nodded and pulled her into his bed.

Andie left the following day for Christchurch, New Zealand. Nick met up with her a week later, and together they flew to Mount Cook and traveled to the Aoraki Mount Cook National Park—a stargazer's heaven. They backpacked into the mountains, where they spent their days roaming the pristine, breathtaking wilds and enjoying their evenings staring into the heavens and making love.

One evening, as they lay in each other's arms, Nick was sliding a strand of her long hair between his fingers and across his lips. Never in his life had he believed that he would find a woman like Andie.

She nudged his side.

"Please. Not another rooster joke."

"I was thinking, Sergeant. Why don't we get married? You know, take the big dive, jump a cliff, hug a tree, bite a snake, wake up a rooster?"

At first, he thought she was kidding, but when he looked into her eyes, he saw that she was sincere. "Andie, I'm an old, worn-out dogface."

She playfully slapped his abdomen with the back of her hand. "You're right. You're not getting any younger. Neither am I. Which means it's time. We can quit the army and go raise chickens, a couple of roosters too. Better yet, I swear, Sarge, I'll make you crow at the crack of dawn."

He laughed. "But you snore as loud as a Howitzer."

She rose up and placed her arms against his chest. Then she nudged her nose against his. "I'm telling you the truth, Nick. I love you. That's enough."

"You don't know me."

"Sure I do, Soldier Boy."

Something inside him snapped, and he reached out, grabbed her wrists, and squeezed hard. She'd never called him that before. Donnie, the kid he'd grown up with, had called him that. Nick had always hated that moniker.

"Hey, let go, Nick. That hurts."

He'd never shown that type of fast-twitch aggression toward Andie. He shut his eyes and let go. "Don't ever call me Soldier Boy again."

She held up a hand in submission. "I'll only call you Sergeant from now on, like I always do. But you hurt me. I never thought . . ."

"Andie, I don't know what got into me. It'll never happen again. The war . . ."

She ran a hand down his chest. "You sure are fucked up, Sergeant." She giggled. "But I get it. And I'm hooked on you. Baggage and all."

He drew in a deep breath and gently stroked her cheek. Images of fallen soldiers passed through his mind. He could see faces, their expressions of horror in the last moments of life. He shook his head. Because she was a soldier too, she understood why he would react this way. She, if anyone, would be able to see past it. And it would never happen again, he vowed. "Why would you want some old guy like me?"

"I want a real man for a husband. Is that so wrong?"

"There are plenty of younger, less damaged men out there."

"Boring. Little boys. I want a man who's really seen the world. One who understands the value of life. Someone who likes to play hard. A big, sexy hunk. That's you, Nick."

"So those are the criteria? Isn't it the man who usually proposes?"

She laughed. "Who cares about that traditional junk?"

"I suppose you don't want a ring either?"

She shrugged. "I'm not a material girl. You know that."

"Every girl wants a ring."

She smiled. "Just don't make it a diamond. I want a pearl so I can always remember how my little parasite burrowed his way inside my shell to make nature's perfect little jewel."

He laughed aloud. "So I'm a parasite now?"

"Well, I might call you my proverbial grain of sand." She feigned a shiver. "Can't stand sand in my bathing suit bottoms. It's like being pecked to death."

"I'll remember that for the honeymoon. No sandy beaches. Or maybe beaches but no bottoms."

She laughed. "I like both ideas."

CHAPTER 26

Margo reached the snowshed sooner than she believed possible, a surprise, because she thought she'd traveled farther away from it. The truth was, she'd meandered back and forth across the terrain and hadn't gone a great distance at all. There was enough daylight left that she could still see to build a fire. She'd watched Nick do it, and she could as well.

Just before she entered the shed, a dark figure from within moved. She recoiled and raised her stick. God, no.

Nick appeared at the opening. "Good job getting yourself out of that creek bed."

It took a moment for comprehension to set in. "You were following me? And you didn't help? That is so fucked up." This was the type of perverse game her father would play just to teach her a lesson.

"You're lucky you aren't seriously hurt," he said. If he'd even so much as smirked, she would've hit him with the stick. But his face remained as impassive as the tone of his voice.

She laughed, surprising herself. There was nothing funny about what she'd been through. "You're an asshole. I don't need you. I don't need your screwed-up games. And I certainly don't need any more of your lessons."

His expression hardened. "You did need a lesson. And you still need someone out here who can take care of you."

"What I need is water."

When he took her hand, she burst into tears.

"Come inside," he said. "I'm starting up a fire. When it's ready, I'll boil some snow."

"I'm sorry. I . . ."

His expression remained unyielding. He stood and waited for her to say more, but she couldn't. What could she say? That she'd made a mistake? That she was a fool for not trusting him?

"Apology accepted," he said.

She nodded and followed him inside the shed. Once seated, she wiped the tears from her face and watched him build the fire. Its warmth was a real comfort, but the sight of the leftover pheasant was an even greater treat.

When the fire burned down a bit, he placed several pieces of the pheasant in the pan, along with the tail. "You need a little fat to keep the baby healthy. The tail is loaded with that."

Once she was settled, she began to consider Nick's behavior. Why the games? Why hadn't he just guided her down the mountain? Why sneak alongside her in the woods? The only explanation was that he wanted to keep her close, that despite his tough exterior, inside he feared being alone, dying alone. He wore no ring, said he had no family. He was a lonely soul. In this wilderness, the two of them formed a makeshift family.

He looked at her as if again reading her thoughts. "What's on your mind, Margo?"

"You can't really think I'm unhappy about my pregnancy," she blurted out.

"I shouldn't have brought it up."

"Because it's not true. I don't know why I care what you think, but I want you to understand the facts."

No response.

"Nothing to say?"

He turned the meat over in the pan. "You seem to want to talk about this. So be it. You strike me as an unhappy person. If that's the case, maybe you're working your problems out in your dreams. It seems that something beyond our predicament has you worried. Probably been there a long time. And as I said, it doesn't seem like you really want to be a mother."

She was momentarily speechless. Did this man really think of himself as some kind of armchair psychotherapist? "You have no idea what you're talking about or what I went through to have this baby. This is my only chance to have a child. I went into premature menopause. My time was running out, and I had to make a choice. I chose to have a child. Did I want a husband and a family? More than anything. But sometimes you don't get dealt a winning hand."

"Loneliness is dangerous. It's dangerous for a soldier. I know. I think it's just as dangerous for a mother."

Over the last several years, she'd maintained her own space. It hadn't been easy, but being alone was better than getting hurt. It had been like a mathematical theory of opposites: the closer someone tried to get to her, the harder she pushed them away. Usually she pushed because of deceit—a foible characteristic of so many men in her life.

"You're alone too," she said.

He poked the fire. "You shouldn't use a baby as a cure for loneliness. You have a full-time job. Who's going to be the real parent? The child's nanny?"

The anger inside her burned hotter. How judgmental. The man was an arrogant jerk. Despite what he said, there was nothing wrong about wanting to have a baby to avoid being alone, or about wanting to experience the joys of motherhood with or without a husband. This was the twenty-first century. Single parenthood happened all the time, had throughout history. Parents died young, parents left. And so what if she hired a nanny or used a daycare? A lot of married couples did that when both of them worked full-time. She was no different than a divorced woman with custody of her children. Having a child was part of life, the natural order, and she for one knew that all too well, especially in her daily life at work. The hard, cold truth was that she didn't want to have a baby alone, that she'd planned to marry Matt. The best laid plans.

CHAPTER 27

For a long time Margo believed that the relationship with Matt would work out—or maybe she'd fooled herself into believing it would. Out of convenience, she bought a townhouse near Lurie Children's Hospital and farther away from him. The distance kept them apart, although they promised it wouldn't. But life got busy. They stopped meeting for lunch, no longer went out on weeknight dates. They saw each other a few weekends a month.

On a late Saturday afternoon at Margo's place, they sat in silence, gazing out at Lake Michigan. It was summertime, and plenty of people were out sailing and windsurfing.

"I wish I were on a boat right now," she said.

"We should get a boat."

She laughed.

"No, I'm serious. Sail around the lake, take in the breeze, drink plenty of beer. Of course, you'd have to earn your keep as a crew member." He grinned.

How appealing. They'd do something that didn't involve medicine. They'd spend more time together. But where would they find that time?

"It would give us a way to unwind on weekends, something to take us into retirement," he said, then reached over and took her hands in his. "I don't just want us to sail together, I want us to live together. We'll get married, if that's what it takes."

An odd mixture of joy and disgust raced through her mind. How perfect would that proposal have been if he'd left off that last bit. "Was that a marriage proposal? Because if it was, it wasn't very romantic."

"I'm being myself, which is a good thing. You thought it was once. Look, we both have the same goals. We're great together." He reached in his pocket and pulled out a jewelry case. "Marry me, Margo Pratt Fletcher."

The floor underneath her feet caved in. She stared at the ring and then up at that irresistible grin of his.

"Yes, I will marry you, Matthew McCann."

They kissed, and he went to the refrigerator and opened a bottle of champagne that they'd been saving for a special occasion.

"I'd call this the perfect ending to a rough week."

"Why so rough?"

She sighed. "A ten-year-old needed a kidney transplant, and he didn't get it in time."

"Yeah, that's rough. Exactly why I don't ever want to be a parent."

She sat back and stared at him. "You're telling me this now? That you don't want children?" It struck her that when they'd spoken about kids, he had always been vague. But he'd never said that he didn't want a family. And he was so good with the young patients in the hospital. They loved him.

"You always say kids are great when I talk about my work," she said. "Why haven't you ever told me this before?"

"It never came up. The truth is, I thought you felt the same way."

"What gave you that idea?"

"You're so career oriented. Like me. And you never really talked all that much about having kids."

"True, but you're wrong, Matt. I want children. And you led me to believe you did too."

He exhaled impatiently. "I wasn't sure. When you're young those possibilities seem to be so far off in the future, but now that we're getting older . . ." He shrugged. "Children change everything."

"Yes. That's the whole point."

"They swallow up your life. Margo, you have your kids at the hospital."

"That's not a family. That's a job, and they're my patients, not my own children."

"The truth is, I wouldn't be able to live without constantly worrying about whether my kid would show up at the ER on any given day."

"That's absurd. Most kids grow up strong and healthy."

"There are no guarantees. Look at what you see every day in your job."

"The human race has been having babies for thousands of years, and the population is doing just fine. As far as injury and illness go, that's everyone's concern. Any of us could get hurt or become sick any day. We still live our lives."

"Maybe so, but do you want me to lie about my feelings?"

"No, but . . ."

"We're not in our twenties any longer. Chances of birth defects rise with age."

Her face flushed hot. She was only in her early thirties—young for a professional woman. Or at least average age. "You're a doctor, so you really can't think this way, Matt. We cure sick people. My God, if you were this paranoid about driving, you'd never leave the house."

"I'm losing this debate, okay, I admit it. Is there any room for negotiation?"

"No, it's not a business deal. You either want children or you don't. If you don't, then we're too different to be together for the long haul. Do me a favor and think about it."

He shrugged, said nothing more, and she left the ring on her finger. She convinced herself he would change his mind, that this was only their first real talk about children.

❄

Now, as Margo considered Nick, yet another man who was telling her that she didn't need to have children, she couldn't let it go. "What about the hand you were dealt, Nick? Did you get a bad one too?"

"Something like that. The only thing you can do after life doesn't give you what you want is make your own luck. You like platitudes, so here's one you'll appreciate—there are no guarantees in life. Ever."

She folded her arms across her belly and felt the baby move— that was no platitude. Inside, she was carrying life, all that mattered in the world. Nick and Matt were so much alike. She knew she should drop the subject and stop talking, but she couldn't, so she asked, "I'm just curious, Nick. Were you able to make your own luck? Because I sure did."

He didn't reply, although his silence was as loud as the wind beating against the sides of the shed or the sizzling and popping of pheasant grease spitting from the pan.

Still she didn't drop it, her questions almost taunting. "Just why don't you have a family, Nick? Can you answer me that, or have I asked too much?"

He looked away and then met her eyes. "It was stolen from me. The war."

She didn't understand his vague response, but she realized that she'd gone too far. She muttered an apology and dropped the subject. They were back to their familiar silence.

After they finished eating he said, "Time to get ready to go up the mountain."

Her stomach clenched. "How will anyone find us up there?"

"The shelter up the mountain is our only safe haven. This shed exposes us not only to the cold, but also to more wild animals. Plus, we don't know how sturdy this structure really is. It could go down in a strong wind or from the weight of the snow on top of it. We go up the mountain and wait it out. I'll reconnoiter daily when the weather is clear, and we'll meet the rescue squad when they arrive."

She nodded. This was no longer a plan she could argue with. "It's late, so I assume we'll leave first thing in the morning."

"No, we set out right now."

"What? It's dark outside, and soon it'll be pitch black. We can't possibly climb a mountain in the dark, not after what I've been through today. You wouldn't go last night, so why now?"

"The snow is accumulating—almost two more feet since the train wreck. If we don't get moving, you won't make it up."

"All the more reason *not* to go up. What if we get stranded on the way? It's not just me. You have an injured leg."

He waved a dismissive hand in the air. "I'm fine. The cold helps. I've packed the leg in some snow from time to time. You might not have noticed, but I'm getting around fine."

It's true, he wasn't limping as badly.

"I'm too tired," she said.

"Pace yourself, and you'll do fine." He stood, gathered up the cooking implements, placed the leftover pheasant in his bag, and shook out the pan. "I'm going outside to clean up and get rid of the bones."

She waited, doing her best to regain her composure. When he returned, he sat down, keeping a formal distance between them, then said, "I didn't say this right away because I don't want to frighten you, but you're entitled to know. Here's why we have to leave now. During one of my tours in Afghanistan, our unit went on a search-and-kill mission up in the mountains of the Zabul Province, looking to take out some key Taliban leaders. We set up camp on a plateau for the night about thirty kilometers from our objective. One of our men left the group to relieve himself and never came back. We assumed some hostile fighters ambushed him. I wish that had been true." Nick looked down and scuffed his boot on the ground. "I'm sure you've never seen the remains of a man eaten alive by a leopard."

"You're not seriously telling me—?"

"There's a snow leopard near our location. I found the tracks."

Margo gasped. "Snow leopards in Montana?"

"I'm sure the cold brought him down. A lot of animals move to lower locations when it gets this cold. That's why I've been able to catch our food so easily."

"How do you know it's a leopard?"

"Smelled the markings of his strong urine spray where I dumped the coyote remains."

"Not a bear?"

He shook his head.

"So we'll stay here and keep the fire lit."

"That cat's hungry, and he's ready to kill. Without a real weapon, I absolutely cannot fight off an animal like him, not a cat that weighs upwards of a hundred pounds. He can take down prey three times his size, animals like elks or boars. Our situation is far more dangerous now than facing a rabid coyote or even a healthy pack."

She stared into his eyes, hoping for some indication he was joking. He wasn't.

"Leopards usually shy away from humans, but we don't want to take a chance. Like I said, you're pregnant and hormonal. Which makes you vulnerable."

She began to shake.

He rose and extended a comforting arm. "We have to make for the shelter now."

She stood but remained in place. "Cats hunt at night. Your story about the soldier confirms that."

"When the fire dies down in the middle of the night, the leopard might get brave. It's already sniffed out the coyote remains, and I'm sure he smells the pheasant."

"What if we get rid of the rest of the bird? We maybe could take shifts tending the fire."

"I plan on using the leftovers to get the leopard off our trail when we leave. It's our only diversion."

He walked over to the woodpile and retrieved a stick about four feet long and three inches thick—far too large to stoke the fire. He gathered vines and twigs, secured them with sheets of bark to one end of the stick, and coated the binding with the fat left over from the pheasant. Holding up the staff with a flourish, he said, "A makeshift torch. The fat will help light the fire and keep it going."

She examined the torch. It was an ingenious contraption. "It's like a giant match."

"Precisely."

He lit the stick, and they left.

Don't look back, don't question the decision, just keep moving.

He set the pace, and to her surprise, she kept up with him. He was a good guide, which she never doubted. He knew how to avoid the larger mounds of snow and the many pitfalls, like possible sink-holes and iced-over streams. That said, within an hour, she needed rest. Adrenaline had been her friend, but now the lactic acid was breaking down and her extremities were beginning to burn. Still, she forced herself to go on.

When he stopped abruptly and reached a hand back to block the way, she stumbled forward but quickly righted herself. Waddling a few steps more, she walked up alongside him. What she saw made her heart sink. A massive, impassable mound of snow blocked their way—too high and too steep for Nick to climb even if he hadn't had a pregnant woman in tow. To the right was a sheer drop-off. To the left was denser forest.

So, Nick wasn't perfect in his quest for survival. He could get lost too. She got no schadenfreude from this; she wanted him to be perfect.

"This was passable earlier," he said, sounding perplexed. "There must have been another avalanche, smaller but large enough to block the way."

"Do we have to turn back? I've already turned back once today."

"We can't go back. We'll have to go through the forest and make our way around it."

Part of her was relieved not to retreat, but retreat might've been easier than continuing to climb. She bent over at the waist, clasped her knees, and drew in air, trying to oxygenate her muscles. If only they could sit down. But she might not get up if she did.

"Let's take a break, Nick."

"We can't."

"Five minutes."

"I know it's tough, but we have to keep moving. It's not only the leopard. We have get out of the cold."

They continued the climb, navigating through the forest and back around to a narrow path. The snow wasn't as deep on the trail, which meant it was likely a deer trail. That meant they were heading someplace and, she hoped, that place was the cabin and not barren wilderness.

Cold air burned her lungs. She had to do something to keep her mind occupied or she'd go crazy. She thought of seeing her baby's face, hearing its first cry, watching the child take its first step. Repeating the scenarios from earlier that day, she imagined the years passing, the times she and her child would spend together, all the simple but precious joys motherhood brought. And yes, she'd keep going until she dropped. She owed that to herself and her child. One day she'd tell the child about this harrowing experience, about what hell she went through to save them. What a family story that would make, though not one she'd wish on anyone.

But eventually, not knowing whether they would survive became overwhelming. When the stories in her mind became muddled and she couldn't put two thoughts together, she began repeating a *duruum* sound in her mind, like a child comforting herself while lying alone in bed in a dark room, or a marathoner pursuing the runner's high, or a speed-reader clearing the mind of distracting thoughts. The mantra propelled her forward, helped her forget the pain radiating through her limbs and lungs, and helped her forget how this journey might really be the last.

Nick stopped again and glanced around in front of them.

"Are we close?" she asked.

He shook his head.

Stopping was a mistake. Her legs wobbled and turned to what felt like congealed jelly. Another step forward and she'd fall. "I can't do this!" she shouted. "I can't. I just can't do this!"

He looked back over his shoulder but kept walking. "Save your energy. Worry and panic will drain it from you."

Too late. She dropped to her knees and shoved her hands in her coat pockets. She couldn't control the tears. As a doctor, she'd learned to endure long, hard hours. But she'd never learned to hike through the wilderness like a soldier at war—certainly not at eight months pregnant. She looked up at the sky. Snowflakes landed on her face and eyelashes. Their coldness tingled against her skin. She closed her eyes and bowed her head as if in prayer, but she wasn't praying—not conventionally. More like communing with her unborn baby, seeking strength and at the same time imparting her strength. Nick made no attempt to coddle her, and she was glad about that. He did crouch down nearby, as if to let her know he was present and ready to help.

Finally, a wave of eerie calm shrouded her. Or was it hopelessness? She lifted her head and in that moment saw that the clouds had parted to reveal a sliver of sky and the twinkle of a few stars. There it was, the hopeful sign she needed. A little beauty among all the brutality. Her shoulders slumped as the clouds came together again. The starlight was gone.

"Oh," she sighed. But she didn't cry this time.

Nick came over and kneeled down on one leg. "Margo, your eyelashes are frozen. Are you warm enough?"

She wiped her eyes, then felt her neck and wrist. "My body's warm. I think I'm all right. How much farther?"

"We're almost there."

"You just told me we weren't." Why was he messing with her mind?

"I didn't want to tell you because I wanted you to continue to conserve your strength. Needless emotional toil wastes energy. Starving people die when they try to feast right away."

She stood. "Let's go. No excitement. I'll be a true ascetic."

"You're a student of Greek philosophy. Good." He clasped her hand without asking and pulled her along. When they came to a clearing in the trees, she saw it.

"That's a fire tower," she said. "Not a cabin."

"I didn't use the word cabin, you did. Anyway, same difference."

CHAPTER 28

Afew weeks after the trip to New Zealand, Nick's unit was assigned to visit a schoolhouse in a small village located thirty miles from camp, where the Taliban had threatened the teachers for educating girls. Andie entered the schoolhouse. Nick ordered his men to hang back at a safe distance and not to intimidate the locals, whose cooperation Andie sought. Nick remained at the door. Once inside, Andie was greeted by the headmaster, an Afghan woman who spoke passable English. Andie removed her helmet to reveal her long hair, spoke to the headmaster in elementary Pashto, and followed the woman to an interior office. Nick remained in the hallway within earshot.

"How many girls came to school today?" Andie asked the headmaster.

"Only three. Two are mine, one is a neighbor whose mother works because her husband was killed."

"And boys?"

"Five. The families are terrified to send the children, the girls in particular. Families have been threatened. I have been threatened. Last night at my home, two men came late in the night. My husband and I woke to guns pointed in our faces. The men threatened to kill us and our two children if we did not obey them and close the school."

"Who are they?"

"I cannot risk telling you. These men will kill us. They have killed many others."

"You have to understand that these murders won't stop until the brave people of Afghanistan, with the help of our coalition forces, resist the oppressors."

The woman thought for a long time, clearly agonized. Then she nodded her head resolutely. "Your American soldiers will protect us?"

"Absolutely," Andie said. "Our guarantee."

Ten minutes later, Andie had the names of the Taliban insurgents, who were holed up in a safe house. When nightfall came, the unit, using night-vision gear, moved into a stronghold in the foothills. Once inside the targeted stone building, the unit split up. Nick and Andie entered a room where a mother was sleeping, cradling an infant in her arms. Nick's antenna went up—this was no Taliban safe house, not with a woman and child there.

"It's an ambush!" Nick hollered. "Move out!"

Before they could evacuate, there were loud footsteps, followed by gunfire and the sound of men shouting. Nick's unit had been set up by the headmaster—she'd probably believed cooperating with the Taliban was the only way she could save herself. The woman in the bed awoke, and the baby began wailing. Nick readied his weapon and pointed it at the door.

The woman in the bed tried to stand, but Andie said, "Stay down!"

The woman didn't listen but instead ran for the door—leaving her child in the bed. What kind of people were these to put an infant at risk?

Two insurgents burst into the room, guns drawn. Andie dropped down and used her body to shield the child. Nick began firing, taking out the two men, but not before they fired their own weapons. Nick looked over at the bed. A large stain of blood had sullied the bedsheets under Andie's head. Beneath her body, the baby continued to cry.

From the deep recesses of his brain emerged a dark urge—an urge he thought lay buried in Arizona. He ran into the other rooms and fired at anything moving that wasn't an American soldier. Nick had killed all the insurgents, but nothing would avenge the death of Andie. He wanted to keep killing, until he remembered he had to see Andie home. No soldier left behind.

He cradled her lifeless body in his arm, her arms dangling free.

He held her close to his chest as if she were a stillborn babe. If only he could breathe life back into her.

"Sarg," a medic said. "Put her on the gurney."

Nick knew someone was talking to him, but his ears were ringing from all the gunfire. No matter. He didn't want to listen, he didn't want to talk. He wanted to walk off the edge of the world to a place where no harm existed. He remembered that place where he felt no pain. A place where he would be free from physical pain, from his father's wrath, from his mother's berating. A place where no one existed but Nick and JJ. His friend had reassured him that the door would always be open. That Nick only had to step through it, and all the world would be right.

Light flashed. Nick blinked hard in the glare. Was he hallucinating? That door was now open, only feet away.

"This way, Nicky. Bring her to me, I'll make her alive again."

Nick's heart thrilled. He began walking toward the light that glimmered behind the door.

"We'll all live on the farm together," JJ said.

Now he remembered. Andie would be safe there.

He hadn't comprehended the depth of his feelings for Andrea White. He thought he had, but his attachment to her was far deeper than anything he had ever felt. It hadn't been he who'd burrowed inside her shell to form the perfect pearl. Rather, she'd made her way into his soul. She was only supposed to be a helicopter pilot attached to his unit, another cog in the machine, serving alongside the elite Special Forces. Anyone could die on a mission. All too many of his men had fallen. But he'd never expected Andie to die. They were supposed to retire from the service and raise chickens together, a few roosters as well, she had said. They were supposed to have a child together.

"Sarg," the medic said louder. "It's over, Sarg. Protocol. Sir."

Nick heard nothing, only the ramblings of a soldier performing his duty. He moved closer and closer to the door, feeling a lightness. Only a few feet more and he stepped through that door and into another world.

"Stop!" a man ordered.

Outside the house, three soldiers stepped in front of Nick. The door slammed shut. Which one? From the house or Nick's refuge?

Men spoke to him, shouted in his face, and suddenly, Nick was aware.

"Sergeant," his commander said. "It's not your fault."

The following morning, at approximately 0600 hours, a soldier banged on the door to Nick's quarters. "Sergeant! Are you awake?"

Nick woke with a start. How had he managed to fall asleep? He glanced at the clock on his bedside table; he wasn't due to report in until 0700. For a moment, he'd forgotten about Andie, thought he would get up and see her directing maintenance of her chopper. Then he remembered, and the morning came crashing down.

"Sergeant Eliot," the soldier called out again.

Nick didn't respond but rolled over. If the soldier tried to come in, Nick might not be able to control his rage and would kill the man.

"Orders from the Lieutenant. You're needed right away." The soldier paused and then said, "There's something you have to see."

When had Nick heard those words before? Long ago. The soldier refused to go away and pounded louder. Nick rose and answered the door. The morning light assaulted his eyes, making him squint.

"Lieutenant's orders, Sergeant. There's something he wants you to investigate."

"What is it, Private?"

The Private took a deep breath and tried to talk, but the words didn't come. Nick threw on his uniform and boots and followed the Private outside.

Nick got into the Private's Jeep, and they drove to the schoolhouse. He parked the car out front. On the front porch, hanging from the rafters, was the body of the headmaster who had betrayed Nick's squad—who had caused Andie's death. Her vacant eyes stared out at the village, a gruesome warning. Flies swarmed on and around the body. The stench of rotting flesh was already filling the village square. What was more remarkable about the headmaster's corpse was that the face was the only part that remained intact. The woman had been scalped and skinned alive.

The Private gestured and looked away. "The Lieutenant wonders if any of our people know who's involved in this."

Nick shrugged and looked away.

"Sarg?" the Private asked again.

"It's obvious, Private. The Taliban got her for educating girls. I have to admit, it's a very effective technique."

But Nick's thoughts were elsewhere. He was wondering what had become of Donnie Hollis. He hadn't thought about Donnie for years.

CHAPTER 29

Another break in the cloud cover exposed just enough sunlight for Margo to see the fire tower when she and Nick emerged from the dense forest. The tower sat on the peak of a hill. It had a three-hundred-and-sixty degree vantage point and was like no watchtower she knew of in Washington. Back home, the structures she'd seen sat on stilts and had ladders for access. But that wasn't to say she hadn't heard of elaborate watchtowers like this one—her father mentioned them during family dinners while talking about his cross-country skiing trips, which he'd taken with a group of faculty members. She'd never paid that much attention, but some of what her father said had sunk in. This watchtower didn't seem completely foreign to her.

This structure, a weary backpacker's dream, stood two stories high. She was grateful it wasn't the other kind of tower that sat on stilts because she suffered from mild acrophobia. Besides, a ladder would prove too treacherous to climb, especially in her condition. The tower's lower level was made of stone bricks. The top level, which had a balcony surrounding it, was constructed of wood, and windows overlooked the mountains from every direction. Now her reluctance to climb up the mountain seemed entirely foolish. This place looked like heaven. Why did she ever doubt Nick when all he wanted was to find them safety and shelter? Yet why hadn't he described this place to her? The whole truth would've made all the difference.

Only one more obstacle remained. The watchtower was perched on the apex of the mountain; the pathway to reach it followed a narrow ridge that dropped off precipitously on both sides.

As they approached the pathway, Nick said, "Take my hand."

That was a surprise. Now he was going out of his way to help. Why? She tried not to fear the worst, but she couldn't rid the odd thoughts from her mind. He was a strange one, but would he really have brought her all the way up there to shove her over the edge? If he wanted to kill her, she'd already be dead.

She smiled appreciatively and took his hand.

They walked with care, taking one step at a time. Too far to the left or the right and they could stumble and fall to their deaths. It would take only a tiny misstep.

About twenty feet away from the tower, Nick stopped. "Wait here, Margo."

The pathway had narrowed quite a bit. It was now a trap even for the cautious because, with the snow cover, there was no way to gauge the width of the path by looking at it. Nick handed her the torch, which was barely flickering. That he'd kept it lit at all was amazing. He slowly treaded the twenty feet, testing the snow with each step. Then he returned and took the torch.

"You're going to have to do it without my help. If I hold your hand, you might misjudge your step. If you lose your balance, do your best to keep your weight forward." He gestured with a circular motion of the arm. "Fall forward if you stumble or slip. Whatever you do, don't fall sideways or backward."

She no longer had his comforting hand to help her. How remarkable that the simple touch of his hand had given her courage. No matter. She would do this on her own. She looked off the ridge, a mistake because a bout of vertigo caused her to wobble. She righted herself before she stumbled. "Maybe I should crawl."

"No. If you crawl, you won't have any momentum to swing back if you start to slide or fall. Hold your arms out to each side like a tightrope walker. It's a cliché, but do not look down again. And take your time."

Navigating those twenty feet to the entrance to the tower was going to be like walking an *icy* tightrope. Not a chance she'd look down a second time.

"Show time," he said. "I'll go first."

He started across, and she followed. With each step, she made sure of her balance. Her foot slipped a time or two, not enough to send her over the ridge, but certainly enough for her stomach to drop and her pulse to quicken.

When she was about ten feet in, Nick turned around. "Slow down!"

"I'm not—"

"Yes, you are. You're going much too fast."

Only then did she realize just how right he was. With safety only feet away, every bone in her body wanted to run to its door. So close but so far away. Her adrenaline pumped on high. She felt like a cartoon character whose big red heart was bouncing on a spring in and out of her chest.

"Slow," he said, softly but firmly.

She started forward again, forcing herself to move at a snail's pace. Nick was waiting at the entrance to the tower—only a few feet away. He'd already cleared the snow off the steps that led up to the landing and inside.

A gust of wind blew hard. Out of reflex, she brushed away a few strands of hair that had gotten in her eyes, an action that caused her to misjudge her next step. That slight indiscretion threw her off balance and she pitched forward. Quickly, she reached out with her arms and righted herself but felt no ground underneath her right foot.

She looked up and whispered, "Ni . . . ?"

He reacted before she finished saying his name. He grasped her hand and kept her upright and on the mountain, but at the same time he went down hard on one knee—on the side of his injured leg. He winced in pain, then stood up gingerly like a gymnast performing an arabesque on the balance beam.

"Oh God, I'm sorry," Margo said. Once they were inside and settled back into their own brand of civilization, she'd have to examine his wound. His reaction revealed that it hadn't healed.

Waving off her apology, he helped her take the final steps to the base of the stairs. At the landing, she looked up and took a satisfied breath. Almost there. When they ascended the last steps up and she was standing on the stoop, she wanted to throw her arms around the tower and hug it. Instead, she clung to Nick, who stiffened for a moment but then patted her back.

"Be cool," he said. "Don't move." He disengaged and tried the door. It was locked, but, in a matter of moments, he jimmied it open.

"Thank God," she said as she crossed the threshold. "So worth the climb." Relief washed over her body. Safety at last when it seemed so impossibly near and yet far away. If ever there were an oxymoron, she'd just lived through one. Now in the arms this watchtower, it felt as if they'd been adrift on the ocean in a dinghy and had somehow stumbled upon an island with fresh water and lush tropical fruit trees. Heaven.

"Let's get upstairs," he said. "It'll be very dark once I close the door, so grab the railing. Take baby steps."

As soon as he closed the door, any light from outside was gone. Fortunately, though the torch had become faint, its dying light was enough to cast a glimmer on the stone staircase. Standing still a moment, gripping the arm rail, she all at once realized that the wind was no longer slapping her in the face. She'd become so accustomed to its insult that she'd forgotten what calm air was like. What a contrast to her sailing days, when she looked forward to that warm breeze flowing through her hair and across her face, caressing her skin with an almost sensuous touch. Now, the cold, still air inside this tower was just as comforting.

"I hope there's a generator," she said and then half-stumbled on the first step.

"Be careful, Margo!"

She raised a hand in apology.

When they reached the top floor, she was amazed. The moonlight streaming through the windows cast a silver glow throughout the room, bright enough to allow her to make out the furnishings. The large one-room apartment had a table in its center, on which was mounted a map of the area and a sky watcher's chart. A small kitchenette was located near one wall. On the other walls were a narrow table and two chairs, an extra-long twin bed, and a thin mattress with no covers atop it. Best of all, there was a wood stove in the corner of the room.

Nick began looking around. "No wood up here. I'll go downstairs and see if there's some. Sit down so you don't fall over anything." He limped away. He hadn't limped like that before he'd fallen near the entrance a few minutes earlier.

She sat in a chair and looked out the window. No sign of civilization, not a trace of humanity anywhere in sight. Just mountains and snow-covered trees cast against the dark-gray night sky. So this was what true isolation felt like. It wasn't long before she heard Nick coming up the stairs. As he rounded the bend, the red light from the torch glowed and flickered inside the room, the contrast between its light and the size of Nick's shadow a little intimidating. When he reached the top floor, he was carrying a couple of logs he'd tucked under one of his arms.

"We're in luck," he said. "We have enough for the evening. Tomorrow, I'll have to head out for more. This won't be enough if we're stranded for more than a day or two."

"What do you mean a day or two? There must be a communications device in here, a two-way radio. We can call for help. How else would a lookout watcher be able to call in a fire?"

"It's winter. The park service wouldn't leave anything like that up here. They don't want to encourage thieves."

He couldn't be serious.

"You're safe, for the time being." His eyes bore into hers. "Why can't you settle for that, Margo?"

Sure, they were safer than they'd been since this nightmare began. But this was still a nightmare, and like all nightmares, she just wanted this one to end. "If we can find a way out of here right away that's what we should do. Why would you balk at that?"

His glower was so intense that she turned away. She could never predict what would irritate him.

Margo hated settling. It never worked out. She'd had plenty of past experiences with that. Matt for one. She tried settling for Matt, even when he said he didn't want kids. She didn't rescind her agreement to marry him that day he'd proposed, so, officially, they were engaged. And for a while, they seemed to be doing okay at treading water. Their jobs filled most of their waking hours, and when they were together they didn't talk about the children issue. She hoped if they stayed close, he would change his mind without her goading him. Then, on a brisk but sunny afternoon in late May, they set out sailing on his new boat. She lay back sunning herself as he maneuvered the boat's sheet. The leading edge of the luff began to flutter slightly in and, so he pulled the sheet in just enough for the fluttering to stop. He was a natural at trimming the sail, and he constantly toyed with it. Then he joined her, and together they enjoyed the warm air gliding across their faces. That day with Matt, she thought of her father and how he talked about the harmony he felt inside when he would take cross-country ski trips. She'd found the same joy sailing with Matt.

Perhaps because she was in the warm, comforting sun, or perhaps because of the effects of the beer, she blurted out, "Did I ever tell you I caught my father fucking one of his grad students?"

"Wow, no," Matt replied.

"It was horrible. Still is horrible to think of. I actually caught them screwing in our old station wagon. In a parking lot. I was sixteen. It still gives me the creeps."

"That was a long time ago. Your parents are still married, and from what I can tell, quite happy with their lives. I guess your mom forgave him."

Margo brushed away a strand of hair and adjusted her sunglasses. "My mother never knew."

"Good that you didn't tell her."

"I hated my father, and don't kid yourself, I really wanted to tell my mother. So many times I almost did. But she was so good, so kind. I could never hurt her."

"People are human, Margo. Affairs happen. Now it's only ancient history, as if it never happened, meant nothing. Probably did mean nothing. Have you been obsessing about this all these years? What a burden. You should let it go for your own peace of mind."

"That's an insensitive thing to say. I was a kid, and I had to . . ." My God, her father's sin of adultery had resurfaced as a blight on her own life. She couldn't forgive her father. She'd reacted to his indiscretion by becoming indiscreet herself, and she'd ended up pregnant. Yes, they were human. But that didn't erase the pain of the past, nor the hurtful emotions she secretly carried all these years. She'd learned to co-exist with her father's sin. When she became an adult, she understood that all people made mistakes, and as an adult one had to get past not only their own but also other people's foibles. But for Matt to dismiss her emotions as petty or obsessive felt like a betrayal. He should've been the one person who listened, who understood.

The wind shifted, and the sail began to flutter and the boat to rock.

"I've got to adjust the line. Watch the boom." He deftly adjusted the lines, and they were back to smooth sailing.

She couldn't shake her anger. She was deeply wounded by his lack of sensitivity, but she didn't purse it. Maybe Matt was right. *Let it go*, she thought. *Let everything in the past go.*

When he returned, he sat beside her. Once, he would've kissed her. They no longer kissed passionately the way they used to, not even when they were making love.

The sun blazed hotter, and she began to sweat. But was it the sun? The alcohol? She sat up and took a couple of beers out of the cooler. They drank and watched the clouds float by. They used to like to create imaginary pictures and laugh about what they were seeing—stupid talk, silly games. Where had all that gone? Now, they struggled to make conversation, and the silence felt awkward, like two strangers with nothing in common. They must've lain this way for over an hour, because the colors in the sky were now beginning to change.

"Where are we on having a family?" she asked. "Children."

He shifted his weight. "Nothing's changed given where we are in our relationship."

"What do you mean, 'where we . . .'" Then it hit her. She sat up. "Are you having an affair, Matt?"

He hesitated, then wrinkled his brow—the analytical doctor's look. The wind swept his hair from his face as though blowing away a mask of deceit.

"Are you?" she repeated.

"Margo, you're only projecting what you told me about your father."

"That doesn't answer my question."

He inhaled, then looked at her with a combination of sadness and resolve. "What do you want me to say? The important thing is that I love *you*. We just have to, you know, work on . . ."

The undersides of her eyelids flashed scarlet. She grabbed her stomach and retched. She wished she'd thrown up on him. "You're an asshole!" she hollered. She wanted to ask who the woman was, wanted to cry, wanted to shove him overboard, but she did none of that. She turned away and looked out at the horizon and rippling blue water.

"I never see you," he said. "You're always working. Do you realize we saw each other only one evening last month? One evening. And you didn't even stay the night. Some excuse about having to be to at work in the morning. That never stopped you from staying over in the past."

She stood and went to the railing. She turned back and glared at him. "You think the best defense is a good offense? Fuck you, Matt."

He folded his arms high across his chest. "Frankly, I" He caught himself.

"Go on, say it."

"I wondered if you were seeing someone else."

She laughed bitterly. "I never cheated on you. I was out of town a lot last month, and at work, and—"

"Exactly."

"No, *not* exactly. I did not cheat on you. It never occurred to me." She tugged at the ring on her finger, not knowing whether she would give it back to him or throw it overboard. But her finger was swollen from the heat, and her sailing chores and the beers, so she couldn't get the ring off.

Only then did he soften, his stoic defensiveness crumbling like a child's fortress made of sand. "Please, Margo. Forgive me. It was a mistake, meaningless. You're the woman I want to marry, to spend the rest of my life with. We work, you and I."

She shook her head. "Not anymore." She turned her back on him and moved as far away as the boat's size would allow.

Later, Matt married the woman he cheated with—an intern at his hospital. Now, they had an eight-month-old son. It made no sense. She'd always wondered whether things would've been different for them if she'd told him sooner about her father and how it had affected her, and about the baby that was taken from her. Perhaps Matt would've understood her better. Perhaps not. It was ancient history now.

CHAPTER 30

Margo sat watching Nick as he started a fire in the wood stove. This was the first real opportunity that she had to study him without fear of running from more danger. When the flames brightened the interior of the space, she saw that his face was mottled with patches of deep crimson and pure white. The ice in his disheveled hair was beginning to melt, and water droplets were forming at the top of his forehead. He hadn't complained once about being cold, but with only a short collar and no hood on his coat, he was obviously suffering from exposure to the frigid temperatures. His hands were patchy with red and white spots. Had he not kept his hands in his coat pockets or beneath his sleeves, his fingers would surely be frostbitten. Maybe they were, and he was hiding it. While the stove heated up, he found a large pail in a closet on the first floor, went outside, and returned with a bucketful of snow. He put the snow in a pan, boiled it on the stove, and searched through the kitchen cabinets.

When the water cooled, he handed her a filled glass. "Drink."

"Thanks," she said. "I will, but my stomach is in knots."

He wasn't taking no for an answer, so she accepted the glass and drank. Nothing in the world compared to fresh water and its healing properties.

He worked diligently, focused and taciturn, not seeming to care if she watched him or not. There was nothing self-conscious about the man. It was already a foregone conclusion that he expected her to remain in step with him, to do as he commanded. The military had taught him well, but there was more than that. He was a self-made man who relied on no one except himself. Everything he did was part of a larger plan; nothing was random or wasteful. His organizational skills comforted her, felt familiar. In a way he reminded her of a surgeon preparing for a major operation.

She looked away from him and out the window. Her mind wandered down that dark lane again, playing its games, taunting her. If the snow continued to accumulate, they might find themselves stuck in this tower—a death trap. Nick must've realized that before they headed up the mountain. No one would ever think to look for them at a tower. When rescue workers weren't able to locate the remains of their bodies with the other people listed as passengers on the train, what would the authorities think? That they were buried somewhere deep in the snow, somewhere inaccessible? That would mean that the rescuers would give up all search efforts until spring when the snow melted.

Margo's insides felt hollow. She didn't want to continue to think negatively, but she couldn't control her dark thoughts. What if she was missing something? What if Nick had some ulterior motive for insisting that she come up the mountain? She glanced at him and then back out the window. He didn't appear insane or suicidal yet, how could she know what was inside his mind? Her idea of going down the mountain, not up into the remote wilderness, still seemed the more rational choice. Maybe Nick had lied about the leopard. What if he was a serial killer and she was his target? He knew how to kill, had done that for a living. Did he want to torture her, cut the baby from her belly, and kill them both?

The acid rose in her throat. She shook her head, trying to dispel these weird and horrid thoughts. One minute she was comforted by him, the next she was questioning whether she could trust him. They were strangers, true, and though he'd saved her life, she couldn't just disregard her own instinct, surrender herself to him as his prisoner or foot soldier. She clamped her eyes shut. It was only the cold affecting her, messing with her mind. If Nick were more personable, more conversant, she wouldn't be this paranoid.

Within the hour, the small room began to feel toasty, and he said, "You should rest, Margo."

"I'm sorry I haven't been good company," she said.

"You're not here to entertain me. You need to rest."

"Maybe you're right."

She met his eyes. There was no maybe about it. She'd been ordered to rest. She removed her coat, and for the first time since she got on the train a few days ago, she lay down on a bed and felt real warmth.

Her mind cleared. Peace finally. That proved short lived when thoughts of her family intruded. What would they think when they learned the train was missing? Would they give up hope? Would they be glad she was dead, out of their way?

Her stomach growled. They had to eat, but the pheasant was gone. Nick couldn't forage in the forest again until tomorrow. She closed her eyes. She could think only of food, a steak-and-baked-potato dinner. Like counting backward from one hundred, she began preparing the meal in her mind and fell into a deep sleep.

Sometime later—five minutes, an hour, two hours—she emerged from slumber. Her mouth was as dry as baked clay. She opened her eyes and felt a strange weight on her. To her surprise, Nick was lying beside her. Of course he had to sleep on the bed. She couldn't expect him to sleep on the floor. But how they were lying was dumbfounding. Once again, he had his arm wrapped around her belly. She tensed, her first real movement since she woke.

"What's wrong?" he asked.

Did she wake him, or had he been awake all this time? She couldn't tell by his voice and wasn't about to ask. She licked her lips and tried to swallow. "I'm so thirsty," she replied. "I can't swallow."

Without another word, he rose and moved toward the kitchenette. He returned with a pan, not a glass. "Drink, slowly."

She pushed up and took small sips, though the urge to gulp was almost irresistible. But she didn't want to vomit. When he returned the pan to the kitchen, she fell back to the mattress, and the next thing she knew, light was streaming in through the windows and dancing in her eyes. Nick's body was no longer pressed against hers. His arm was no longer wrapped around her stomach, nor was his hand pressing against the baby. He was gone and not upstairs. There was no sound indicating that he was downstairs.

She pushed her body upright and sat on the side of the bed. Odd how one could sense another person's presence even when that person remained silent and sat perfectly still. That was silence. But it was nothing like the silence of being in a room devoid of another person. That was deafening silence.

To be sure he was gone, she called out, "Hello, Nick?"

No response.

"Nick," she cried louder. "Are you down there?"

She sat for a while, looking out the windows and taking in the panoramic view while listening to the undulating beat of the wind striking against the tower. The tower was surrounded by mountains and valleys seeded with evergreen forests that sparkled like diamonds. The sky was dotted with white rippling clouds. At the eastern edge, the sun was beginning to rise, casting off faint hues of orange and red. A beautiful sight to behold indeed, but so very dangerous.

Margo had been a city girl for so long that she'd forgotten the beauty of nature, except for what she saw through the eyes of the children she treated. The young looked at life through pristine eyes. They believed in fairy tales, and some did even to the end of their days. It was that magic that pushed Margo to try harder, to be a better doctor. Sometimes very sick children became mature beyond their years, comforting their parents. No child should be cast into an adult role. Margo understood that all too well. She'd had to grow up much sooner than she should have. She'd come to understand that her firstborn child, Olivia, wasn't a mistake; she was a gift. A gift stolen from Margo and given to her sister.

CHAPTER 31

Margo's sister Heather and her husband, Charles, had been grateful at first. Her sister often wrote describing how Margo's "niece" was doing. She'd even sent pictures of the child. Heather said Olivia's arrival had made her life complete, that she had the perfect daughter, the perfect life. The baby was getting the best possible care, was a member of their family. But Margo still felt empty. She wondered if she would've felt the same emptiness if anonymous strangers had adopted Olivia. Would out of sight, out of mind have spared her the anguish?

According to plan, Margo stayed in Birmingham to separate herself from Heather and Olivia. She didn't want to live with her parents anyway. Not until the summer after her freshman year at Duke University in North Carolina did she return to Spokane for two weeks. Her bedroom had been converted into a sewing room, and she had to sleep on a cot among the threads and bobbins and assortments of fabrics. Her school friends had grown apart from her, so she spent most of her time hanging out with her younger sister, Blanche.

When Margo first set eyes on Olivia, a precocious two-year-old, she fell in love with her. Since the time of the birth, Margo had convinced herself that she was only Aunt Margo, but that changed when she saw Olivia's eyes. They were as brilliant blue as the eyes of her biological father, the boy who'd gone by the silly name Keystone. Maybe she should've found that disturbing since she never once tried to look for him or tell him about the child. Her parents hadn't either. No one seemed to care one ounce about him. At the time, it was too complicated to bother with anything like that, which was exactly what the Fletcher family convinced themselves of. Another skeleton in the closet, one not to be exhumed. Other than those blue eyes, Olivia looked like Margo, not like her sisters. If the child had only looked like Heather or Blanche, it might not have been so troubling. But the child's physical resemblance to Margo only made her seem more like Margo's child again.

On their first meeting, Margo kneeled down and said, "Hey, sweetie, I'm your . . . Aunt Margo." Except she almost swallowed the words Aunt Margo.

"Momma," Olivia said, and grasped Heather's leg. Heather smiled. Margo wanted to die.

Margo steeled herself and forced out the next words. "Grandma Emma and I made you a little blanket. To play with your dolls and to sleep with if you like. Grandma Emma likes to quilt. You'll see it has pink hearts and purple butterflies. We didn't know which color was your favorite."

"Pink," Olivia said in a precious, small voice.

When Margo handed Olivia the blanket, the child's eyes sparkled.

"What do you say to Aunt Margo?" Heather said in a firm voice that reminded Margo of her father's.

"Thank you, Aunt Margo," Olivia said.

Margo hugged the child and told her that she was welcome. Was it her imagination, or did Heather's posture stiffen when Olivia hugged Margo back?

A few weeks after Margo left, Blanche told Margo in a phone conversation that Olivia had become so attached to the blanket that she took it with her everywhere she went. She also told Margo that Heather had several times tried to take the blanket from Olivia—resulting in hysterics from the child—until Charles convinced Heather to relent.

Now, from the forest observation tower, Margo prayed her

unborn child would have the chance to carry a favorite blanket or stuffed animal.

She rose and stretched. The smell from her soiled clothes permeated her nostrils. She'd have to find a way to bathe. Then the baby moved a limb, the ripple visible through her shirt. Thank God her body took care of the baby's needs.

She walked from window to window, studying the surroundings. No telling how long Nick had been gone. Then she saw traces of footprints in the snow that led down the incline they'd climbed to get to the tower. Nick was right—one misstep would've been deadly.

She went to the kitchenette and scrounged around. Inside a cabinet below the counter, a few pans were tucked up on a shelf. In an upper cabinet, she found some dishes. Inside one of the drawers, she found utensils and packets of salt and pepper and a pack of matches with three matches left. Those three meager pieces of paper with a minute amount of explosive on each tip had the potential to save a human life.

A gust of wind beat hard against the windowpanes, sounding as if a pane of glass had broken.

Margo flinched and dropped the matchbook, which slid behind the counter. She reached for them, but the girth of her belly stymied them. Nick would have to deal with that later.

She walked to the center of the room and studied the map table. From a faded red dot marking their location, it appeared that they were on top of Scalplock Mountain, about five miles from the highway. A doable walk without the snow but now seemingly impossible. She traced her finger along the trails, memorizing the pathways to fill the time.

Then the sky darkened, which meant more snow. The room was also getting cold, and the wood was gone. She walked downstairs to look for more, but it was too dark to see, so she headed back up. When she rounded the corner and the surface of the top floor came into view, she noticed a radio sitting on a low shelf cabinet. That she could reach. It wasn't a two-way radio but it still served as a connection to the outside world. She pumped the handle for power, but before the radio powered on, the door downstairs opened, and footsteps echoed up to the second floor.

She set the radio back on the shelf, "Nick?"

"Be right up," he replied and soon mounted the stairs.

As he turned the corner, her eyes widened when she recognized what he was carrying. The sight made her both ravenous and nauseous. "You killed a deer?"

He set the animal down on the counter near the sink. "Baby elk."

"I hope you don't plan on butchering it in here."

His eyes narrowed in irritation. "We can't leave the carcass outside. It would attract predators."

"Of course, you're right. As usual. What can I do to help?"

"You can get out one of those pans, and we'll cook some of this meat."

"I want to ask how you killed this animal, but a part of me really doesn't want to know."

She met his questioning eyes.

"Okay, so tell me then." She needed to praise his efforts, not act like a schoolgirl. It might be the way to loosen him up. Then she added, "No reason girls can't become good hunters."

"I set a trap, something for the animal to fall in. The key is knowing how to find a herd and then spook them into running in the right direction. The hard part is avoiding the adult animals."

"What did you use as a weapon?"

"I found a shovel downstairs. How much more do you want to know?"

She raised a hand.

"I didn't think you'd be so squeamish after having worked in an emergency room."

Margo tensed. She'd never told Nick she worked in an emergency room. Had she? No, she certainly didn't remember that.

Who was this man?

CHAPTER 32

The day after Andie's murderous death, someone tapped on Nick's barrack's door.

"Sergeant, it's time," a soldier said. Nick rose from his chair and headed out toward Andie's casket, which was sitting next to the cargo bay of the transport plane. The base chaplain, a tall, lanky, youngish man who looked more like a college basketball player than a member of the clergy, said a few words, all scripted—the same script he'd used for other fallen soldiers who had shipped out earlier that morning. After the *God rest her soul* part, the pallbearers began wheeling the casket toward the ramp to place it inside the cargo hold. "Wait, Chaplain," Nick said as he walked toward the casket. "Please open it."

"I'm sorry, Sergeant, we can't do that," the chaplain said. "Her wishes were for a closed casket."

"Do it, sir," Nick said, with a tinge of menace in his voice.

The soldiers in attendance fidgeted nervously. Not only was Nick making a morbid demand, but he was also challenging a superior. Enlisted men didn't talk that way to captains, chaplains or not.

The chaplain stared at Nick and nodded. "Open it, Corporal," he said to the soldier in charge of the depressing task.

The corporal complied.

Nick walked over and looked at Andie. There was no more blood, no more ripped flesh. She was laid out in her dress uniform. Her body had been cleaned, her hair styled in a tight bun. How beautiful she looked, like a doll in a package just waiting to be opened.

Suddenly, he couldn't breathe. It was as if a massive wrecking ball had slammed into his chest. His mouth went dry, and his knees were about to go weak, but he dug down deep for that reservoir of dispassion he'd first found in grade school and forced himself to hide his distress. He stood more erect, and saluted Andie.

"Close it," the chaplain said.

Nick couldn't bear it. He took a step closer and touched her hands, which lay folded gracefully across her chest. He'd always marveled at how her hands could be strong and delicate at the same time. Those hands had protected the innocent, had killed those who were evil. Her flesh was cold and warm at the same time—cold clay of death, warm from the scorching sun. How was that possible? The temperature was already in the nineties, and he was perspiring profusely like everyone else, so undoubtedly the others would confuse his tears for sweat. Sergeant Nick Eliot didn't cry. He wanted to touch her face, but that, like his tears, would show weakness, would reveal something about himself he had to keep hidden. Instead, he slipped the pearl engagement ring he had purchased in New Zealand onto her finger. He'd been waiting for the right romantic moment, but that time would never come. But she would forever be his.

"Step back, Sergeant," the chaplain said to Nick. "Let her go. It's not your fault."

"I never said it was," Nick replied.

CHAPTER 33

Margo and Nick sat together at the small table, eating cooked elk and drinking sterilized water. She wanted to ask him about how he knew she was an ER doctor. But she couldn't. Maybe if she could get him to talk more, he would reveal something that would ease her mind. But even in repose, he wasn't much of a talker. He hardly uttered a word unless she prodded it out of him. It was almost as if her presence was the cause of his reticence.

"You're still limping," she said. "More, actually, since the fall on the steps. Now that we're warm, I really should take a look."

"It's fine. Just a scratch."

"I'm worried that you haven't been able to keep it clean, and it'll get infected."

He looked up. "There isn't much I can do about that at the moment."

"Yes, there is. We can make soap from the animal fat."

His eyes widened, and he shook his head slightly, as if he were wondering why he hadn't thought of that himself.

Finally, he seemed to understand that she could be helpful.

"We've got a pan; we just have to mix the fat with cold water and refrigerate it," she said. "We can set it out on the balcony. When the fat hardens, we discard the water and keep the soap frozen until we're ready to use it."

He nodded and stood. "I need to clean up the dishes."

"I have some news."

He set the dishes on the counter and looked at her with a curious expression.

She pushed her weight forward and got to her feet. She walked across the room and found the radio where she'd left it on a shelf. "A radio," she said, holding it up.

"Interesting," he said, his tone even and not excited as she'd expected.

"I thought you'd be happy."

When he didn't respond, she returned to the table and sat down. "It's not a two-way radio, unfortunately. It's the kind you power up with a crank."

"Let me see it."

When he sat down, she handed the radio to him, and he began turning the crank. A few minutes later, he tried switching it on. No luck. He located the battery compartment and slid off the lid.

"Battery's corroded." He brushed it against his pants, got up, and went over to the kitchenette. After rummaging through the drawers and cabinets, he found a long nail. Returning to the table, he began shaving off the corrosion. Once the battery was shiny, he put it back into the radio and cranked the handle again. This time, the radio powered on.

Her heart soared. Finally, a taste of the outside world.

He turned the dial back and forth slowly at first, but got no reception, only static.

"Let me try," Margo said.

To her mild surprise, he handed the radio over without objecting.

She played with the dial until she heard faint voices. There was too much static to get clear reception. She rose and walked around the room, holding the radio high and ultimately finding a sweet spot in the room. Country music, Clint Black's "The Hard Way," was playing, still accompanied by a lot of static, but recognizable. She closed her eyes and sang along, gently swaying to the soft melody. She only knew a few of the country artists. Her father detested the style of music. But her mother, an Alabama girl, had her favorites—Patsy Cline, Tammy Wynette, Emmylou Harris.

When Margo was a kid, her mother, when not driving with Professor Fletcher, would tune the radio in the car to the classic country station. *All the times I reminisce* . . . She knew this song, which seemed to tell the story of her life . . . *finally realizing this.* She lost herself in the music, becoming one with it, so much so that she felt truly connected with the outside world. *Until it's gone it can't be missed* . . . She imagined reaching an arm over the mountains, away from the ice and snow, and pulling her body back home to safety. . . . *I'm finding out the hard way.*

The song ended, followed by more static. An announcer said the local news and weather was up next. Still more static.

A loud boom pounded on the floor, as if a tree had fallen inside the house, but it was Nick stomping his foot.

He shouted, "Stop it!" and knocked the radio from her hand. The device smacked the ground with a horrible crack-thud, and the crank-handle broke off and slid across the floor.

Margo froze as she watched the handle come to a stop. Then she cut her eyes toward Nick.

His chest heaved as he stood glowering.

Anxiety slammed into her chest. As if a massive wave had engulfed her body, she felt as if she'd been forced below water. Her fingers and toes instantly numbed and began to throb. She slowly stepped back, trembling. There was nowhere to go. Even if she'd wanted to run, he stood in the path to the door.

He looked away and turned toward the window. Had he cracked under the pressure?

She forced herself to maintain control when all she wanted was to fall apart. This couldn't escalate, couldn't go any further. He needed reassurance. That was all.

Keeping her voice low, she managed to say, "What's going on, Nick?"

He gaped at her, wild-eyed. Moments later, he shook his head. "The static. It got louder, and I . . . It doesn't happen often, but the static. IEDs the Taliban use sound like this, I lost four of my platoon."

So, he was suffering from PTSD. From her ER experience, she knew that the smallest, most inconsequential occurrence could bring on a manic or psychotic episode. She'd seen former military vets lose it and have to be taken down by orderlies or security guards and then sedated. When she worked at Marshall General, a disabled vet went on a rampage in his neighborhood, banging mailboxes with his fists and threatening to kill his neighbors and anyone who stepped on his property. The event was triggered by the postman coming to his door with a piece of registered mail. After the vet's wife was able to calm her husband, she brought him to the ER and had his hand stitched up. He looked in control at first, but when a nurse asked him what had happened, the episode was re-triggered. Before all hell broke loose, the attending nurse was able to stick him with one hell of a powerful sedative. Margo didn't have the luxury of attendants nor the medications to calm Nick down.

Her hands were shaking, so she clasped them together to conceal the tremors. Whatever she did, she couldn't appear frightened. She should have expected this, should have seen it coming. It was all too clear now. Nick's tough exterior was just that—an act. All along, he had been bottled up with dynamite looking for a fuse. His quiet but hard nature, his directness without much compassion, his need to be in control were all evidence that he was fighting demons. And yet, he'd done nothing before this to reveal his instability. Usually there was a hint. Not with Nick Eliot.

He raked his hands through his hair and exhaled. "We're in a life-and-death situation. I'm doing the best I can to keep you safe. But you just keep on and on with your insubordination and your nonsense." This episode had far from passed. She was no longer simply his pedestrian foot soldier, she was a soldier in his platoon who'd crossed the line and disobeyed. Worse, she had become his enemy. If he became any more manic, anything might happen.

"Of course you're doing your best, Nick," she said in an even voice. "Thank you. Sincerely. I'm going a little crazy here myself."

His face hardened again, and he advanced on her at lightning speed, stopping inches from her face. How foolish of her. She'd used the wrong words.

"You think I'm crazy? Is that it? Crazy?" he spat.

She took a few steps back to put space between them.

"Answer me!" he said.

"No, of course not. I'm sorry. You've been remarkable, getting us through this. If not for you, my baby and I would be dead. I'm so very grateful. I just want to go home. I know you do too." She paused, then tried a technique that sometimes worked in the hospital. "Tell me about yourself, Nick. After all we've been through, I really want to get to know you better. So I can be better help to you. Please. I'm sorry if I've made the situation worse. I just want to help."

"Give it a rest, Margo. I'm not an idiot. Don't try to manipulate me. The more important question is how's the baby? You haven't mentioned anything today."

Had her head just spun three-sixty? Yes, he was angry, still manic, but what a time for him to ask about her baby's welfare. Her heart skittered, and more fear inched up her spine.

Don't go there. Think positive. Be brave. Don't let him see inside.

"I think everything is fine," she replied. "But I'm certain my blood pressure is up."

He exhaled, and the anger in his face drained. Turning, he walked over to the broken radio, squatted down, and gathered up the pieces.

Was the episode over?

"I think I'll rest, if that's okay with you," she said. "Unless you need me to do anything, or want to talk, or . . ."

"Yes, you do that. I'll see what I can do to fix this radio. And then make us some soap."

She lay down on the bed and watched him take the radio to the table, where he sat down and fiddled with the pieces.

After ten minutes, he shrugged and said, "No luck. I'll work on it later."

He seemed almost back to normal—almost, but not quite, since his eyes had a residual glassy sheen. Part of him was still somewhere else. He would only stew if left to his own thoughts. She needed to get him talking, get him to do something that he was good at, so he would find solid ground below his feet.

"We need a plan," she said, hoping that thinking proactively would bring him all the way back. "This may sound silly, but what if we make a fire outside and send up smoke signals? The Native Americans did it."

"Indians?"

"I'm just thinking smoke could get someone's attention? Maybe a passing plane?"

He bolted up from his chair and took a step in her direction.

She cringed. Then, all of a sudden, he turned back toward the kitchenette. When he reached the counter, he braced his hands on its edge, his knuckles turning white. Maybe he would get through his frustration by taking charge again. In his mind.

"Okay, Margo. Let's think about that for a second." His tone was patronizing. "Do you know how high commercial planes fly? Never mind. Take it from me, if a plane flew over us right now, no one on it would see a fire down here. And you sure can't expect a low-flying prop plane to be out in this weather."

"So what do we do? You can't keep hunting day after day."

"Wait! We wait, Margo. We stay here for as long as it takes. And don't ask how long that'll be. It'll take as long as it takes. Days, weeks, whatever it takes."

And then it was her turn to lose control, and she began to weep. He wasn't thinking rationally. He wasn't thinking about the rescue workers arriving at the scene. Someone would definitely come looking for that train and the survivors. The train wreck affected hundreds of people who would demand a rescue effort.

She tried to suppress the tears. But her chest heaved.

He turned around. His expression was now intense and hard.

She was rocking to soothe herself, to get control.

"Stop it," he said.

"I'm sorry. My hormones are a mess. I'm afraid for us. I know you're taking care of us, doing everything possible. I feel vulnerable."

His harsh expression faded. "You rest. I'm going to add more wood to the fire. If it eases your mind any, I've been in much harsher conditions than these. There's always a way to survive. We'll just have to find that way."

She nodded and then had an epiphany. Maybe this would give him a peace of mind. "Hey, you know what? I think it's Christmas Day. Merry Christmas, Nick."

When he didn't respond, only looked perplexed, she closed her eyes, rolled over, patted her belly, and whispered, "Merry Christmas" to her child.

She'd counted on the baby to make Christmas a happy time again. The holiday hadn't been festive ever since the year that Olivia had turned sixteen. That was six years ago.

CHAPTER 34

Heather and Charles had wanted to take a Caribbean cruise over the winter holiday break, and Olivia would finally be allowed to come to Chicago and stay with her Aunt Margo. Yes, she'd finally been granted permission to visit. Margo had just broken up with Matt. She welcomed the chance to play Fun Aunt Margo, the cool, sophisticated, single woman Olivia didn't see much.

When Olivia arrived at Chicago O'Hare, Margo waited anxiously for her to walk out of airport security. Her heart melted when she saw Olivia. She'd grown up so much. She wore a short, form-fitting denim dress with leggings and a pair of boots, had a cross-body bag slung from one shoulder to the opposite hip, and wore her hair up in a hippie-style bun secured with a bandana with strands of loose hair pulled down and around her face. Her makeup consisted of heavy eyeliner, mascara, and bright pink lipstick on her plump lips. She was stunning, simply beautiful, and Margo couldn't have been more pleased. The moment she saw her standing there waiting, Olivia's face lit up like a bright star, and she put an extra hop in her step. Margo waved, and instead of waiting for Olivia to reach her, they raced to each other and hugged.

"Aw, it's so good to see you, Olivia," Margo said. "You look like your pictures—no, even more beautiful." She didn't want to sound too sappy, but she couldn't help herself. So much for the cool, sophisticated aunt. "So did you have a good flight?"

Oliva nodded, and her bun bobbed up and down. She rolled her eyes like a typical teenage girl and said, "It was a great flight, except I had to sit next to this guy who wanted to talk the whole way. When he got up for a few minutes, I finally had the chance to put my earphones in and face the window. There's glory in a window seat. Such glory."

"How's everyone back home?"

"Mom and Dad are off on their big, fabulous, disgustingly gross trip. Imagine sitting on a ship for a week, getting seasick, and eating the same food over and over again."

Margo laughed. "I don't like cruises either. But sailing, now that's entirely different. I'll take you one day."

"Mom said if I didn't get my homework done, I'd never get another trip away during the holidays."

"Homework during the winter holidays?"

"Journal project, English lit. No biggie. And yeah, I'm doing fine in school. Mom said you'd ask and to tell you that we didn't need to be running all over the city. That we should stay in and read and eat healthy."

"Very funny."

"No, I'm serious. She said you were the wild child, that you might be a doctor now, but, you know, whatever. She's so freaking strict it's ridiculous. Thinks everyone is out to get me. I must have heard fifty lectures before this trip alone on how I shouldn't talk to strangers, shouldn't walk on the street by myself because someone could snatch me. Jeez, I'm not four years old. It's a wonder I ever got to go to preschool."

"That's just normal parental concern. No one wants anything bad to happen to their kid."

Olivia shook her head. "I'm looking forward to a little fun for a change. I'm a little wild child myself. No offense, Aunt Margo."

"None taken. Anyway, you know how things get blown out of proportion. We all grow up, and we all have our moments. I never did anything bad. Your mom is probably thinking about her own dirty deeds."

Margo wrapped an arm around Olivia's shoulder, and they shared another laugh.

That week they visited museums, went shopping, to lunch every day—and then did more shopping, because Olivia was definitely a fashionable Fletcher woman and had to have all the new styles. Plus, her father had given her a credit card and a hefty allowance.

They'd just come in from a long day of shopping. Olivia kicked her shoes off, plopped down on the couch, and kicked her legs up. Then she looked up at Margo. Margo sensed that Olivia had been trying to tell Margo something all day. But if she'd asked, Olivia, like most teenagers, would've shied away. Margo was now the designated Fun Aunt, so she got to hear the stuff that Mom didn't.

"I'm seeing someone," Olivia said.

"That's good, Olivia. He's nice, of course?"

"Chase is the best. But I ... My parents don't know. They won't approve. He's a sophomore at Gonzaga."

Margo understood why her sister and brother-in-law wouldn't approve. "Olivia, that makes him, what, nineteen? I mean, you're only sixteen, so—"

Olivia got that look of disappointment and borderline disgust that only a teenage girl can get. "I thought you'd understand, Aunt Margo. The high school boys are immature. Chase is really sweet. A really good guy. And very, very cute. Awesome guy."

"You should tell your parents," Margo said. "If he's as nice as you say, they'll understand." Margo knew this wasn't true.

"No, they won't. They got upset last year when I was interested in a senior in high school. And he was only seventeen." She swung her legs around, sat up, and leaned forward. "So, you're a doctor and my aunt. I was wondering." She blushed. "You could write me a prescription for birth control pills, right?"

"Oh, Jesus, Olivia. You should talk this over with your mom.

Heather will—"

"She won't do it. She'll think I'm some kind of slut. My God, it's the twenty-first century, and my parents are like—like Grandma and Grandpa."

And so, Margo was put in a position she never wanted to be in.

"We're doing it already!" Olivia blurted out.

And in her eyes, in that face which so resembled Margo's own, she saw the same defiance that she'd shown had at the same age. Aunt? Mother? What did it matter? Margo was a doctor, and if Olivia had come to her as a patient, she would've written the prescription.

"Oral contraceptives are not enough," Margo said, trying to sound clinical. "You should be using a condom. STDs are—"

"We have been, but the last time it broke. Oh my God, I was so scared, because I was a week late. I thought I was . . ."

Margo wrote the prescription, which Olivia filled at a chain pharmacy that had a store in Spokane. It took Heather all of a week to discover the pills—which of course on the label showed the prescriber as Margo Fletcher, MD.

"You had no right, Margo," Heather told Margo over the phone in a tone as calm and analytical as their father's.

"I'm a doctor, and she came to me for help."

"I don't believe you did it because you were her *doctor*." The mockery on the last word was also worthy of their father. "Be that as it may, Charles and I feel that you betrayed our trust."

Of course, their parents were aligned with Heather. Blanche, the Switzerland of their family, stayed neutral. And while Olivia and Margo kept in touch for a while through emails and texts and the sporadic phone call, Olivia gradually withdrew and went on with her life, and why not? She was young.

Margo hadn't seen her family in six years. This trip home was to be a reunion and Margo hoped, a reconciliation. Now, she hoped she and her baby lived to see Spokane—to see Olivia, her niece, her biological daughter, get married.

CHAPTER 35

Nick didn't protest when he received the transfer stateside to Fort McNair in Washington, DC. He'd killed the henchman who'd murdered Andrea White, but he hadn't gotten to the bosses, who received protection from many internal factions. Because he couldn't root out the leaders and kill them, he wanted to come home. Besides, he needed a rest, perhaps a permanent rest, from the army. He had a decent job waiting for him back in the US. The army had a high demand for instructors qualified to train soldiers to fight in mountainous terrain. Few had better qualifications than Nick Eliot. So he continued on in the military when he was ordered stateside and became a training instructor for Special Forces.

Four months after he'd returned to the United States, his commander, a Colonel Dwyer summoned Nick. Dwyer was prematurely gray with a face so leathery that he could've passed as a seasoned veteran well over fifty. The fact was, the officer was only forty-eight, eight years older than Nick.

"We have a job for special ops which requires your survival skills and talent with weapons," the colonel said. "In Afghanistan."

"I'm done with that, sir. I'm no longer a kid." The part about age was convenient to say but, in truth, Nick didn't feel old. He didn't want to fight anymore.

"Hear me out, Sergeant," Dwyer said. "This involves an operation to destroy a compound housing chemicals to be used in warfare."

Nick snapped to attention.

"We have reason to believe the insurgents have successfully weaponized chemicals and are planning an attack on the Bagram Airfield." Dwyer went on to tell him that the compound was located underground outside a small settlement near Azrow. The military couldn't bomb the facility without risking civilian casualties. The operation was delicate and dangerous, in need of expert handling.

"Your experience is critical, Sergeant," Dwyer said. "You know the area."

"If you order me back to Afghanistan, of course I'll follow orders, sir," Nick said.

"This is hazardous duty, Sergeant. Strictly voluntary."

Nick thought for a moment, then shook his head. "I've served my time, sir." This offer was the test, and his reaction proved that he no longer wanted to fight.

Dwyer folded his hands on his desk and leaned forward. "There are two unique factors you should consider before making a final decision. First, Specialist Andrea White has a stake in this. We believe the insurgents who are in control of the compound are the people who planned the ambush that killed her."

"If I may, sir, what leads us to believe that's true?"

"We detained and questioned the husband of the school headmaster who attacked your unit. At first he said he knew nothing about the attack, but after some effective interrogation, he provided intel about the insurgents who ambushed your unit that night. The leader of the insurgent group is a Taliban mullah named Hamid. His group has control of the chemicals."

Nick's heart rate accelerated. The fight was returning.

"The second factor, Sergeant, is this: Specialist White's autopsy revealed she was three months pregnant at the time of her death."

Nick felt as if his skull had just been pried open and his brains pummeled. He had not a moment of doubt that the child was his. Had

Andie known? She must have known. The way she looked at him, the ambiguous smiles she gave him. The proposal of marriage. The story of the pearl. A metaphor for a child.

"She put in for a transfer back stateside with pregnancy as the grounds," Dwyer continued. "She made you her medical proxy, the secondary beneficiary of her life insurance policy and military benefits. Her grandparents were the primaries." Of course they were. Nick could support himself.

He and Andie had thought they'd hidden their relationship. So much for stealth and discretion. The military had known all along that they'd violated the rules. Why had the army brass looked the other way? Probably because of their effectiveness in combat.

"I appreciate your telling me this, sir."

"I'll give you some time to think about this mission," Dwyer said. "Purely voluntary."

"I don't need to think about it. I'm in." Nick saluted and left the room in a daze.

After the initial astonishment passed, he realized it was time to do something he'd been dreading. He dug through his desk drawer and found Andie's letter, the one he'd never opened. Since her death just months ago, he hadn't found the strength to read the letter. He unsealed the back flap and began reading Andie's last words, her last thoughts.

She started the letter with a rooster joke. Of course she did. Then she reminded him of how she'd grown up on her grandparents' farm in the heartland of Nebraska. She asked that, if he was reading this letter, he go see her grandparents in person and tell them about what kind of soldier she was.

Nick wanted to beat himself unconscious. How could he have procrastinated about opening this letter until now? It was common for soldiers to write letters and give them to someone else for safekeeping and delivery if necessary. The unspoken code was that these letters were to be opened and read. He'd violated that code. In his cowardice, he'd stood by and let her grandparents learn about Andie's death from a dispassionate messenger and hear nothing else.

He read on, hearing her voice in his mind. Her last few lines might as well have been a cold dagger penetrating his heart. *Pregnant with your child . . . was to be my gift to you . . . dearest, Nick, you are my one true love. I know your family history, but think of it this way, Sarge. You'd be a great father because you know what it is to be a bad one.*

He'd never thought of a kid in those terms. But her words resonated.

No matter what, if you truly loved me, you must honor my life and go on. Find happiness and a family. Complete yourself.

Rage coursed through every inch of his body. He tucked the letter back in its envelope, raced out the door, and began running as hard and as fast as he could. When he could run no more, he returned to his office, dripping wet. There was no time to go to Nebraska. He had to get ready for war.

Nick returned to Afghanistan a week later. The mission, code name Operation Dragon Claw DC-10, would be more dangerous than any he'd been on. He handpicked the soldiers who would accompany him. The squad consisted of seven men, two women, and himself. Afghan forces would sit this one out. It was always risky to trust Afghan soldiers. Too many potential Taliban spies.

An advance team of more than one hundred coalition troops traveled toward a province south of Kabul and southeast of Kuh-e Soltan Saheb, near the Pakistan border, where intense fighting was beginning to break out. These additional troops would, the Americans hoped, draw out the Taliban soldiers from Nick's target village where the terrorists had stored the chemicals. This diversion would allow Nick's special ops unit to make a foray the following day into the village and destroy the chemical cache while the insurgents were gone. Eight hours after the coalition troops had set out, Nick got the word—Operation Dragon Claw DC-10 was a go.

The likelihood that he would kill the people who shot Andie, or kill Mullah Hamid, was almost nil. But he would make sure those bastards couldn't engage in chemical warfare, and that would be a measure of revenge.

A Hellfire chopper dropped Nick's unit at an altitude of 7,800 feet and ten miles from the target village, which was located north of Azrow in the mountains. The squadron began its trek up the hillside and along narrow valleys toward the remote village. Each step was a calculated decision, because there was no guarantee that the trail was clear of IEDs, even though a team had swept the area in advance. Each soldier carried a backpack jammed with sixty to a hundred pounds of supplies, including communication gear, weapons, first aid, clothing, and personal items. They climbed higher and set up camp on a flat, narrow ridgeline. The observational rally point had a bird's-eye view of the village where the chemicals were being stored. Day and night, two members of the unit observed the activities of the village through high-powered binoculars and infrared lenses. The squadron wouldn't move in until they were sure that most, if not all, of the Taliban fighters near the compound had left the target village to join the other insurgents caravanning south to join the ongoing battle. That happened three days later.

Nick and a ranger named Arnold Raker went out for a closer look. Before initiating the Operation Dragon Claw DC-10 objective, the squad had to confirm that the chemicals were still in place. The target point, a hut, lay on the sparsely populated outskirts of the village. If Nick and Raker worked quickly, they'd get in and out without the villagers noticing them. Around two o'clock in the afternoon, Nick and Raker entered the village alone. They made their way inside the hut, which, according to army intelligence, provided access to an underground tunnel.

Nick stood guard while Raker checked the entrance to the tunnel. When Raker found the door locked, he pulled out a small lock kit from his rucksack and jimmied the door open. Moments later, Raker went inside the tunnel. When he emerged, he reported to Nick that he'd found barrels that, according to intelligence, contained the toxins.

They left the hut, headed back to their encampment on the ridge, and reported in to command. Operation Dragon Claw DC-10 replied that the operation was a surefire go. The soldiers suited up in masks and protective clothing.

Talented Pakistani scientists sympathetic to the Jihadists had developed the binary nerve agent that the squad had to destroy. The agent was designed to be mixed with an igniter just before use. The precursor was more stable and less hazardous than the finished agent. To counter the effects of exposure during the neutralization process, the soldiers took a pre-dose of galantamine, along with atropine.

The squad headed down to the village and made their way inside the tunnel. Two soldiers set up a portable stove and began boiling water. Three others opened containers of hydrogen peroxide. When the water was hot, a soldier named Schmitz, a weapons disposal specialist with a degree in chemistry from Rice University, added hydrogen peroxide, then poured the mixture into smaller containers. This created the neutralizer that would be dispensed into the barrels containing the toxic powder. The soldiers would pry open one hundred tight-head steel-drum fifty-five gallon containers with bolt-ring closures, add the neutralizer, and seal them again.

The scientific team went inside while Nick and Raker, weapons poised, guarded the hut in case Taliban soldiers or villagers showed up. Nick waited patiently, hoping the process would go smoothly and efficiently.

The entire process took six hours, which seemed like an eternity. Schmitz assured Nick that the barrels had been properly resealed and looked as if they'd never been disturbed.

The team evacuated the site and helicoptered back to their military installation. The mission had come off perfectly, or so everyone believed. And then, that night, Raker awoke from his bed, vomiting blood. Despite the best efforts of the medical team, he suffered a brain seizure and died. Thirty minutes later, Nick fell victim to the vomiting and seizures. He suffered paralysis as he alternated between consciousness and oblivion.

No one else on the team got sick.

What had gone wrong? Neither Raker nor Nick had gone inside or gotten near the open canisters during the neutralization process. They'd only taken a quick look inside the tunnel to make sure they had the correct target and not some residence or feed-storage shed and to confirm that the Taliban hadn't moved the barrels.

The cause of their illness remained a mystery. It clearly wasn't the result of poisoning from the toxins in the barrels. Nick suspected that when he and Raker entered the hut or when Raker opened the storage-room door, they'd triggered a booby trap, which blasted them with something, God only knew what. Nick had hung back, watching the perimeter, so he hadn't gotten as close as Raker to that unknown toxin.

Nick was ready to die, wanted to die. He'd accomplished his mission, prevented further loss of life for his fellow soldiers, and had at last avenged Andie's death, at least in a fashion. There was nothing more for Nick to live for. He told every doctor and nurse caring for him that he wanted to die.

CHAPTER 36

While Nick went out to forage for more firewood, Margo stayed in the bed. Her legs throbbed, and the truth was, she did need rest. The baby was dropping more each day, causing increasing pressure in her pelvic region while also allowing Margo to breathe more easily. All of this meant that the birth date was getting close.

It had been foolhardy to travel to Spokane, but she'd wanted to try, probably for the last time, to reconcile with her family. What could be more healing than a wedding and the gift of a new grandchild—probably her parents' last grandchild? Blanche still insisted that she didn't want kids. Heather would've liked to have given their parents another gift or two, but the fertility doctors long ago told her that any chance of having children of her own was nonexistent. Margo had been so estranged from the family that Heather didn't bother to call her with the news of the Olivia's wedding. Margo heard about it from her mother.

Her mother's call came in early December. Margo had made no plans for the fast-approaching Christmas holiday. After she and Matt broke up, she'd spent most of her past holiday-seasons working at the hospital. A few colleagues had invited her over to their homes, but the one time she went felt awkward and out-of-sync. After the birth-control pill fiasco with Olivia, Margo's family members didn't reach out to make her a part of the holidays, and she didn't push back.

She was just as upset at them as they were with her. The long-dormant wounds from her teenage years had festered. She was glad she hadn't aborted Olivia—of course she was—but she still resented her father's dictatorial intrusion on her rights and then her parents' prudish demand that she cede her baby to her older sister without even a pretense of a discussion. She resented Heather's selfishness. And she was angry at herself for behaving like a compliant child, even though she was, at the time, still a child. Her decision to get pregnant again, triggered by the premature onset of menopause, would give Margo a child to love. And, she hoped, give the Fletcher family a chance to put the past behind them.

In early December, during her eighth month of pregnancy, her mother called. After asking Margo how she was feeling—she'd never bought into her pregnancy the way most prospective grandmothers did—she announced, "I have some news. Your niece is getting married."

"That's cool," Margo said, struck again by contending emotions. She'd lost track of the family except for phone calls and texts and occasional visits with Blanche, who would come to Chicago. Through Blanche, Margo knew that Olivia, now twenty-two, was dating someone, but Margo didn't know it was serious. The first thing that crossed Margo's mind was that Olivia was too young. But how did she know that?

"She's getting married Christmas Eve at our home," her mother said.

A year away—par for the course these days. "Plenty of time for Heather to plan a great wedding," Margo said.

"Christmas Eve of this year, Margo."

Margo prayed that Olivia wasn't pregnant. "Really," Margo said dispassionately. "Either this has been planned for a long time, or it's sudden."

"I know what you're thinking. Don't. She's not pregnant, and this isn't sudden. The kids want something small and intimate."

So, the wedding had been in the planning stages for a long time. Even Blanche didn't have the heart to tell Margo—or had promised not to.

"It must piss Heather off," Margo said. "She's not a small-wedding girl."

"Please, Margo. No unpleasantries. I called with some nice news. Olivia would like you to be there. So would your grandmother."

"But not you and my father and my older sister."

"We're not the only ones responsible for what's happened in this family. You haven't reached out, either. And our concern is Olivia. She's grown up with certain assumptions. No one has a right to change those."

"As if that's ever been a risk."

"We can't know how you'll react to an important event like this. You like to speak your mind. What I'm doing is extending an invitation to the wedding. It's a nice gesture from your niece. You're in your last month, so I assume that you can't travel."

"Who's the lucky groom?" Margo asked, articulating sounds just to blunt the intense emotional sting of her mother's thoughtless words.

Her mother went on to describe Olivia's fiancé, checking off all of the requirements—educated, CPA, nice family, good-looking—in other words, parent and grandparent approved even though he was five years older than Olivia.

"Thank everyone for the invitation, Mother," Margo said, trying to sound sincere and not sarcastic.

"Take good care of yourself, Margo."

Margo hung up believing that there was no chance she could travel to Spokane in her condition.

A wise teacher in medical school once told Margo that *normal* was what your parents tell you was normal. It didn't matter that your family did things differently from most of the neighbors, that your father took your dinner off the table if you arrived ten minutes late, that you and your sisters couldn't date until seventeen when most of the other kids had been going out in groups since age thirteen, that you couldn't give money to door-to-door solicitors even if they were high school football players from the neighborhood selling cookie dough to buy playoff team jerseys, that any profession that didn't rely on mathematics wasn't worth a damn, that you had to follow the tenets of the church even if your father had slipped. The Fletchers were normal—until, Margo realized after she left for college, they were not.

Now, she had a more immediate problem. She needed to get the circulation moving to lessen her aches. She went over to study the map table. The map was circular for reasons she understood when she looked out the windows—the tower had a three-hundred-and-sixty degree view. Margo thought of the forest watchers and the many times they must've studied this map each day. And after that, what did they do the rest of the day—stare at the mountains, read books, write poetry, let their hair grow long?

She paced around the room until she remembered the broken radio. Nick couldn't fix it, but what would it hurt for her to try? Looking around, she didn't find it anywhere upstairs and so headed downstairs to look for it. The light coming from upstairs was dim but enough to see to make her way downstairs to the small foyer.

It was too dark to see much of anything, so she went to the front door and opened it. Cold air rushed in, but the daylight allowed enough light into the small hallway to see. She walked to a door and opened it to find a large room, maybe ten by ten—a combination workshop and storage room.

What she saw made her stomach lurch. She stepped back and surrounded her belly with her arms.

This is nothing. Or is it?

The remains of the baby elk lay splayed in an odd configuration atop a workbench. The meat had been separated and set aside. The skin and fur had also been separated and was pressed flat. The severed head of the animal, its dark eyes open in a lifeless stare, was placed above the bones arranged in a seemingly ritualistic configuration. A sobering and odd sight. Why had Nick kept anything other than the meat on this counter? Why not put the remains in the trash can next to the bench? As she stood perplexed, her skin began to crawl, and it wasn't from the grotesque sight she was taking in. She recalled Nick's childhood story about the skinned animals that the kid Donnie had mounted on trees.

Was her mind playing games?

Maybe. Nick did say the remains of the animal would attract predators, which explained why he'd kept them inside. It just didn't explain what he'd done with them.

In the opposite corner of the room, various small, rusted tools, some tattered rope, and an empty cardboard box filled the shelves. She searched among the items, but the radio wasn't there.

The front door banged, and a strong breeze sailed inside, a stark reminder of the cold that lay just beyond. How fast one forgets discomfort in the arms of a warm room. Back inside the foyer, she opened the door to the latrine. Of everything in this tower, she was most thankful for this room. She started to sit but looked down first and gasped. What the fuck?

The front door slammed shut. The lavatory door closed. Everything went dark.

"Nick?"

No answer.

So she braced her hands against the walls of the dark room and attended to her more immediate needs. A moment later, the entryway door opened, and a cold breeze rushed underneath the lavatory door.

Footsteps.

"Nick, is that you?"

"You shouldn't leave the door open, not for any reason, not for a second."

"I couldn't see down here. I needed the daylight."

"It only takes one wild animal to come in and attack you and the baby."

A moment later, she opened the door. Nick stood in the hallway not two feet away, waiting. Disturbing yes, but not as disturbing as what she'd just discovered.

"I know you don't like me to ask questions," she said. "But answer this one. Why is the radio sitting at the bottom of the latrine?"

CHAPTER 37

B ack upstairs, Margo sat on the bed and stared at Nick, who stood by the window. Although it was still the early afternoon, the sky had turned dark, the precursor to yet another storm. Would they ever stop?

"Why, Nick?" She didn't try to suppress her anger, although she knew she was playing a dangerous game. At some point, you have to stand up for yourself—even in the face of insanity.

"I took the radio down to the storage room to fix it," he said in an even tone. "I planned to take it outside to see if I could get reception and maybe figure out what the current situation is with the train wreck, to see if any rescuers have arrived on-site. I couldn't fix the radio. I got frustrated and threw it away."

Given his meltdown yesterday, the answer was plausible. But that didn't mean it was true. The tower's waste can would've been a more logical place to dispose of the radio , not the latrine. Was he intentionally keeping her away from the news, from civilization? If he got rid of the radio to keep her from the truth, what else had he lied about? Why would he lie? He didn't act irrationally before this psychotic event. On the contrary, he'd been the model of rationality, albeit aloof and often irritable, even harsh. She'd attributed his abrupt, domineering behavior to his long career as a soldier, not some psychological problem. If he'd meant to do her harm, he wouldn't have rescued her from the train in the first place. He could've hurt her a hundred times in the past days, killed her and hidden her body in the wilderness. He'd done the opposite. He'd saved her more than once, twice, and at great risk to his own well-being. Without her as a burden, he probably could've found his way down the mountain.

"The radio might've told us whether the rescue team is at the accident scene," she said. "We could've learned more about our situation, could've figured what our alternatives are."

He shook his head. "Doesn't matter if they've arrived. The snow just keeps accumulating. It's hazardous out there. We can't make it down the mountain yet."

"The longer we sit here doing nothing the more trapped we become. You said it yourself. The snow continues to accumulate."

His frown threatened to turn into a scowl. "This is an exercise in survival. You want to live, you better soldier up and follow my lead."

"Nick, I'm no soldier. I'm a pregnant woman. Frightened and vulnerable."

When he turned on his heels and walked away, she clasped her hands together, bowed her head, and prayed.

In the kitchen area, he placed his hands on the counter as if to brace himself, and looked out the window. He wouldn't apologize. Throughout this entire ordeal, he had never apologized, never said *thank you*. Not once.

Her lower abdomen cramped hard, as though she was having menstrual pains. She hugged her belly and leaned forward. Too much stress, too much physical exertion. Just Braxton-Hicks contractions. Nothing more. It wasn't time. She walked to the bed and lay down.

The blizzard had raged on for most of the day, but now the wind blew even harder. There was a low rumble in the distance—not wind, however, but something altogether different. With some difficulty, Margo rolled off the bed, waddled over to the east-facing window, and listened.

"Nick! A helicopter!"

The juddering of the helicopter got louder, which meant it was heading in their direction. Nick sprang to his feet and rushed to the window, while she started toward the door out to the upstairs balcony. The deck was covered with ice and snow, so she'd have to hold onto the railing with one hand to make sure she didn't slip while waving at the helicopter with the other. Just as she was about to turn the door handle, Nick grabbed her wrist.

"Stop, Margo! You're not going out there."

She struggled to free herself from his grip with her free hand, but he was much too strong.

"What the hell are you doing, you son of a bitch? We've got to get out there so the pilot sees us. Let go of me!"

He pried her hand off the doorknob and squeezed his body between her and the door. She tried to push him aside, but it was like trying to move a massive block of granite. She balled up her fists and started hitting him on the chest, but he didn't flinch. He simply grabbed both of her wrists and held her arms apart.

"Why are you doing this?" she screamed. "If you're some sick pervert, just tell me!"

"It's not a helicopter," he said.

"Bullshit."

"No. Listen."

She listened. The rumble persisted, got louder, but it no longer sounded mechanical. The upper floor shook, and the windows rattled so loudly they might've actually broken. The word *tempest* came to mind. Nick was right—again.

"We've got to get downstairs!" he shouted.

Bolts of lightning struck so fast the sky looked like a strobe light on a discotheque dance floor. For a moment, she thought she was imagining things.

"Keep moving, Margo!"

Once downstairs, Nick pulled her into the storage room and toward the bench. Once he helped her get down on the floor they scooted underneath the bench and pressed themselves up against the stone wall. The wind's roar was deafening. The building shook as if it were made of tinker toys, and Margo feared that it would break apart into little pieces.

"Oh my God! What's happening?"

"I don't know. Maybe a bomb cyclone."

"What's that?"

"A winter storm, hurricane-force winds, snow. Not the time to talk. Hunker down!"

She tried to curl up protectively, and he wrapped his arms around her. His body against hers felt both welcome and repugnant.

Again, the tower shook even harder.

"No!" she screamed. "No, no, please God."

"Andie, it's all right."

Was he confusing her for a man?

He pressed his body against hers and pulled her closer. Then the unthinkable happened: he kissed her.

She jerked her head away and gagged as he clung to her. She didn't want this. "Nick! I'm not Andy. I'm Margo Fletcher."

He didn't hear her over the din of the storm, or didn't want to hear her, because he stroked her hair and said, "Andie, it'll be all right."

Margo struggled to free herself but, given his superior strength, that was impossible. She prayed that his assault would stop with the kiss. If he realized what he'd done, if he became aware of how much she'd loathed that kiss, he could easily snap and kill her.

CHAPTER 38

After the bomb cyclone—or whatever it was—passed, Nick rolled out from underneath the bench and helped Margo to her feet. The storm had lasted twenty minutes and the kiss had lasted seconds, but it was the kiss that had her in turmoil. Neither of them spoke about what had just occurred. Was he even aware of what he'd done? He'd called her Andy. Was he gay? Or maybe Andie was short for Andrea. Either way, he'd confused her for someone he'd cared about. Earlier, he'd mentioned that he'd lost someone dear to him. Andie? Why hadn't he told Margo about him or her?

"Wait down here while I go check things out," he said as if nothing had happened.

She nodded, glad for the time alone. He truly didn't seem to remember the incident. Or if he did, he knew how to keep up a good front.

He came back a few minutes later. "There's a broken window, but the wood stove is still lit, so you can come up."

Upstairs, the wind seeped in through the shattered window.

"Have any idea how to fix the window?" she asked.

"I'm going to use the wood from one of the chairs to board that window up," he said. "It could've been far worse. I'd bet that this particular window was already compromised, and the winds just finished the job. Pretty sturdy construction, though. The cyclone would've leveled most places." The Nick she'd come to know had returned—affectless and all business, as if nothing had happened in the storage room. There was comfort in that. But she couldn't let her guard down.

She turned toward the bed. "I need to rest." She tried to behave normally, but for Margo Fletcher and Nick Eliot, there was no normal. Not since the train's crew applied the emergency brakes only a couple of days earlier. That train ride seemed like it had happened in another lifetime, and in a strange way, it had.

"The baby?" he asked.

"Fine, and I want to keep it that way. I'm exhausted and a bit crampy. Kind of freaked out by the whole thing."

Once in the bed, she rolled toward the wall and closed her eyes. She did her best to focus on the wind and snow slapping against the windowpanes. When Nick began breaking up the chair, the sounds of the wood cracking and splintering called to mind the breaking of bones. She tried not to flinch, but she couldn't help it. She wanted to cover her ears and block out all the noise from this world. But she feared that doing so would only alert him that something was amiss. He might become annoyed or agitated. He worked for a long time, as if trying to find an excuse to stay out of Margo's way. Or, that was one explanation for his preoccupation with the repairs.

Yet again, Margo's thoughts drifted back to her family. How delighted her parents and Heather must've been that her pregnancy made it impossible to attend Olivia's wedding. And no guilt necessary for a breach of etiquette—they'd graciously extended the invitation, but Aunt Margo declined.

Three days after the phone call with her mother, while Margo was holed up in her condo watching *Casablanca* on cable—Ingrid Bergman had just asked Sam to play "As Time Goes By"— Margo got a text from her sister Blanche.

In town on business. Can I come by and see you?

Wow. Margo responded, then put a "thumbs up" emoji in the box. *Where r u?*

Outside ur condo.

Margo shook her head. Her weird little sister showed up unin-vited, which was fine, but then didn't just ring the buzzer and ask to come in. More Fletcher formality filtered through Blanche's wonder-ful ditziness.

A few minutes later, Blanche was comfortably seated inside Margo's condo.

At first, they only acted like sisters, talking about babies, work, and more about babies. Margo put Blanche's hand on her belly, and Blanche shrieked in excitement when she felt the baby move. It hit Margo that hers was the only pregnancy in the Fletcher family that Blanche could experience. Margo made popcorn, and they watched the rest of *Casablanca*. After they both wept at the last scene, Blanche maintained that Ilsa should've gone off with Rick and left Victor Laszlo to his own devices. Whatever. Only then did Blanche reveal why she'd really come all this way to see Margo.

"Mother says you're not coming to Olivia's wedding."

"Look at me," Margo said. "I'm a whale. And whales can't fly."

"There are other modes of transportation. Olivia really wants you there."

"I have work, and I only heard about the wedding recently." Margo averted her eyes.

"Sorry. I was sworn to secrecy."

"Yeah, our dear old father would throw you in the brig if he heard you violated the rules."

"He . . . It's not only that, Margo. I've got to survive in this family, too. And I didn't want to hurt you."

"I'm pretty tough. Anyway, the whole thing is bullshit. So what if I prescribed birth control pills to a sexually active sixteen-year-old? Heather should've thanked me."

Blanche hesitated for a moment "The whole fucking morality thing was only an excuse, Margo. A pretext to keep you away. Heather took Olivia to the Spokane OB-GYN that week and got her a pre-scription from her own doctor."

"Why cut off communication?"

"Because Heather has always been scared that you'll tell Olivia the truth or, I don't know, that maybe Olivia would bond with you in a way she hasn't with Heather. She's jealous of you."

Margo was stunned. "She's jealous of me, and she's raised my daughter as her own? I never came close to telling, Blanche. I wouldn't fuck up Olivia's life like that. There's been enough of that in our family." Margo shook her head. "I don't get it. I truly was acting as an aunt and a physician. Protecting Olivia, and if you think about it, Heather and Charles."

"I agree with you. And, I think, if you can find a way to come to the wedding, we can all get through this." Blanche put her hand on Margo's belly. "I have a feeling this little one is going to help. You know how babies can bring a family together." Blanche smiled wistfully. "In most cases."

Margo thought for a moment, then shook her head. "It's not wise to travel. Even on the ground."

Blanche inhaled deeply, and her fair cheeks turned a bright red. "There's something else that might change your mind." Her jaw flapped, but she couldn't get the words out. For a moment, Margo worried that someone was terminally ill. Their grandmother? One of their parents?

"Just say it, Blanche."

She took a deep breath. "A couple of weeks ago, Olivia came to me. She wanted to know what the deal was between you and Heather. I . . ."

"Jesus, girl, spit it out."

"I . . . I told her you were her biological mother. I fucking just told her."

Margo's mouth dropped open and didn't close for a long time. Blanche had flung open the secret door to their family closet, and the bones had clattered to the floor. Part of Margo was glad that Olivia now knew the truth; the other part was terrified. What would this do to her? What would this do to Heather and Charles and their parents? Margo hoped Olivia wouldn't hate her, that the family wouldn't shun Blanche. She wanted to scream at Blanche; she wanted to hug her sister in gratitude.

"Did you hear me, Margo?"

Margo released the air in her lungs. "Jesus, Blanche. You, the dispassionate one? Ms. Switzerland?" Then Margo started laughing, almost uncontrollably.

"What the fuck is funny about this, Margo?"

Margo suppressed her giggling long enough to say, "Heather and Charles disowned the wrong fucking sister."

Blanche shrugged and grinned. "I was sick of the lies. And the unfairness. They've never been fair to you, and they've never been fair to Olivia. It's always there, and it's eaten this family up. You're mistreated, and you're like a saint. Keeping that secret. Well, I'm no saint."

The urge to laugh passed as quickly as it had come. Margo didn't know what to think, what to feel. There was fear, guilt, relief—most of all relief, because Olivia still wanted her to come to the wedding. "I'm no saint," Margo said. "How did Olivia react? I mean, what did she say?"

Blanche reached out and took Margo's hand. "She said somewhere inside her, she knew. I mean, who wouldn't, she looks like you and Mother, and a story about recessive genes can only go so far. But Olivia also said that it doesn't matter. That Heather is her mother, always will be, that you're her fun aunt."

Margo thought for a moment. "Good. That's good." And it was good. "Does anyone else know about this?"

Blanche shook her head.

"Did she ask why I gave her up?"

"Yeah, I told her, and she gets it. She's twenty-two, so seventeen is young to her now. She understands you were too young to raise a baby. That you were practically still one yourself."

But Margo hadn't wanted to give up Olivia. Not after her father burst into the clinic and certainly not after her daughter was born. By then, she'd desperately wanted her baby. Margo was too young to understand she had that choice. She feared losing her family if she didn't do as she was told. The reality was, she lost her family anyway. No, she didn't lose them. They discarded her. She was packed up and shipped out, never to return, out of the way.

"Does Olivia know the circumstances? That our parents forced me to give her up, didn't give me a choice?"

"No. That wasn't for me to say. I couldn't crush the kid."

Margo nodded, feeling the agony of old bones being sent back inside the closet. Perhaps it was best this way.

"Olivia wants her aunt to be at her wedding," Blanche said. "If there's any way you can travel, please try to come. Please."

Margo thought for a while. "I've always wanted to take a train ride and see the countryside. I'll check with my obstetrician and see if he'll sign off. I doubt it, but . . ."

She spoke with her doctor and booked the train tickets the following Monday. Then she sent a text to her mother with the details.

Now, the snow beating against the tower windows lulled Margo to sleep. She woke right before dawn. Nick was lying beside her. She sat up, but he didn't wake, which was unusual. Most of the time, he was so attuned to her every move that she couldn't so much as make a peep without him noticing. She pushed her body to the edge of the bed and scooted off. She walked to the kitchenette and drank some water.

Despite her naps, she still felt queasy. Then a hard, agonizing cramping struck. She keeled over and grabbed the counter, trying not to groan. Maybe the elk meat had gone bad and she'd contracted food poisoning. If so, the dehydration that followed would place the baby at risk. But, as quickly as the cramp came, it passed, along with the queasiness.

Nick rolled over, opened his eyes, and looked at her.

"Sorry to wake you," she said.

"It's cold in here. I'll add some fire to the stove." He got up, and as he approached he seemed so hulking, so intimidating, that she shuddered. Fortunately, he didn't seem to notice, because he walked past her and stoked the fire.

Another wave of nausea rolled over her, this one worse than before, and there was no stifling a deep groan. A moment later, her water broke.

CHAPTER 39

Nick looked at Margo with a kind of impatient bewilderment and pointed to the floor beneath her.

"Is that what I think it is, Margo?" he asked.

"Yeah, my water broke. I'm in labor." Using the wall to brace her back, she slid down to the floor.

His eyes widened. "Is the baby all right?"

"God only knows. It's coming so fast." She should've known it would be like this. It had been so long since she'd delivered the first baby and she'd been so young, that she'd forgotten how the birth process felt. Of course, every pregnancy and birth differed. Her mother always said that she'd birthed her children in a matter of hours. That wasn't true of Margo's first. Once she became a doctor, she doubted the truth of her mother's claims, thinking how easy it must've been for the older woman to look back and repaint a difficult reality into a more palatable fantasy. And yet, the signs were there. But with all the chaos and physical exertion, she'd missed the signs indicating the process had started much earlier, maybe even a day or two prior.

Nick hobbled over and squatted down at her side. "Come on, let's get you in the bed." He reached out a hand.

"No, don't touch me."

"What can I do to help?"

"Find a helicopter and fly me to a hospital."

"Come on, I'll rub your back. It'll help the pain."

Any touch from him was repulsive. "No thanks." She stood up using her own strength. With wobbly legs, there was only one place to head—the bed. Then it happened—the baby moved. "Oh Jesus. This can't be happening." She keeled forward.

"What's wrong?"

She probed her stomach and located what she believed was the baby's head. "The baby turned. It's breech."

"What does that mean?"

"Not the desired position to deliver. Too much can go wrong. I might need a C-section, but that can't happen. Obviously."

"What can we do?"

She reached the bed and sat down.

"I need to elevate my hips above my head. Let's put some ice on the top of my stomach. Heat at the other end. Babies don't like the cold. Maybe it'll work to turn the baby back around."

As he broke ice from around the ledge of one of the window-sills, she made her way across the room and toward the wood stove, where she eased to the floor and lay on her back. She lifted her legs and spread them apart to feel the heat between them and her lower abdomen. Modesty couldn't be a consideration.

He returned to her side, carrying shards of ice.

"Hold it on the top of my abdomen."

He did as she asked. When a contraction came, she lowered her legs. When the contraction passed, she repeated this process of lifting of legs and placing ice on her belly.

After the third time, he asked, "Is it working?"

"No. We'll have to try another approach. Let's get ready for the birth first. So we're ready when the time comes. Go look around the room for anything we can use to deliver the baby."

He found only a few rudimentary utensils in the kitchen.

"Grab the bucket, go downstairs, and get some snow. Then boil more water."

When he returned, he set a pan on top of the wood stove. Once the water reached a full boil, she had him sterilize the knives, forks, and spoons.

"You'll have to use the table knife to cut the umbilical cord. Dump that water and get some more snow. I'll need sterilized water to wash the baby and for drinking to stay hydrated."

Another contraction came and went. They were coming closer together. Her cramps intensified, coming every five minutes. This pattern persisted for at least an hour. It indicated she was still in active labor, the first stage.

"We need to try and move the baby. I can't do it alone. I need you to perform an ECV. It normally takes two experienced hands. Go clean your hands in the snow. Break off some of the soap you made from the fat. It's outside the window. Keep the other part of the soap clean. Hurry. I'll get back in bed myself."

Returning shortly, he said, "Just tell me what to do."

"I'm going to take a deep breath, and when I exhale, you'll need to lift the breech out of my lower pelvis."

He shook his head. "Say it another way."

"Slide your hand down to the bottom of my abdomen, where you can feel the bottom of the baby."

He did as she asked.

"When I exhale, gently push your fingers underneath the baby. Try to get a firm hold on the baby's buttocks, the lump of flesh at the lowest point. Keep a firm hold. I'll try to manipulate the baby by pulling the head from the top counterclockwise. When I stop, you push upward in the same direction. We'll alternate."

He nodded.

She took a deep breath and let it out. "Now." She groaned as his fingers delved deeply into her abdomen.

"Got it."

"Push, gently. Until . . ." Barely able to speak, she groaned, the pain intense. "Hold it!"

When he stopped, she used her hands in a push-pull movement, urging the baby to move.

The baby began to turn after several attempts. When the baby had turned forty-five degrees, he announced, "I lost my grip."

"It's okay. Move your hands up to the side and push."

Nick pushed.

"Not so hard, damn it!"

He reduced the pressure. Finally, the baby made the rest of the turn.

"Is it okay?"

"Yeah, we did it." Silently, she thanked God.

For the following few hours, the baby held its position. To endure the pain, she tried singing every stupid song she could remember. Nick, the steadfast soldier, just stood and waited for her to give orders. But there were no orders. This was the time to breathe and get through each contraction, some of them excruciating. There would be no epidural or other medication to ease the even more intense pain yet to come. That she dreaded.

The baby continued descending and didn't flip again. Margo's body shifted to the second stage of labor—the transition stage, they called it. Her stomach rippled up and down, forming a peak at the height of the contraction, making it easy to judge the stage by the formation of the stomach. The strong contractions came on faster, every couple of minutes, and each lasted at least a minute. It was time to get ready for the actual birth, so she removed everything except her shirt for warmth.

She walked around the room until the next contraction hit. When that one passed, she began to shake and shiver and was now nauseated, on the verge of vomiting. Then it was time.

Back in bed, she propped her body up against the wall and raised her knees. "I'm getting pressure on my pelvis. I can't see if my cervix is entirely effaced and dilated. The opening needs to be a full ten centimeters." Another contraction hit hard. "Oh, Jesus. I don't want to push until it's time."

The contraction passed. But another one was just around the corner. "Are you a good judge of centimeters, Nick?"

He shrugged. "I learned the metric system in the army. One centimeter is about the width of a pencil."

"Very good. I need you to feel inside. Slide two fingers to the end of the vaginal canal and you'll find the cervix. It should be flat, not fleshy, and shaped like a donut. See if you can assess how much it's opened." Though she was directing Nick clinically, and he was cooperative, he was still a stranger and she wanted nothing to do with him. But she couldn't do this alone and had to tolerate him.

He kneeled down, placed a hand upon her inner thigh, and grimaced. He slid two fingers inside her vaginal canal and probed. "Not sure, there's . . ."

"Can you identify the cervix?"

He nodded.

"You're looking for an opening in the cervix. Think of the inside of a donut, how wide the opening is."

"It's more than two fingers, more like the width of a baseball. Maybe eight centimeters. And there's something round, is that . . . ?"

"Yes, the baby's head."

"Sure it's not the rump?"

"Let's hope not."

Over the following few hours, Nick improved his nursing skills. He held Margo's hand and rubbed her back during painful contractions. When the baby had fully descended in her uterus and she had the strong urge to push, the next stage of labor began.

"Before I start pushing, I need you to check the cervix again."

He didn't wince this time but almost gleefully did as she asked. "Looks like you're there."

A contraction came on, and the urge to push was powerful. "Good! Here we go." She bore down. "See anything?"

"No, just bulging."

She rested and waited for the next contraction. Then she pushed again. The process repeated itself more times than she cared to count. So much for birthing babies with ease like her mother.

The next time Nick checked her progress, he cried, "I see the head."

Her tissue stretched, causing an intense burning. She needed an episiotomy, but no way would she let Nick perform one, not with a mere table knife. Finally, the baby's head crowned. Again the unthinkable: Nick's face exploded with an exuberance she didn't think him capable of. On the next big push, the baby's head emerged.

"Make sure the umbilical cord isn't wrapped around the neck. Check the mouth to make sure nothing is inside it."

Nick waited a beat. "All clear. But the head's turning to the side. Is that all right?"

She nodded. "When the baby's out, cut the cord." Then she pushed, fighting the pain. At once, her baby emerged and began a marvelous wailing.

Margo opened her eyes. Nick was smiling so broadly that her heart skittered. The strangest thoughts invaded her mind, but she couldn't quite articulate them.

"Is the baby a girl or a boy?" she rasped, wanting to weep. She was so exhausted, she was shivering, but also elated.

"A son."

CHAPTER 40

After Nick was exposed to the toxic chemical in Afghanistan, he was ordered back to the United States for rest and recuperation. The paralysis subsided after a few weeks, but it had weakened him, and the physical therapy—hours a day in the facility—helped him regain muscle mass. Three months later, he was reassigned to Fort McNair, Washington, DC, again to train soldiers. At age forty-two, he'd served twenty-four years, and that was enough. He was realistic—he couldn't go back to Afghanistan, hunt down Andie's killers, and destroy them. By participating in the destruction of the chemicals, he'd avenged her death as best he could. There was nothing more he could do, so he retired from the military.

He wasn't qualified for much except war, so he took a job consulting with a private defense firm located in Virginia just outside of Washington, DC, which designed and manufactured weaponry for sale to the government. If he couldn't be on the battlefield, he would at least keep those who could fight safe.

Andrea White's memory was never far away. Sometimes, out of nowhere, he would find himself remembering one of those corny, ribald rooster jokes. He would hear Andie's deadpan delivery in the clipped, no-nonsense Nebraska twang and see the slight upturn at the corners of her mouth and the mischievous glint in her eyes as she neared the punchline. Life plays dirty tricks by stealing the people we love and then taunting us with their memories.

Late one Friday evening, Nick arrived home at his condo. He'd just pulled a cold beer from his refrigerator when his cell phone rang. He glanced at the caller ID. It read US Government. He set the phone on the counter. When it rang for the second time, he answered.

"Nick Eliot?" a man asked. "I'm Captain Keith Stone, with the Judge Advocate General's Corps."

Nick's stomach clenched. A military lawyer. What was this about?

"What can I do for you, sir?" Nick asked. "Is there a problem?"

Stone was silent for a moment. "So it seems. But nothing to do with your military service. Your record is spotless, Sergeant. I'd like to meet with you in person about another matter."

In person without explaining? In this day of texting and emails? He sighed. Only in the military would this be required. Just like the time Colonel Dwyer called him in about that final mission to Afghanistan.

"Let's say Monday, Fort McNair, JAG Office, 0900," Stone said.

It wasn't an order, but it sure felt like one.

CHAPTER 41

Margo had given birth to a son! All along, she'd assumed the baby would be a girl because girls ran in her family. When she began labor, she feared that the baby's lungs would be underdeveloped, given the early delivery and the ordeal she'd gone through in the past few days, but there was no question about his lung capacity. He bellowed so loudly her ears hurt. But those bellows were the sounds of pure joy.

However, her joy was tempered at the moment by a serious medical problem—she still had not birthed the placenta. If it didn't come soon, she would have a medical crisis neither Nick nor she could overcome.

Nick had cut and tied off the umbilical cord with no trouble whatsoever. She expected as much, considering his ability to tie knots.

She groaned as another contraction hit.

"Be quiet, Margo. Don't upset the baby."

"I can't help the contractions. Dammit. The placenta hasn't birthed." If her uterus didn't expel the placenta and harden, she could die—would die.

He cradled the baby in his arms, comforting him. "I'm going to clean him up."

"Wait." She held her arms out and toward the baby. "Let me hold him first."

"I don't think that's a good idea; you're still having contractions."

"Give him to me! Please."

Nick faced her but didn't bring the baby. "You're out of control. Get a hold of yourself."

"Now!" she demanded.

"I'm going to clean him up first. You better stay focused on what you're doing."

Damn him. She stood up to go get her baby, to wash him off herself, but she was dizzy and fell back down to the bed.

"Get control of yourself, Margo," Nick said as if commanding an underling on an army base. "I've got everything handled."

Why was he speaking like this? She began to weep. "Just please let me hold him."

"Stop acting like a fool. You'll only upset the baby. You're too weak to hold him."

Maybe Nick was right, maybe she was so weak that she might drop . . . no, she would never. Another contraction came on. Why was it so painful? This was the afterbirth, which was supposed to be easy, to feel like nothing, to literally just slide out. She cried in agony.

"Quiet!" Nick said.

"Are you fucking kidding me?" she moaned.

"I don't tell jokes. And I don't like foul language from a woman. You're upsetting the baby."

Completely abandoned, she could only watch the pleasure Nick was taking in cleaning the baby—robbing her of the joy *she* should have felt. She was so angry. Her baby belonged in *her* arms, especially right after the birth, so he could bond with *her*. He needed to suckle, even if her milk hadn't yet come in. That was how it worked, how it was supposed to be.

Nick began to sing to the baby. "Hush little baby, don't say a word, Daddy's going to buy you a mockingbird—"

"It's Mama, not Daddy!" she screamed.

Nick turned back. "I'm not going to tell you again, Margo. Get control of yourself. If you don't . . ."

"What's that supposed to mean, 'If I don't?' You've lost your mind,

Nick. No, it's clear you've never had it to begin with. Did we really have to go up the mountain? Did you bring me up here because you wanted to avoid the rescuers?"

He only glowered, incongruously rocking the baby in his arms.

"This is *my* baby, not yours," she said.

"You're wrong about that, Margo. You stole him from me."

And then, it hit her. This man was one hundred percent insane. And she was his target. She'd heard of women stealing newborns from their mothers, but she'd never heard of a man doing it. No amount of screaming or swearing would change his warped mind.

He calmly walked over to her, cradling the baby in his left arm. For a moment, she thought he was going to hand her the baby. She extended her arms. But her relief lasted a nanosecond, because he slapped her face hard, so hard that sparks of light obscured her vision. Rage exploded inside her. She started to come at him, but he shoved her back down to the mattress.

She gasped and grabbed the sides of her head.

"You don't believe me, do you, Margo? But it's true. This is my son."

"How is that remotely possible?" she asked through a moan, wondering why she was again playing his twisted game.

"Think about it, doctor."

Could Nick be the biological sperm donor? The sperm donor's identity wasn't provided. Only the genetic and biological data about the donor had been released. Anything was possible, but this was so farfetched that she couldn't buy it.

Who cared? If there was a scintilla of truth in what he was saying, it didn't matter. The baby was hers.

"If that was true—and I know you think it is—then why would you deprive your child of a mother?" she spat.

"He'll have a father."

"He needs a mother, goddammit!"

Nick pointed a threatening finger at her. "I said get control of yourself. Are we clear?"

The baby started to wail.

"We're not at war, Nick. Give me my baby."

His face hardened, and she recoiled in fear. He was going to strike her again. Another contraction came, and she grasped her stomach. She moaned like a wounded animal experiencing pain, and also from the rage building inside her. He backed off.

After the pain subsided, she moaned to herself, "Come on. Come . . . on." There was no indication that the afterbirth would expel.

Nick walked to a chair, sat down, and began rocking the baby back and forth. The baby gurgled. It was all so horrifying. She'd kill this man. She didn't know how, but she would.

The baby quieted.

The pelvic bleeding had not subsided, and the pain was excruciating, causing her to moan no matter how hard she tried to stay quiet. "Don't you even care about what I'm going through?"

Nick didn't react, didn't even blink an eye, and offered no words of comfort or support.

"If I die, the baby dies," she said.

"He's healthy. He'll make it."

"Bullshit. He needs to suckle, he needs to work the colostrum out of my breasts, and he needs nourishment. That's what he needs. Not songs."

"You're not getting the baby until you've birthed the placenta and gotten ahold of yourself. I see no signs that you're in a rational state of mind or anywhere near it."

She screamed.

"Shut up, Margo!" He got up and took the baby to the stairs.

"Where are you going?"

He ignored her.

Then she understood. He was leaving with the baby. She could feel it. She was too weak to pursue him. "No!"

But she was wrong. He didn't leave. He came back upstairs cradling the baby in one arm and the filthy elk skin in the other.

"You can't put him in that skin," she said. "It's filthy, full of bacteria." Her entire body was now shaking.

He paid no attention to her but took the skin, placed it in a pan filled with water, and set the pan on top of the stove. Then he returned to the chair and began rocking the baby again.

This could not be happening.

The contractions spaced farther apart. Too tired to fight, she lay on her side, hoping her body would birth the placenta. After boiling the elk skin for about a half hour, Nick removed it from the pan and hung it to dry near the stove.

"Andreas is a nice name, Margo. It's the name of a member of my squadron who died in the line of duty. Well, she was a woman, so her name was Andrea. Why don't we name him Andreas?"

Margo wanted to leap from the bed and choke the life out of Nick. Now it was clear why he'd called her *Andie* during the bomb cyclone, why he gave her that disgusting kiss. Even so, whatever he'd experienced in the war, whatever had happened to Andrea, there was no *us* to this equation. The baby would be named Michael, after her grandfather.

"His name is Michael, as in the angel who is like God," she said.

"My father was named Michael. He was an evil man."

Catch more flies with honey, her mother had always said.

Margo had to play this game according to Nick's rules if she had a chance to survive and get out of there alive with her baby—Michael. "So we'll compromise and call him Gabriel, the Messenger."

"His name is Andreas," Nick insisted.

She couldn't get the upper hand with this madman. He had the physical advantage, and more than that the army had trained him to kill. Except . . .

"Your leg's infected, Nick. Isn't it?"

"No, it's only a scrape. Nothing."

"Show me."

The intensity in his eyes returned. "I told you. It is nothing." He growled, the tone more animalistic than ever before.

"May I feed the baby now?"

"You haven't birthed the placenta yet."

"Nursing him will help me do just that. He needs me."

The baby woke up and fussed. Then Nick did another unthinkable thing. He placed his finger in the baby's mouth and let him suckle it.

"Don't do that! You'll confuse him. Please, please don't. If you're really the father."

"Which I am." And then, in an instant, she believed him. Tragic. Maybe if things were different, if Nick were different . . .

She was too weak to stand, too weak to take Nick on—incapable of it even at her strongest. She continued to weep and rock. So tired. She closed her eyes, listening to the sounds of her baby fussing.

CHAPTER 42

When morning light broke, the mental fog slowly subsided. Margo had survived the night without hemorrhaging to death. Her body was fatigued, but thankfully, the cramps were gone. Her abdomen was hard, a good sign, which meant her uterus had contracted and, she hoped, the placenta had been expelled.

With all the strength she could muster, she lifted up on her elbows and used her hands to push up to a sitting position. She looked down at the mattress. It was a bloody mess, but there was no sign of the placenta.

The room was cold. Too cold. Goose bumps rose on her legs and arms.

Gripped with panic, she glanced around. Nick and the baby were gone. She didn't cry or scream or panic. She now had a weapon—angry determination.

Just as she started to stand, a slick mass slid out from inside her vagina—the placenta. It had indeed detached, which of course was why she was alive. She placed the afterbirth on the mattress, got dressed, and walked to the wood stove. A quick touch revealed that it was only lukewarm.

How long had the fire been out? And where was all the wood? No longer in the corner where it had been stacked. Not a single piece was left. It was gone—all of it. The pan used to boil the animal skin was overturned and lying beside the stove. Inside the kitchen, the pot holding the potable drinking water was upside down inside the sink. That madman had left no drinking water. He'd left her to die.

She needed water. She needed warmth. She needed sustenance.

She knew what she had to do. Women had done the same for as long as they'd given birth. But she didn't have the strength to rub sticks together to make a fire.

She stood, feeling noticeably lighter since the baby's birth, and walked over to the kitchen. Down on all fours, she ran a hand under the counter until her fingers brushed by the matches that she'd dropped the previous day. Now, she was just slim enough to reach them. She set them on the counter, took the pan, and headed for the stairs. Outside, she went into the snow, filled up the pan, and headed back toward the stairs, but then on impulse made a detour inside the storage room.

The animal bones were still lying on the bench. She went to the shelves and, with all her might, tried to pull out a board. Impossible. She glanced around the room. The old line of rope was there. The shovel was in the corner. Nick had made a mistake in leaving it. He wasn't infallible, the perfect killing machine after all. The implement was too thick to break the wood apart, but her adrenaline kicked into high gear, and she was able to use the shovel to hack away at the shelves, beating them mercilessly. First, splinters chipped off, and then larger pieces broke away. Before long, she had enough of what she needed to build a small fire in the wood stove.

She returned upstairs with her snow and wood. With only a few matchsticks, she had to succeed right away. As soon as the first match brushed against the ignitor, fire rose at the tip. And when its heat touched the tinder, the small pieces of kindling lit. The fire spread quickly, and before long heat radiated out of the stove.

She heated water to a boil and removed some for drinking. Returning to the bed, she picked up the placenta and carried it to the kitchen countertop. Using the table knife, she cut the placenta into sections. Once the organ pieces were prepared, all that was left was to boil them. She scooped the flesh out of the pan and placed some on a plate and the rest outside the window to freeze.

She sat down at the table, stared at the plate for a long moment, picked up the flesh, and raised it to her mouth. It would be like eating calves' liver. Many modern women, many of those who had birthed their babies at home, had eaten the placenta. Many women swore that after consuming the afterbirth, they regained energy and avoided postpartum depression. Nothing to be squeamish about.

After taking a deep breath, she sunk her teeth into cooked flesh. The taste was not offensive at all, palatable. Was that hunger talking or sheer determination? No matter. She was content, so content that she had to stop herself from eating too much too quickly. But the truth was, she'd never been more ravenous or so satisfied by a meal, a meal in which she was devouring her own flesh.

Once she'd consumed the placenta, she found her strength returning. Maybe the myths weren't myths. Never again would she dismiss homeopathic remedies.

It was time to get moving.

She cut sections from the mattress, used the material to wrap up the rest of her placenta, and placed the bundles inside her coat pockets. Not only that, she was also able to use the material from the mattress for bandages to help absorb her vaginal bleeding. It wasn't that she was simply hormonal after having given birth, she was still continuing to ooze blood. She got the shovel, applied soap made from elk fat to the wooden end, and lit the tip to serve as a torch. She closed the door to the stove, walked downstairs, and made a stop inside the storage room, where she grabbed the rope and a few of the dead animal bones to use as makeshift weapons. Then she walked out the front door of the watchtower.

Anger coursed red-hot through Margo's veins, but she kept the rage in check. She needed to focus on the long, hard chase.

CHAPTER 43

The Monday after Nick received the call from Captain Stone, the military lawyer, he drove to Fort McNair. He couldn't imagine what this meeting was about.

He signed in at the reception desk and was taken to a conference room. Moments later, Stone entered the room.

Nick rose and started to salute, but when Stone extended a hand, he recalled he wasn't a soldier anymore. The men shook hands. The gesture felt odd.

"I'll get right to the point," Stone said. "The army made a serious mistake at your expense. We'll do what we can to compensate you."

"What mistake?" Had something happened in combat? If so, that something could only have related to his last mission.

"I know that before your last mission, Operation Dragon Claw DC-10, you made a sperm deposit, as many combat soldiers do before deploying. So did Arnold Raker, the ranger who died on your mission to destroy toxic chemicals." The lawyer took a deep breath, as if choosing his words carefully. Nick resisted the urge to tell him to get on with it.

"Like you, Raker wasn't married. Several weeks ago, the facility where his—and your—sperm were banked got a call from Raker's mother, a Laura Raker. She asked whether her son's sperm had ever been donated. I'm no expert here, but I understand that a sperm bank can disclose a donor's identity if the donor gives permission. The administrative assistant at the facility responded that they would need Arnold Raker's permission to discuss the matter. When Raker's mother told the assistant that her son had been a casualty of war, the assistant asked if she could call Mrs. Raker back. Anyway, bottom line, it seems that the initial army combat report mistakenly indicated that *you* were the soldier who died and that Raker was the one who became ill. The mistake was recommunicated to the sperm bank as part of the soldier's last requests. The mistake wasn't discovered until the mother called."

Nick felt as if he'd been hit by shrapnel from an IED.

"Where is this going, Captain?" Nick asked.

"You'll recall that on the consent forms, you checked the box allowing your sperm to be donated in the event of your death?"

Nick didn't recall. He'd hurriedly filled the form out, didn't care one way or another what they did in the event of his death.

"Your sperm was purchased and transferred to an out-of-state hospital. Donated."

"What do you mean *donated*?"

"Gone. Used. All of it."

Nick's face flushed with anger and confusion. "How does something like this happen?"

"Mistakes like this are more common than you think. There have been a number of custody lawsuits arising out of mistakes and misappropriation." Stone went on to talk about lawsuits in Utah and in Orange County, California—a law school lecture that Nick had absolutely no interest in.

When the lawyer finished, Nick said, "Captain, are you aware of my situation?"

"I am."

At one point in his life, Nick wouldn't have cared that he was sterile. He'd even considered a vasectomy. Then Andie came along, and everything changed. She'd told him to have a family if she died in combat, to go on with his life. So, before he went on that last mission, he'd banked the sperm in case he was injured, in case he decided to honor her wishes. When he came into contact with those chemicals, he'd been injured in that way.

"There's something else that you should know," Stone said. "Our investigation revealed that your sperm donation resulted in a pregnancy."

Nick sat back in his chair. "Who's the woman, Captain?"

"I'm sorry I can't share that, Sergeant Eliot. I wish I could. The damned HIPAA laws. I shouldn't say this, but I'd suggest that you retain an attorney and bring a lawsuit against the military and the private facility. I could recommend a law school classmate who is a good family lawyer."

"You mentioned other custody battles," Nick said. "What would my chances be?"

Stone closed his eyes. "I'm no expert, but the way it usually goes, the biological mother almost always prevails. Sometimes even without visitation rights from the sperm donor."

Nick stood. He had to get out of there before he beat the name of the woman out of Stone. "Thank you for your time, sir."

"I'm sorry, Sergeant," Stone said. "Do you want that recommendation?"

"No, sir."

As soon as Nick left the facility, he called Colonel Dwyer, the officer who'd sent him on the mission to destroy the chemicals. Dwyer took the call immediately, a good sign.

"I assume you know why I'm calling, sir," Nick said. "I've just been talking to the Judge Advocate General's people."

"I do," Dwyer said solemnly. "I was aware that you had an appointment with the JAG representative today. I'm sorry, Nick. We'll make it right. Especially in light of what you've given to your country."

"There's only one thing you can do to make it right, sir. I need a name. The name that Captain Stone said he can't give me."

There was a long silence. "I'll get back to you, Sergeant," Dwyer said.

Nick didn't hear anything more for several days, thought he might not hear anything at all. Then Dwyer called. The woman who was carrying his baby was named Margo Pratt Fletcher, a physician in Chicago. Nick then went to get back what was his.

CHAPTER 44

Before leaving the watchtower, Margo quickly studied the table map one last time. She had a fairly good idea where the path down would be. But looking at a map didn't mean she could find her way down mountainous rugged terrain in blizzard conditions. She'd combine her knowledge and a mother's instinct to find her way.

She stood just outside front door and scanned the perimeter, keeping the important landmarks imprinted in her mind. She felt weak and energized at the same time, but she didn't think about the cold or about the sun when it disappeared behind the clouds or the fact that she'd just given birth a short time ago. Nor did she think about the snow when it began to fall again for the umpteenth time. She simply pulled the hood of her coat up around her head and face and drew the toggles tight. Carefully, she traversed the narrow, hazardous ridge and, once below it on safer ground, continued along on more compacted snow until she got to the forest. As the snow continued to fall, the ground became soft again, her legs sinking a foot or two down, which made walking slow but not impossible.

She'd worried about tiring quickly, but the farther down the mountain she walked, the more empowered she became. The shovel gave her confidence that she could avoid sinkholes and stay on solid ground. She actually felt thankful her father had insisted that she learn how to ski—both downhill and cross-country. Not that Margo enjoyed skiing, much less excelled at it. She took after her Southern mother, who would rather sit in the snow lodge drinking hot rum and listening to piped-in music than venturing out into the cold and damp winter air. Now, as Margo walked deeper inside the forest, her father's words on those ski trips took on a new meaning. He'd speak of the musical sounds of nature, of the brand-new symphonies created on each new trek through the wilderness. Her father was a hard man, unduly strict, and a hypocrite. She hadn't seen that he was also a romantic, a man seeking the poetry of life and finding it only outdoors, away from the pressures of his job and supporting a wife and three girls. Yes, he'd interfered when she was about to have the abortion, but that interference resulted in a good thing—Olivia's birth. As for his fling with Greta? People make mistakes. Margo had carried his burden long enough. His mistakes were not her own. These peaceful thoughts, so anomalous given the events of the past days, helped drive her forward in pursuit of the madman.

The trail switched back and forth in what seemed like a random direction, but according to the circular map, it led down to the railroad line. Her makeshift torch wasn't as effective as Nick's had been, but the tip still smoldered, remaining hot enough to fend off potential predators. The soap she'd brought along with her acted as additional fuel and kept the torch going.

As the snow continued to fall, the ground became softer, and sometimes she sank down to mid-thigh. Still, she pressed forward, downward in the direction of the railroad tracks, all the while searching for only one thing—any sign of Nick and baby Michael. Soon, she could barely trudge along. Too slow. She had to move faster somehow—had to.

She surveyed the landscape while she caught her breath, then muscled her way to an evergreen tree and pulled and tugged on a thick, low-lying branch until a large section broke loose. She tore off another piece, then another and another, grunting and squealing each time from the exertion. Next, she took advantage of another one of

Nick's mistakes, pulling and twisting individual strands of twine from the fraying rope she'd taken from the storage room. Eventually, she had enough longer pieces to serve her purpose. With sections of the rope, she tied the evergreen branches on the soles of her boots and ecured a knot to hold the greenery in place, fashioning a pair of crude but surprisingly effective snowshoes. She faltered a bit at first until she got the rhythm and the feel but, within minutes, she was able to move along the upper surface of the snow at a decent pace.

In her haste, she ignored her homemade torch, and the ember at the end of the shovel had died out, leaving her without fire Fortunately, she still had a couple matches in reserve.

When the hunger got too great, she ate a piece of the frozen placenta, all the while continuing on her crusade.

After an hour—or was it two or three?—she stopped in her tracks. A red line dotted the snow. *Don't jump to conclusions.* She bent over and examined the material. Unmistakable to an emergency room doctor—blood. Good, because if this were human blood, she might be close to Nick and her baby. Bad, because whose blood was it? She refused to believe the worst. It had to be Nick's from the wound in his leg.

The snow was falling, hadn't stopped, so that meant if the blood was still visible, she was getting close. So she hoped.

Using the shovel as a ski pole, confident on her evergreen snowshoes, she followed the bloody trail until it disappeared, and then she stopped and listened. The wind howled, causing the branches to creak and rustle. Then she heard something else, or so she thought—barking? Growling?

Coyotes? Wolves? A bear?

She waited a moment more, listening. The barking stopped. Maybe there hadn't been barking or any sound at all. Maybe the forest had played tricks with her mind, just as Nick had played tricks with her mind these last few days.

Just ahead, off the main trail, a narrow path led into the forest but continued downward. The trail was visible only because the snow was more compact. Maybe manmade, but more likely a deer trail. If there had been barking, it had come from that direction. It was risky—she might never find her way back, or worse, might encounter a predator—but she had to follow that path. Energized, she hurried down the deer trail and into the forest. At times, the trees and plants threatened to cover the path entirely, but always the narrow trail reemerged.

Maybe halfway down the mountain, the trail switched back. The wind had blown at her back before, helping her along, but now the breeze hit her head on. She cursed her luck, because the already tough going would get tougher. But the wind wasn't her enemy after all, because it carried the whining and growls and yips of a pack of coyotes—but also a high-pitched whine that did not come from the coyotes.

It was her baby's cry!

CHAPTER 45

Margo had walked with eyes forward before, always looking ahead, but now she looked down to the snow. A new trail of blood. Humans and animals were close by.

Although she couldn't believe she was capable of it, she started running as best as she could in the makeshift snowshoes. When she rounded another bend in the trail, she saw the pack—five coyotes surrounding their prey—a hunched-over Nick Eliot. Nick cradled baby Michael inside his jacket, protecting the infant from the coyotes' snapping jaws. He flailed his massive arms—the arms of a killer—at the animals, but ineffectually this time. Had he ever before been so useless in a battle?

The coyotes jumped at Nick, pulling on his coat, tearing at his flesh.

"Hey!" Margo screamed as she charged forward, waving the shovel.

Some of the coyotes backed away, but the one gripping Nick's arms continued to bite and pull. Unable to fight back, Nick absorbed the attack, while cradling the baby inside his coat as best he could with his other arm.

"Get out of here!" she shouted as she rushed at the coyotes and brandished the shovel. When she reached them, she swung the shovel with every ounce of force she could muster and struck Nick's attacker on its hip with the sharp end of the blade.

Bone cracked, and blood spewed. The animal whined, let go of Nick's arm, and scurried back toward the pack.

Another coyote lunged forward and locked its teeth on Nick's arm. The baby wailed louder.

Margo circled around to the other side of Nick, trying to find a location where she could strike at the animal without the risk of hitting her child. She swung wildly at the animal's head.

A miss.

The blade sunk into the snow, kicking up a shower of ice. She yanked the shovel out, lifted it, and swung again, this time striking the animal's head with the blade and coming dangerously close to Nick—not that she cared if she split that son of a bitch's skull in two. The coyote yelped and fell to the snow, whimpering. Then it stopped moving.

Now wary, the other three coyotes backed off but didn't leave.

Nick lifted his head. His wounds were far more severe than she'd imagined. There were bites all over his face and neck. Blood poured out of his left eye. No doubt, the coyote had blinded him in that eye, perhaps permanently. His shirt was stained crimson at the abdomen. His pants were ripped. His previously injured leg was exposed, and she saw the truth. The wound was festering from an ugly infection. How he'd managed to forage for food and gather wood over the last day or two, to hide the malady from her trained eye, was mystifying.

"Margo," he rasped.

The baby continued to cry.

She raised the shovel again, poised to strike him, the most dangerous predator of all in this forest.

"I thought you were dead," he said, slurring his words. "I wouldn't have left you if I thought you could." He groaned in pain. "Please."

At last, true emotion radiated from his eyes. That emotion was fear.

"Shut the hell up, Nick, and give me my baby."

"Please. You don't understand. Please."

She took a step forward, ready to swing the shovel. His eyes widened. Now he understood a truth about her. She would strike him if she had to—perhaps even if she didn't have to.

With great effort, he opened his coat, revealing the elk fur and the bare arm of Margo's baby. He struggled to unhook the sling from around his neck and, when it came free, he held the sling out. He was so weak that the baby's weight was too heavy for him, and he dropped the bundle in the snow.

She crouched down and snatched the infant.

Just as she was lifting little Michael off the ground, Nick lunged at her. His fist struck the side of her head, and she dropped the bundle. A haze obscured her field of vision, and pinpoints of light flashed against her retinas.

Focus, Margo. Focus. Read and react.

She reached out into the beyond, grasping for consciousness. But she was slipping into an abyss. A weight rolled over her. Paws. Panting sounds. A feral, canine stench.

From someplace near yet so far away, her baby wailed. An electrical awakening jolted her. She opened her eyes. She was lying in the snow. Three coyotes circled her warily, hungrily. She glanced around. The shovel was gone. So were Nick and the baby.

As she rolled up onto all fours, she shouted in a harsh voice that was unfamiliar, a voice that was more animal than human, "Get away from me!"

To her shock, the animals slowly retreated.

She could no longer hear the baby's cry. But his tiny voice was imprinted in her mind. No way would she let that fucking lunatic steal her child. She looked at the coyotes. All three were thin and tall, with thick fur matted from the damp snow. Just wild dogs, she told herself. Dogs are genetically drawn to humans. She needed to stand, to rise above them in height, to threaten them so they would back off.

She reached inside her pocket and retrieved a piece of the placenta. She waved it in front of the animals now huddled together in a small pack. The coyotes sniffed. She flung the flesh as far as she could. The three animals raced to it and fought among themselves.

She stood, stumbling as she struggled to find her balance. Which way did Nick go?

She scanned the ground. A trail of blood led downhill, away from the trail. She needed a weapon. She felt inside her pockets, but the bones were gone. When she reached the trees, she pulled on a branch but couldn't break it free.

Without a weapon, she feared that she couldn't overpower Nick, even in his greatly weakened condition. She surveyed the landscape again, searching. Beyond the deer trail she'd followed to get to this place, the hillside dropped off sharply—just like the drop-off she'd encountered when she ventured down the mountain alone a couple of days earlier and stepped through the ice over the frozen stream.

The memory of her baby's cry, his little breaths, his infant sounds, propelled her forward. She hurried back to the deer trail and scurried down the slope. Where there was a stream, there were rocks. From her earlier trek, she had learned to recognize the contours of a frozen stream. Boulders protruded from this rocky basin over which water, not frozen, flowed. She reached the bank and collected an arsenal of rocks.

As she stumbled forward, the yips of coyotes reached her ears. They hadn't retreated after all, only left her—the strong—to pursue the wounded and weak—Nick and the baby. Hungry predators pursue the frail.

Energized with adrenaline, she made it back up the incline, sometimes scrambling on all fours. She returned to the clearing where she first found Nick and the baby and continued along the bloody trail. No sign of Nick or the animals.

Terror tugged at her core.

The snow intensified, falling hard now. The snow was always fucking falling. Now it covered most of Nick's bloody trail. But vestiges of his footprints remained visible. She moved along, and with each step her anger mounted.

Thunder rumbled. The sky darkened to a black-gray. The snow fell even harder, pelting her body like bullets. She tightened the hood of her coat to cover her face. She stepped into a shallow sinkhole, but righted herself. She wouldn't stop.

Soon the snow obscured the trail of footprints and blood. She wanted to scream but resisted.

Where was Nick?

She studied the ground and visualized the circular map, assessing this location. She'd gotten off the path she'd been following. The only option was to keep moving down. That was the only direction Nick could go in his condition.

The wind howled, but she wasn't afraid. Mother Nature was her protector, her baby's protector. Suddenly, the wind again carried to her another sound, a wonderful sound—her baby's cries.

She rounded the bend. Nick Eliot moved ever so slowly. With each step he looked as if he might fall. If only he would. He used the shovel as a crutch. His other arm hung at his side.

Where was the baby?

She hurried after Nick, staying hidden just inside the woods. She had no plan, but she was driven by rage. He started moving faster. Why? Had he sensed her presence? He was a soldier after all, trained to avoid hidden enemies.

She stealthily moved closer, within twenty feet, then ten. So close she could hear him pant. His breathing was labored. How could he possibly remain upright with all his severe injuries?

Where was Baby Michael?

Not with Nick. Now was her chance.

Her heart skipped a beat. Reaching inside her pockets, she gripped a rock in each hand. Then all at once, she bolted out of the woods, charged the enemy from behind, and with all her remaining strength struck Nick in the head, over and over again. He staggered forward, dropping the shovel. She continued pummeling him, on the head and the face and the neck, and especially on his damaged eye.

He wobbled and stumbled around to face her, a look of hatred and rage on his face. He came at her far more aggressively than she'd expected. She tried to hit him again with a rock, but it was too late. He knocked the rocks out of her hands. Before she could get away, he was on top of her, his hands reaching for her neck.

She thrashed, trying to avoid his grip. Her thick coat was her savior, forming a kind of barrier.

She pulled at his arms, but he was too strong. She flailed her legs to try to kick him, but it was no use.

Then her hand struck a rock—not one of her weapons but one that had lodged in beneath the snow. She grasped the rock and, with all her might, kneed the infected wound in Nick's leg. He groaned in pain and anger and relaxed his grip on her neck—just long enough.

She lifted the rock and struck Nick's injured eye again, cracking the orbital bone.

He shrieked in agony.

A predator who sensed his weakness, she kicked his wounded leg again. When his body began to crumple, she shoved him away using the snow's softness to roll out from underneath him.

She scrambled to her feet and kicked his leg again. And again. And again. When he seemed subdued, she picked up the shovel.

He tried to lunge at her, but he was too weak. He whimpered and curled into the fetal position.

Margo looked around. No sign of the furry bundle swaddling Michael.

"Where's my baby, Nick?"

"I . . . I . . ."

She kicked him more, unable to control her rage, which only grew when she recalled how he'd slapped her when she was most vulnerable.

"Answer me!" she said.

He groaned.

"Where did you put him?"

No response.

She raised the shovel. "If you don't answer me, I'm going to hit you until you can't move and skin you alive. Do you understand me?"

His uninjured eye shifted to the left. She followed the path, and there it was, fifty feet away. The furry bundle lay just off the trail. A tiny arm was outstretched from the bundle and lying still on the snow. How could she have missed it?

Her heart dropped ten stories. She raced back toward the bundle. When she reached it, the baby was still.

She screamed.

Suddenly, the baby fussed, and his tiny arms flailed and reached out for her. Momma was there. She fell to her knees and scooped him up. He was alive and seemingly well.

"It's okay, it's okay, sweet Michael," she whispered. "Mommy is here." She placed the baby inside her coat, stood, and started back down the deer trail, which would lead to the main trail and back to civilization. She gave Nick a wide berth as she circled around him. The man would be dangerous until the last glimmer of life left his body. When she was ten feet past him, there was a crunching of snow and a groan. Electrical currents of fear shot through her body. Was the madman up and on his feet again? She turned back to see him lift his head and try to prop his weight up on his elbow.

"Let me explain," he said.

She wanted nothing more than to run as fast and as far away from this place and this maniac as possible. But something inside her made her stop and listen. "Explain? There's no explanation for what you did."

"I'm the baby's father."

"Go to hell, Nick."

"Let me explain, Margo. Please."

His wounds were fatal. Not her concern. He would only try to kill her again if she came close.

"In Afghanistan, I was exposed to chemicals," he said, struggling to get the words out. "A man died. The army made a mistake." He panted hard, trying to speak. "They donated my sperm. You got it. A mistake. The boy is mine. I swear."

She gripped the shovel even tighter. She did believe what he was saying, had since he'd told her in the watch tower. So what? Because she was perimenopausal and her clock was ticking, she'd gone to a fertility doctor, and she was artificially inseminated.

"You stole him," Nick said.

"How can you be sure it was your sperm, Nick?"

He laughed, but it sounded more like a groan. "The army. How do you think I found you?"

"Even if it's true, I didn't steal from you."

Another pained laugh.

"You followed me onto the train. Did you plan to kill me all along? Was the avalanche just a stroke of luck?"

"I never intended to kill you. I wanted to get to know you, to work something out. He ... I tried to save everyone in our car ... I saved you—the baby. That's what I wanted. But when you went down the hill by yourself, you defied *him*, risked the baby's life. *he* convinced me you weren't fit. To eliminate you."

She knew better than to engage Nick and his insanity, but she couldn't help herself. This would be the last opportunity to learn anything more about this man. "Who did I defy? Who convinced you, Nick?"

"I'm a soldier, but *he's* the killer. He told me to take what was mine. To protect the baby. He told me to take you up the hill, to wait until you gave birth, and then ..." Nick hacked and blood spewed from his mouth.

The man was clearly demented, and now he was probably delirious as well. Time to leave.

"Please, Margo."

What did he want from her? Forgiveness? Understanding? Treatment? Another chance? What did it matter? Yet, she felt more than a twinge of sadness for him. "I'm sorry for what happened to you, Nick. You should've come to me, not stalked me like I was some animal. Talked. Don't you understand? I would've wanted the baby to have his biological father in his life. Under the right circumstances. I know what it's like to lose . . ." She shook her head. Enough. She didn't owe anybody an explanation.

"A combat soldier, too long." He gurgled, coughing up blood, the fluid adding to the crimson stains already spattering the snow. "You're a doctor," he said. "Help me."

"I can't save you, Nick. Not both you and the child." She only hoped she could get to safety soon.

Nick held up a hand. "Please, Margo. Think of what I did for you."

"You left me for dead twice, and you tried to strangle me. So you could steal *my* baby."

"Our baby. He's ours. I got on that train to meet you, to get to know you" As improbable as it seemed, he crawled forward.

"No, Nick. He's *mine*. I carried him for nine months." She turned to leave. It was cruel to allow this to continue. Also dangerous.

"Don't leave me," Nick pleaded. "You have to help me."

She kept walking.

"I'm not who you think I am," he said.

She stopped and looked back. "I know exactly what you are."

"Please, Dr. Fletcher."

"Would you have us all die out here, Nick? That's not going to happen. Take solace in this: the baby is going to live. By saving me from the avalanche, you saved the baby." She turned and walked on.

"I didn't try to kill you, Margo! That wasn't me."

She kept going.

"Tell her!" Nick shouted.

She hesitated slightly at these words but continued her march forward.

"Make her understand!" Nick groaned.

She glanced back over her shoulder. Nick was looking at her with pleading eyes, his arms outstretched.

There was a clap of lighting and a loud blast of thunder.

"Tell her!" Nick shrieked. "It wasn't me. It was you, JJ."

CHAPTER 46

M argo continued down the mountain. She comforted the baby as she descended. When she emerged from the cover of the forest and saw the train shed in the distance, her heart and soul resounded with joy—workers were clearing the tracks. She hurried to them, and after their initial disbelief wore off, they summoned help.

In no time, a helicopter landed on-site, and her baby, Michael Pratt Fletcher, and she were escorted to the nearest hospital, where she recounted her story and told the authorities where to find Nick's body.

"All's well," the pediatric nurse said, handing Margo the baby. "We're calling it a Christmas miracle." Then, because the law needed to be served, she handed Margo the birth certificate to sign.

She held the baby to her breast, and he latched on. She took joy in listening to him coo and suckle. She stroked his soft skin, breathed in his sweet smell, and began singing her own version of an old lullaby.

Over the mountain, over the sea,
Back to my home where I long to be,
Oh, light of my life, he shines on me . . .

When the baby fell asleep, she reached for the birth certificate. In the box that asked for the father's name, she wrote *unknown*. That was the first false entry she'd ever made in an official record—she knew very well who the father was. The biographical information of the sperm donor had not included the name of the father, only his basic facts: donor's heritage, blood type, hair color, height, complexion, hair texture, eye color, and weight. She didn't need to know more. Along with Nick's rantings, those facts were enough.

When the baby and she were released from the hospital, the police kindly escorted them to the nearest airport. It was time to start life afresh. The Christmas holiday was about birth, and she'd received a gift—her child.

She hadn't called her family. Would she go back to Chicago or on to Spokane? A part of her just wanted to walk away, but she felt the inward pull urging her to come home.

CPSIA information can be obtained
at www.ICGtesting.com
Printed in the USA
JSHW052203211020
8950JS00003B/13

9 781684 425501